A Blind Eye

ALSO BY G M FORD
FROM CLIPPER LARGE PRINT

Black River

A Blind Eye

G. M. Ford

W F HOWES LTD

This large print edition published in 2005 by
W F Howes Ltd
Units 6/7, Victoria Mills, Fowke Street
Rothley, Leicester LE7 7PJ

1 3 5 7 9 10 8 6 4 2

First published in the United Kingdom in 2003
by Macmillan

A CIP catalogue record for this book is available
from the British Library

ISBN 1 84505 770 8

Typeset by Palimpsest Book Production Limited,
Polmont, Stirlingshire
Printed and bound in Great Britain
by Antony Rowe Ltd, Chippenham, Wilts.

To Joe and Donna Bocco – my forever people.
To ungrateful children numbers one and two.
To Oakland and Jimmy and Rose and Hugo and
Francis,
Eye Sore and Ear Sore and Mr and Mrs
Berkowitz
wherever they may be.

Bless you all,
Gmf

For children are innocent and love justice,
while most of us are wicked and prefer mercy.

– G. K. Chesterton

Mama says we all got a kernel of mean-ness inside us. A place to go and hide where there are no brothers and sisters and mamas and papas and nobody matters but us. A place where we don't ever have to share the cake or ever have to smile when we don't mean it. Where all we gotta do is what we want, and we don't have to answer to no one about nothing. All we gotta do is make sure we're the ones who survive. 'Cause not everybody makes it. Nope. Not everybody can find that hard place in their hearts. And for those who can't . . . well then . . . it's gonna be a long row to hoe. Life's gonna chew 'em up and spit 'em out. Leave 'em nothing but a shell with the nut gone, until, by the time the end rolls around, they're ready to go, 'cause they ain't lived nothing but lies, so nothing they got left at the end is worth fighting for. Might as well be gone is what I say.

CHAPTER 1

I see.' The woman sighed and forced her face into an uncomfortable smile. 'You haven't been listening to me, have you, sir?'

'I've been listening,' Corso said.

'Then you've heard me saying noon tomorrow, sir.' She hesitated. 'At the very earliest.'

'I really need to get out of here.'

She stopped fanning the pile of tickets and reluctantly made eye contact.

'As I've told you *before*, sir, all flights are canceled indefinitely.'

'I've been stuck in this . . . this . . . facility for two days.'

She sighed. 'Sir . . . pleeease. It's inconvenient for all of us, sir, but I assure you there's absolutely nothing that can be done about it.' She gestured toward the windows, shook her head disgustedly, and again used her square white fingernails to pick through the paperwork. Corso jammed his hands into his pants pockets, turned away from the Courtesy Desk, and walked to the window.

Outside, a thin curtain of snow and ice blew in from the west at a thirty-degree angle. Nothing moved. Daylight's footprints and tire tracks lay buried beneath yet another foot of freshly fallen snow, leaving the tarmac a solid, wind-whipped blanket of white.

Inside, O'Hare International Airport looked like a refugee camp. Every flat surface held either a stranded traveler or his baggage. Fifty yards away, at the far end of the concourse, a pair of soldiers, automatic weapons slung over their shoulders, crisscrossed the floor, stopping here and there to check a lock or gaze into the face of a sleeping citizen.

The helmets turned in unison as Meg Dougherty came striding around the corner, her tall laced boots clicking over the floor and her black cape fanning out behind her like a pair of ebony wings. She said something to the boys, but Corso couldn't make it out. The taller of the two gave her a small salute and then dug an elbow into his buddy's ribs. The buddy leaned over and whispered something in his partner's ear. They smiled and bumped shoulders as she walked past.

In the harsh overhead lights, she looked like a vampire queen. Or maybe the angel of death. Pure Goth. Black all over. Cape, tights, boots, nails, lips, and hair. Better than six feet. Betty Paige on steroids, she cut through the artificial air like an arrow.

A muffled groan pulled Corso's attention to the window ledge on his right, where an elderly woman stirred in her sleep, sliding her wrinkled cheek into the small puddle of drool her mouth had deposited onto the side of her plaid Samsonite suitcase.

Dougherty came to a stop at Corso's side. She looked out the window at the winter wonderland. Then turned and threw an angry gaze Corso's way. He noticed, averted his eyes, and began to survey the icy night with renewed interest.

'You enjoy your little jaunt?' he asked.

'Nothing like a jog around an airport to clear the lungs.'

He walked three steps closer to the giant pane of glass separating them from the blizzard. Put his hand to the surface for a moment. She followed him.

'It was a most informative interlude. It really was.'

Something in her tone alerted him.

'How so?' he asked.

'Well, first off, I found out we're probably not going anywhere.'

Corso eyed her. 'Since when are you the weatherman?'

'Weather person.'

'Whatever.'

'Since I met a meteorologist in the bar.'

'Oh, really.'

'Nice guy . . . named Jerry.'

'Jerry?'

'Says this weather pattern is what they call a static low-pressure inversion. Says it's got Chicago surrounded.'

'Hmmm.'

'Says the weather pattern is stalled right here over the Midwest.'

'That so?'

'Yep. According to Jerry, the storm's about a hundred miles across and not moving a muscle anytime in the foreseeable future.'

'A hundred miles, huh?'

'That's what he said.'

Corso turned and walked back to the Courtesy Desk. The woman's eyes were weary and rimmed with red. 'You're not going to be a problem, now are you, sir?'

'What kind of a problem?'

'I'm not going to have to call security, am I?'

'Why would you want to do that?'

'Because, sir, you seem to be the only one having difficulty understanding the situation.'

'I've got to get out of here.'

Her face said she didn't give a shit. 'As I've told you every fifteen minutes for the past six hours' – she shrugged, showed her palms – 'nobody is going nowhere.'

Corso opened his mouth, but the woman cut him off. 'Unless, of course, you'd like to discuss the matter with security.'

'Why do you keep bringing up security?'

'What with the terrorism and the increase in vigilance and all,' she said, nodding at the approaching soldiers, 'I'm given to understand that security checks can be quite lengthy and unpleasant these days.'

Corso heard the scratch of boots and felt the presence of the soldiers. A voice asked, 'Trouble here, Annie?'

She put on a wry smile and looked to Corso for an answer.

Corso held up both hands in surrender. 'No trouble,' he said.

She arched an ironic eyebrow at the soldiers and then turned back to Corso. 'Then what can I do for you, sir?'

'I just wanted to ask a question.'

'What question is that, sir?'

'Where's the nearest airport that's still flying?'

She set the pile of paperwork on the counter and began clicking on the keyboard. Each of her thick white nails had a different Christmas design painted on it. A Santa. A Christmas tree. A candy cane. A reindeer. And a wreath.

'Madison,' she said after a moment.

'How far away is that?'

'Coupla hundred miles,' she said.

Corso thanked her and walked back over to the window where Meg stood, gazing out at nature's carnage. The old woman on the ledge stirred again.

'Let's go,' Corso said.

'I've got a few ideas about where *you* can go,' she said, without turning his way.

He ignored the jibe. 'We'll go to Madison.'

'What's in Madison?'

'Planes that fly.'

Courteous Annie and the soldiers had formed themselves into a tight muttering knot, alternately whispering and casting furtive glances at Corso and Dougherty.

A dry, humorless laugh rolled from Meg's throat. 'A guy with your problem really should try not to attract so much attention.'

When Corso continued gazing out the window, she walked around him. Stood right in front of him, looking up at his expressionless face. 'That was a conversational gambit, Frank. You're supposed to ask me what problem it is I'm talking about.'

His face did mock surprise. 'I didn't know there was a script.'

'I didn't either . . . until about a half hour ago. There I was sitting at the bar, drinking Irish coffee and watching CNN.'

He met her glare. 'With Jerry.'

'Right there on the stool next to me. Hip to hip, as it were.' An uncomfortable silence settled in around them.

'Guess whose face is all over the news,' she said finally. He tried to look bored. 'Honey don't do the guessing thing.'

'Seems reclusive author Frank Corso's got a warrant out for his ass.'

'Really?'

'Bestselling author Frank Corso. Fugitive material witness Frank Corso.'

'Who says?'

'CNN, NBC, ABC, CBS. Pretty much the whole

alphabet soup is in agreement. All that's missing is Tommy Lee Jones and the relentless pursuit.'

'Interesting.'

He raised his eyebrows and folded his arms across his chest.

'Do I detect an issue here?'

She stepped in closer, shifted her weight from one foot to the other, and strained the words through her teeth. 'Of course I've got an issue, you asshole. You hired me under false pretenses . . . on no notice . . . saying you needed me for some more photos of the Manderson thing. Gotta have 'em . . . right away. I need to drop everything I'm doing and get my butt to the airport.'

'You're being paid for your time.'

'That's not the point, Frank,' she growled. 'The point is that I'm a professional photographer. That's what I do. You need pictures for your books, I'm happy to have the work.' She shrugged. 'You overpay me, and I let it happen. I tell myself the extra money is in deference to our former . . . more intimate relationship. But . . . I am not your keeper.' She paused for a long second. 'Remember? This is a discussion we've had lots of times before.' Corso didn't answer. She went on, her voice rising. 'So you'll have to excuse me if I'm a bit miffed when I have to find out from TV that our business trip to buttfuck Minnesota is about avoiding the law . . . and that I'm just along as camouflage.'

Corso swiveled his head, checking the nearby

seats. 'It was just going to be for a few days,' he whispered. 'Then the whole thing would be over and we could go back home and everything would be status quo.'

'A few?'

'The Grand Jury's term expires next Sunday. After that, it's all over.'

'That's nine days.' She stomped the floor. 'You thought you could drag me all over the map for nine days and not have me notice we weren't accomplishing a goddamn thing?'

Corso shrugged. 'I figured you'd last a week,' he said. 'Maybe a little less.'

She shook her head in disgust. 'I should have listened to my voice,' she said. 'The minute I got off the phone with you, I had this voice asking me how in god's name you could possibly need any more pictures from Justine, Minnesota. I was like, "Jesus, what else can that maniac want? I've got pictures of every damn thing in that one-horse town. Hell, I've got pictures of that guy what's-his-name's lungs, still connected and slung over a ceiling beam. I've got pictures of—"'

'It was just supposed to be—' he insisted.

'And your hair . . .' She poked him in the chest with a long red fingernail. 'That's why you cut off your ponytail.' She made a rude noise with her lips. 'And here I was thinking you might have finally grown up.'

'Shhhhhh.'

Her voice began to rise. 'So . . . let me see if I've got this story straight,' she began. 'You gotta excuse me, but I'm a couple of books behind.'

Corso winced. Put a finger to his lips. 'Keep it down,' he whispered.

'In that last book of yours . . .'

'*Death in Dallas.*'

'Yeah.'

'You claimed you knew where that rich guy . . . what was his name?'

'Harding Coles.'

'Yeah, Harding Coles. You claimed you knew where he buried his ex-wife's body.'

'I thought I did, yeah.'

'Thought?'

'Things have eroded.'

'Eroded how?'

'Abrams,' he began. 'A.J. Abrams. The guy who swore he knew where Harding had planted his wife.'

'Yeah?'

'He turned up missing.'

'So? Call that number you call when you really need to find somebody or something. From what I've seen, they can find anything.'

His tone suddenly got serious. 'I've told you before. For both our sakes, you need to forget all about that. That was an emergency. A onetime thing.'

'So . . . you've already tried them?'

He remained silent.

She was momentarily taken aback. 'Really. Even those guys drew a blank.'

'As it stands, I don't have a thing.'

'So make up something, share it with the Texas cops, and get this foolishness over with.'

'I can't.'

'Why not?'

'Think about it. What if they go tramping out to where I tell them to go, and come up with nothing?'

She considered the question for a moment, before pursing her lips and emitting a long low whistle. 'You really don't have a clue where that poor woman's buried, do you?'

'Nope,' Corso said. 'So . . . if I go back to Texas, I either spend six months in jail, or I make up something and end up looking like Geraldo Rivera coming out of Al Capone's basement with nothing in his hand but his dick.' She started to speak. He held up a hand. 'And when it's over, I get sued for the national debt and lose.'

'Again,' she added.

'Thanks for the reminder.'

'You should have thought of that before you started claiming you knew where the bodies were buried.'

'I was on deadline. I thought I was on my way to finding out.' He made a face. 'What can I say?'

'So all this time you've had your platoon of lawyers keeping the Texas folks at bay. Keeping you in Seattle.'

'Yeah.'

'So how in hell did things get so ugly so quick?'

'Barry called,' Corso said, naming his lawyer Barry Fine. 'Seems they're a mite pissed off down in Texas. They decided to send somebody up to get me.'

'They can do that?'

'Only if the local authorities co-operate.' He waved a hand. 'Barry said King County was co-operating with the extradition, and I better get lost until the grand jury's term expires.'

She laughed. 'Because you're such a popular figure with the King County authorities.'

'They're still pissed off about Walter Himes.'

She walked in a slow circle. 'So you decided to hide out, but you didn't want to be alone, so you decided to drag me all the way to Justine, Minnesota, on a fool's errand, where I might end up stranded' – she began to sputter – 'up to my ass in . . .'

Over Corso's shoulder, Courteous Annie and the soldiers were no longer bothering to disguise their curiosity. 'I ought to turn you in,' Dougherty said. 'I ought to march right over there and tell those soldiers who you are. There might be a reward or something.'

Corso pretended not to hear. 'We can drive to Madison and catch a red-eye.'

She gestured toward the window. 'In this?'

Corso inclined his head toward the sleeping woman, then checked the Courtesy Desk, where

13

Annie now had her eyes locked on Corso as she whispered into the phone.

'I can't spend another night here.'

As Dougherty thought it over, the old woman groaned again and turned her spit-glazed cheek toward the ceiling. Dougherty winced at the sight. 'Drive?'

'We'll get an SUV. Four-wheel drive. It'll be an adventure.'

Her eyes remained on the old woman. Unconsciously she brought her hand to the side of her face. 'I don't drool when I sleep . . . do I?'

'Buckets,' he said.

'I hate you for dragging me into this.'

'I'm sorry.'

'Well now,' she sneered, 'at least *there's* something we agree on.'

'You wanna rent the car or fetch the luggage?'

'What I want is to go back to Seattle,' she said. 'You don't need a playmate, and I don't take fugitive gigs. You're gonna have to dodge the cops on your own, Frank. I've got a life to live.'

He started to speak but changed his mind. After a moment he said in a low voice, 'Soon as we get to Madison, I'll put you on the first flight to Seattle.'

'For real? No speeches? No messy scenes in the airport?'

He held up two fingers. 'For real.'

'I still think it would serve you right if I turned your ass in.'

'The car or the bags?'

'I'll get the car,' she said.

Corso dug into his back pocket, pulled out his wallet, and extracted a credit card.

'On me,' he said.

'Damn right,' she said as she snatched it from his fingers and strode away.

CHAPTER 2

It's getting worse.'

She was right. No more fluff floating down from the dome of the sky. Now it was a torrent of ice slanting onto the metal skin of the Ford Explorer, hissing like static and rocking the big car on its springs. What had, four hours ago, been the sharp slap of windshield wipers was muted now. Despite the full-blast roar of the heater, snow had collected at the extremities of the windshield, leaving only a pair of crescents through which they could peer at the deserted freeway ahead.

'How far have we gone?' she asked.

Corso checked the odometer. 'A hundred and fifty-three miles.'

'We should have driven out of it by now.'

'Presuming your friend Jerry was right.'

She shifted in her seat and bared her teeth. 'Don't start with me, Corso. This fiasco was *your* idea, remember? As I recall . . .'

The recollection lodged in her throat as a violent gust of wind buffeted the car, throwing it out of the solitary set of tire tracks they'd been following for the past hour, sending the rear wheels skittering

16

back and forth across the icy surface. Dougherty grabbed the overhead handle.

'What was that?'

'The wind,' Corso said, as the Ford wiggled back into the ruts.

She tapped a long red fingernail on the dashboard. 'You noticed the outside temperature gauge?'

Corso flicked his eyes down to the green digital readout. What had, in Chicago, read twenty-four degrees Fahrenheit was now registering minus three.

'We should have turned around when the snowplow did,' she said, for what Corso reckoned to be the eighth time.

He grunted. As much as it pained him, she was right. For the past hour, the freeway had been deserted. Service areas closed. Snowed-over cars and trucks abandoned along the shoulders of the road. Seemed like the whole state of Illinois had decided to sit this one out in front of the fire.

'When the snowplow gives up and turns around . . . you know . . . I know this sounds crazy to you, Corso, but maybe we should have taken the hint . . . Maybe we should have showed a modicum of . . . of—'

Corso wiped the inside of the windshield with his sleeve. 'Exactly where are we?' he interrupted.

'In the middle of a goddamn blizzard is where we are.'

'I mean like on the planet,' he said. 'Where's the map?'

Dougherty was feeling around on the floor

17

beneath her seat when Corso feathered the brakes several times and brought the Ford to a halt.

Her dark eyebrows merged as she looked up at Corso.

'What?'

Corso inclined his head toward the windshield. She sat up and looked out. Whoever they'd been following for the past hour was gone. While the eastbound lanes of I-90 were a maze of ruts and tracks, the westbound lanes ahead were an unbroken ribbon of drifted snow.

'Where the hell did he go?'

'Beats me.'

'What are we gonna do?' Dougherty asked, as much to herself as to Corso.

'Depends on where we are,' he said.

She started to reach for the floor.

'I think you put it in the door thingee,' Corso said.

He watched as she retrieved the map and snapped on the overhead light. She pulled an emery board from the pocket of her cape and laid it down next to the scale indicator on the map. Using her thumb as a marker, she worked her way up their route from Chicago. 'Presuming the odometer is right, we should be somewhere along the Illinois-Wisconsin border.'

'How far would it be if we turned around and headed due east for Milwaukee?'

She took a measurement. 'About a hundred miles.'

'How far to Madison?'

18

'About half that.'

'We're down to a quarter tank of gas.'

She checked the map again. 'There should be a town named Avalon somewhere up ahead.' Corso clicked on the high beams, but the extra wattage only made visibility worse. Looked like they were inside a Christmas paperweight.

'This was really dumb.'

'We'll get off at the next exit,' Corso said. 'Spend the night in Avalon.'

'How long has it been since we passed anybody?'

'Maybe an hour,' Corso said, easing his foot off the brake, allowing the car to creep forward.

'You know why that is?' she demanded.

'No . . . but I've got a feeling you're going to enlighten me.'

'It's because we're the only people on the planet rat's-ass dumb enough to be out driving around on a night like this . . . that's why.'

Corso pressed his lips tighter and gave the Ford gas. His back ached from leaning forward, squinting into the gale. He took one hand off the wheel and used it to massage the back of his neck. The twin cones of halogen light disappeared about fifty feet in front of the car. The overhead freeway lights illuminated only themselves.

The dull thump of the wipers and the roar of the heater filled the inside of the car. Corso let go of his neck and reached for the radio.

'Pleeease.' Dougherty strained the words through her teeth. 'I don't think I could stand it.'

They rode in silence. A mile and they passed a trio of cars, snowed over and abandoned on the shoulder. Then two more cars and an abandoned bus before Dougherty pointed and said, 'Stop.'

Corso eased the Ford to a halt. Twenty yards ahead, covered with snow, a road sign rocked in the wind. Dougherty popped the door open. The interior was immediately filled with swirling snow. 'I'll be right back,' she said, slamming the door.

He watched as the wind propelled her to the snowed-over sign on the shoulder of the highway. Her cape was pressed tight around her body as she used the flat of her hand to smack the sign, sending a wall of snow slipping to the ground around her boots.

Avalon 2 miles. She used her hands to clean off several smaller signs mounted lower on the post. Blue and white symbols. Gas, food, and lodging.

Halfway back to the car, she slipped on the icy surface, teetered for a moment, and then fell in a heap. Corso jammed the Ford into Park and fumbled for the seat belt. Just as he got the belt loose, she was back on her feet and leaning into the wind with her cape flapping wildly as she trudged back to the car and climbed in.

Her eyelashes were a solid line of snow. Her lower jaw chattered as she spoke.

'Daaamn, it's c-c-c-cold out there.'

'You okay?'

When she nodded, the snow in her hair dropped into her lap.

'Let's get out of here,' she said, brushing snow down onto the floor.

'Avalon, here we come,' Corso said, easing the car forward.

She shuddered. Tried to turn up the heater but found it was already running full bore, and then sat back and refastened her seat belt.

'What's Avalon mean anyway?' she asked.

'It's a Celtic legend. Supposed to be an island in the Western Sea. A paradise where King Arthur and his knights were taken after death. Kind of like Round Table heaven.'

'There's the exit,' she said.

Corso tapped the brakes several times as they rolled down the exit ramp and skidded to a stop. 'Icy,' Corso said.

On the far side of the road, the gas, food, and lodging symbols were accompanied by a blue-and-white arrow, pointing to the right.

They both leaned forward and peered down the tree-lined road.

Dougherty rubbed at the inside of the windshield with her sleeve.

'I don't see a thing.'

'Town's probably just up around the corner,' Corso offered.

Fifty yards and, without warning, the road got steep. The Ford skidded several times as the two-lane road wound down into the valley below. Corso shifted into first gear and allowed the engine to hold the car back as they descended, and still

21

the tires fought for traction. Corso wrestled the wheel. 'Icy,' he said again.

'Town's probably down at the bottom of the hill,' she said in a low voice.

'It better be,' said Corso. ''Cause there's no way we're getting back up in this thing until the snow melts.'

'A problem we wouldn't have if you had just—'

'Give it a fucking rest, will you?' he snapped.

Suddenly her tone matched the weather. 'Is that my employer speaking? Am I being ordered to just take my imaginary photographs on demand and otherwise keep my mouth shut so as not to annoy the famous writer?'

Corso sighed. 'No . . . it's your friend Frank Corso speaking, and he's telling you that we're in this together. Maybe trying to drive to Madison wasn't the brightest idea I ever had, but we're stuck with it now . . . so we might just as well not act like . . .' Uncharacteristically, he fumbled for a word and then gave up.

'I see. You're not telling me what I can and can't say. You're just telling me to stop being such a bitch.'

Corso searched his mouth for a denial, but 'Something like that' came out.

Her face said she should have known. 'How quick they forget.'

'What's that supposed to mean?'

'Whatever you want it to.'

'Isn't this conversation just a joy to be part of on a wintry night?'

'I can remember a time when you thought so.'

'That was then.' He took a hand off the steering wheel. 'We were . . . you know . . . then.' Waved it. 'You know what I mean. It was different then.'

She put on her astonished face. 'I most certainly don't know any such thing. Why doesn't the famous on-the-lam crime writer enlighten me.'

'When you're . . . you know . . .'

'Doing the nasty.'

'Yeah.'

'Go on.'

'When you're . . . you know . . . involved like that . . . the rules are different. You put up with a little more shit than you otherwise might.'

She sat in silence for a moment and then emitted a dry laugh. 'So what you're saying is that when you're getting laid, you'll listen to a lot more bullshit than you will when you're not.'

He thought it over. 'Makes complete sense to me,' he said finally.

She looked at him for a long moment. 'Amazing,' she said. 'Guys are absolutely amazing.' When he didn't respond, she folded her arms across her chest, sat back in the seat, and said, 'You'll be sure to let me know when I'm allowed to speak again, won't you?'

The muscles along the side of Corso's jaw tightened. Ahead, a bright yellow sign announced a 20 percent grade. Corso worked the brakes. Gritting his teeth as the Ford slid around a corner, Corso turned his head toward Dougherty.

She sat stiffly in the seat, staring through the windshield, wearing her most disinterested gaze.

'Why don't we just . . .' he began.

He watched as her eyes opened wide. 'Corso!' she bellowed.

He snapped his eyes back to the road. It took a moment before his brain was able to register and categorize what his eyes were seeing.

Ahead, a snow-encrusted pickup truck lay on its side, blocking both lanes, passenger door open and pointing at the sky. When he tapped the brakes, the Ford surrendered the last of its traction and began to accelerate down the steep incline.

'Do something!' Dougherty screamed as the hill pulled them faster and faster toward the wreck. Corso stood on the brakes, but the Ford was out of control now, gaining speed, turning a lazy circle before plowing headfirst into the wreck.

Inside the Ford, Dougherty's face was a mask of fear. The last image she processed was the bottom half of Corso's face covered with blood. And then the Ford began to pinwheel along the undercarriage of the pickup truck, the scream of tearing metal filling the air, in the instant before they bounced over the guardrail and became airborne.

CHAPTER 3

'Corso . . . damn it . . . get off me.'

She grunted as she tried to push him off, but Corso's unconscious bulk remained welded to her left shoulder. The scratch of the wipers was slower now, the heater a mere whisper at her feet. Her right ear, pressed against the window, was beginning to freeze. She grabbed him by the ears, lifted his head, and looked into his face. His nose was squashed nearly flat. In the eerie moonlight, the twin rivulets of blood running down over his lips and chin shone obsidian black. Using his ears as handles, she gently shook his head. Called his name. Nothing. She shook him again, and he coughed. Groaned. Suddenly his eyes fluttered, rolled several times in his head, and then popped open. He moved a shoulder and brought a tentative hand to his face. She watched as he blinked several times, trying to focus on his bloodied fingers.

'Corso,' she said again. He looked her way with nothing in his eyes. 'I think you busted your nose,' she said.

His lips blew bubbles in the blood as he touched his face and winced.

25

'Nose.' He said it as if he'd never before heard the word.

Without warning, the car began to slide, the sickening sound of ripping metal again filling the air. A silent scream stalled in her lungs as the Ford slid downward, bouncing twice before coming to rest again. From the corner of her eye, Dougherty could make out the rough bark of a tree pressed against the passenger window. 'We gotta get out of here,' she said. Corso was still staring dumbly at his hand. 'Come on, Corso . . . move.' He blinked, trying to clear his vision, and then rolled his shoulders to the left, easing his weight from Dougherty as he grabbed the steering wheel and pulled himself upright in the seat.

She grunted as he knelt on her side and groped for the door handle. She heard the click of the lock. Watched as he tried to push the door straight up and failed. Then tried again, without budging the door from the twisted frame. Blood from his nose dripped like red rain onto her shoulder as he eased himself higher, found the button for the window and pulled it downward. The window squeaked but didn't move.

He banged the window with the flat of his hand and the car began to spin on its axis. They lay perfectly still until it seemed the car had finished moving, and then Corso tried the button again. This time, with a sorrowful groan, the window began to ease open. Slowly, as the dashboard lights dimmed and the wipers slowed to a crawl, the window began to slide down into the door.

Powdery snow swirled into the car's interior. The remnants of the heater output and the collected warmth of their bodies instantly disappeared, replaced by an icy, bone-numbing cold. Corso pulled a knee to his chest, got one foot on the steering wheel, and levered himself up through the window.

Relieved of Corso's weight, Dougherty reached over, grabbed the steering wheel, and began to pull herself sideways in the seat until first her knees were on the inside of the passenger door and then higher until her boots made contact and she could push herself to her feet.

She stood on the door, her toes resting on the armrest. Above her head the open window gaped, velvet black. 'Corso,' she cried. She waited. Nothing. And for an instant she felt the fear rise in her chest. Had he fallen and gone skittering down the hill into the ravine below? Had he, in his stupor, simply wandered off and forgotten her? Again she hurled his name into the darkness. And again his name was swallowed by the storm. The snow stung her cheeks as she sniffed back a tear and mustered her strength. And then suddenly she felt the car move, and the black void above her head was filled with Corso.

He'd stemmed the flow of blood by packing his nose with snow. He stuck his arms into the car and grabbed her roughly by the shoulders. On countless afternoons she'd watched the rippling of his thick muscles as he'd worked on the boat. On countless nights she'd reveled in the controlled power of his embrace as they'd made love in the dark cabin below. She knew he was strong, but nothing like this. He groped around until he had his hands under her arms and then plucked her from the car as if she were a child.

Next thing she knew, she was sitting on the side of the Ford. Snow and her hair swirled around her head, obscuring her vision. She shuddered, pulled her cape tightly around her shoulders, and looked around.

The Ford was lodged against a tree, about fifty feet down the incline. The muted purple glow of a streetlight was visible above. Below, the incline seemed to steepen before disappearing altogether into blackness. Above the roar of the storm, she could hear Corso breathing raggedly through his mouth. He reached over and took her hand.

'Let's go' was all he said, before stepping off the car onto the hillside, dragging her along in his wake as he struggled up the hill, using bushes and trees to pull them upward toward the light. Halfway to the top, he fell heavily to his knees and began to slide back toward her. It seemed, for a moment, they might slip backward into the void below, but he dug in with his feet, stopped his slide, and then began crawling upward, until he disappeared over the guardrail, where he again turned back and reached for her. She gasped as he ran his rough hands over her breasts, feeling around until he found her upper arms and lifted her to his side. 'Jesus, Corso . . .' She waggled her shoulders and brushed at herself. 'If you wanted a feel, all you had to do was ask.'

'I'm blind,' Corso rasped.

'What?'

'My vision's all screwed up. It's like I'm cross-eyed or something.'

Before she could reply, the sound of breaking glass rose above the roar of the storm. They stood on the snow-covered road, wincing as they listened to the Ford bouncing off trees and boulders as it made its way toward the black silence at the bottom of the ravine.

Shaking in the cold, Dougherty reached over and fastened the five buttons on Corso's overcoat. 'We've gotta find shelter,' she said. 'We're not gonna last very long out here.'

'Down,' Corso said. 'We keep going down.'

His words seemed to anger the storm. Above their heads, the trees swayed like frenzied dancers. The snow seemed to thicken, nearly obscuring the over-turned pickup truck forty yards away. She poked a hand out from inside her cape and took him by the sleeve. He pawed at his face, trying to clear his vision, shook his head twice, and then followed her down the slope toward the ghost truck.

They skirted the wreck on the high side. The undercarriage was a solid layer of dirty ice. The open door rocked slightly in the wind. She pulled Corso around the front, bent, and wiped the snow from the windshield with her bare hand. The truck's windshield was completely iced over from the inside. No way of telling if anyone was there. 'I can't see anything,' she shouted above the locomotive wind.

Corso pulled her back the way they'd come. He groped around on the undercarriage with his hands and then stepped back a pace and kicked at the ice. Four times, until a block of dirty ice fell on his boots, revealing a rusting muffler and exhaust pipe. Corso let go of her hand. He grabbed the open doorframe, put his right foot on the exhaust pipe, and pulled himself upward until he could look down into the cab.

He blinked and rubbed at his eyes, trying to put his kaleidoscopic vision back together. An old man lay at the bottom of the cab, squashed against the window. Stone dead. Frozen white and partially covered with snow. Corso levered himself upward, resting his belly on the doorframe. He used his right hand to brush at the frozen driver, as if removing the snow would somehow bring him back to life. He could hear Dougherty's voice chattering with cold as she called his name, asking what was inside.

Corso began to pull himself from the cab when he noticed the odd angle of the dead man's right arm. Held upward and away from his body. He brushed away the snow covering the hand and arm. His breath froze in his throat. The old man had spent his last moments trying to warm himself with a yellow Bic lighter, which now lay frozen in his stiff dead fingers. A voice deep in Corso's head wondered if such an ignominious and futile gesture might not be a fitting metaphor for life. Candle in the wind and all that. And then, for reasons he couldn't explain, Corso reached for the lighter. The old man held it fast in his icy death grip. Bringing his other hand into the cab, Corso prised the corpse's fingers back one by one. The frozen fingers unfurled with a sound like crackling cellophane, until the lighter dropped into Corso's palm.

Corso wiggled himself from the cab, found footing on the undercarriage, and then dropped silently to the ground. Dougherty stood, hopping from foot to foot, pushing buttons on her cell phone. Her hair was completely covered with snow.

'No service,' she shouted.

'There's an old guy inside. Frozen solid.'

She pocketed the phone. 'That's whaaat weee're gonna be if weee don't get out of heeere.'

As if to give her comfort, Corso offered the ice-covered lighter. She grimaced.

'Jesus, Corso,' she said. 'You must have busted something loose in your head. What goddamn good is that gonna do? Come on.' She snatched the lighter from his hand and began pulling him down the hill.

After a quarter-mile and three hairpin turns, the road began to level. They walked shoulder to shoulder, shuddering together in the arctic wind. Half a mile more and they were on the flat, stumbling along beneath an arched cathedral of bare trees, when Dougherty began to falter, to stagger slightly, and finally dropped to her knees in the snow. She looked up at Corso. 'My legs,' she stammered. 'I can't feel them anymore.'

Corso picked her up and set her on her feet again. 'You gotta keep walking,' he said. She nodded. Took a single step forward and pitched face-first into the snow.

Corso dropped to one knee, scooped her into his arms, and then struggled back to his feet. Holding her in his arms, he began to trudge forward, one slow step at a time, weaving from shoulder to shoulder as he made his way down the narrow road.

Dougherty went inside of herself. To the place where the rest of the universe didn't exist. The world where the voice in her head was the only sound and the pictures the voice painted were the whole of creation.

She kept imagining the old man in the truck. Wondering how long he'd held out hope. Whether he'd finally had a moment where he knew he was going to die. Had he taken that last instant to bark out his defiance to the universe? Or had he gone meekly into the frozen reaches of the night? She wondered about hope. About how it was the only evil left in the box after that silly girl removed the lid. She was wondering about how hope had risen from final evil to state of grace when another sound began to intrude.

'Can you see it?' the voice said. 'The purple light? Over there.'

A hand pushed her chin to the left. 'See it?'

'It's a house,' she said. 'Put me down. You can make it. Get the people. Come back for me.'

Instead he boosted her upward with his knee and again began staggering forward down the road. His ragged, frozen breath burst out before him as he fought his way forward. They were at the driveway now. All she could see was a single light and the shape of a house through the swirling snow and ice.

'Put me down. Go get the people,' she was pleading, but instead he lifted her higher and began to trudge through the knee-deep snow of the driveway. Every step was an exercise in agony. She was beating his chest and screaming. Crying. 'Oh, god, Corso,' she was yelling. 'You gotta put me down. Something's broken inside your head. You're bleeding to death through your nose. Please. I can make it on my own. Really I can. We gotta stop the bleeding. Please, Corso, please.'

Corso was making a noise now. A low keening sound, almost a chant, as he forced himself forward, his puzzle-picture vision growing dimmer and dimmer, the pleading voice fading to silence as he moved onward. Then he stumbled and fell forward, pitching her out onto something hard.

33

CHAPTER 4

First time Corso opened his eyes, all he could see were flames dancing across a stained ceiling. The only sound to reach his ears was the groan and crackle of the fire. Unable to raise his head, he experienced a moment of doubt, wondering if perhaps he hadn't died and gone to hell. He was still pondering this possibility and trying to move his extremities when the ebony wings folded around him and again the world turned black.

Second time he opened his eyes, dawn had begun to trickle in the side windows. He was able to raise his head far enough to prop it with his hand. His head felt as if someone were driving a sixteen-penny nail between his eyes, with measured rhythmic strokes, driving the point deeper and deeper into his brain. He was unable to breathe through his nose but remembered where he was. The old house with the No Trespassing sign tacked onto the door with roofing nails. Deserted. Front windows boarded over. He recalled Dougherty kicking in the door. Recalled her half dragging, half carrying him inside. And then lying there on

34

the frozen floor and the candle in the darkness. The single flickering flame and the empty room. And then closing his eyes to make the hammering in his head go away. And then . . .

The third time he opened his eyes, he sat straight up and winced as a brain-tumor headache nearly threw him back to the floor. The fallen snow reflected halogen-bright through the side windows, and then he remembered it all. How Dougherty saved his life. He looked around. She lay at the other end of the fireplace, huddled in a heap beneath her cape. He remembered how she'd used the lighter he'd found to make her way through the deserted house looking for something to burn. How she'd found long empty drawers in the kitchen still lined with fancy paper. How she'd leaned the drawers up against the hearth and stomped them to splinters with her boots. He could see the violent shaking of her hands as she lit the crumpled paper and waited for the splinters to catch fire. And then the larger pieces of the drawers and then the kitchen cabinet doors, and then it started to get warm. And how he'd tried to get up but couldn't and her soothing voice telling him to stay on the floor. How they were going to be all right. After that, things got spotty.

The fire was now reduced to a glowing bed of ash. One segment at a time, Corso levered himself from the floor, until he stood unsteadily on his feet. The air was warmer at the top of the room. His head reeled, and for a moment he thought he might pass out and crumple back onto the cold boards. Unsteady, he staggered over and put a hand on the brick fireplace. To the right of the fireplace opening, several thick brown boards lay stacked and ready, their ends splintered and spiked.

Moving slowly, Corso pulled back the rusted screen and piled the remaining boards onto the glowing embers in a crisscross pattern. For a moment nothing happened, and Corso feared he had smothered the fire. The new material did nothing but smoke and hiss. Then the thick, dusty smoke began to swirl up the chimney and, after an anxious moment, a single yellow flame poked its head from among the boards. A couple of crackles and, with a whoosh, everything caught fire at once. Corso closed the screen.

At his feet, Dougherty stirred but did not waken. Using the wall to steady himself, Corso made his way around the corner into the kitchen, where it was noticeably colder. His breath swirled about his head as he looked around. She'd burned everything that could be torn loose and fed to the fire. All that remained was the frame of what had once been a modest set of kitchen drawers and cabinets along the north wall.

Sliding his hand along the countertop, he crossed the kitchen to the back door. His reflection in the wavy glass upper panel of the door stopped him in his tracks. He didn't recognize the face that peered back at him. A seeping green bruise ran completely across his forehead like a bloody head-band. His eyes were blackened and nearly swollen shut. Everything below his nose was a solid sheet of thick coagulated blood. He pawed at his nose and was rewarded with a jolt of pain. He rested his forearms on the countertop and bowed his head, breathing deeply, somewhere between sleep and wakefulness, until a voice from the other room startled him. 'Corso,' it called.

He had to clear his throat three times before he could rasp, 'In here.'

'You need to lie down.'

'I'm okay,' he said.

'You're nowhere in the vicinity of okay,' she insisted.

As if to prove her wrong, Corso pushed himself off the countertop and staggered back into the front room. She was kneeling on the floor with pain in her eyes, rocking slightly, as if the repetitive movement might somehow distract her from her suffering. Corso sat on the hearth, bringing his face close to hers. 'You okay?' he asked.

She nodded, without meaning it. 'Except for my hands,' she said, bringing them out from under the folds of her cape. Her hands looked like they'd been boiled. Swollen and red, they seemed to have a life of their own. 'I froze them last night. They burn like hell.'

'Keep them warm' was all Corso could think to say.

'You should see yourself,' she said through her

teeth as she slipped her hands back under the cape.

'I have.'

She started to get up, but Corso put a firm hand on her shoulder.

'You saved my ass,' he said.

She tried to elbow his hand from her shoulder, but he held firm. 'You gotta lay down, Corso. You got something busted up in your head. For a while there I was afraid you were gonna bleed to death on me.'

'You saved me,' he said again.

'We saved each other's asses,' she said. 'You carried me half a mile through a blizzard.' She winced at the memory. 'Craziest damn thing I ever saw. All I did was start a fire and keep it going.'

As if on signal, the fire in the hearth collapsed upon itself with a rush of sparks. 'Where'd you get the boards?' Corso asked.

'There's a barn outside.' She shrugged her shoulders. 'There was nothing left in here to burn, so I decided to try out there. I fell through the floor. That's when I froze my hands. Ripping up the old floorboards and dragging them inside.'

Corso got to his feet. 'We gotta keep the fire going. That's how somebody's gonna find us.'

Dougherty began to protest and get to her feet.

'Stay still,' Corso said. 'I'm a little fuzzy, but I'm okay.'

He brought one hand to the top of his head, as if to keep it in place, and then eased across the room and pulled open the door. The bright white reduced his eyes to slits. He stood in the doorway gulping the frigid air. The storm had passed, leaving behind a wind-whipped blanket of white reaching nearly to the tops of the fence posts lining the driveway. He stepped out onto the porch and drew the door closed. His shoulders shuddered inside his coat. He rubbed his hands together.

For as far as the eye could see, the only marks on the surface of the snow were a ragged trail of footsteps leading to a leaning barn thirty yards north of the house. He walked slowly, lifting his knees high, trying not to jostle his head. Above him, boxcar clouds raced across a bright blue sky. The air twinkled with wind-blown snow crystals.

It was more of a shed than a barn. No more than a dozen feet across. Listing heavily to starboard. A rusted split rim and a broken rake hung from the right-hand wall.

She'd burned almost half the floor. Corso stepped inside and grabbed the broken end of one of the boards. The rotting wood crumbled in his hand as he forced it upward, prised it loose from its ancient nails, and then tossed it out into the trampled snow.

Wasn't until he tried to kick the nearest full board loose that he realized the other half of the floor was newer. No dry rot here. Just solid lumber nailed on two-foot centers along its length.

Corso stepped carefully over the exposed floor joists, reached up over his head, and grabbed the rusted split rim hanging from the wall. Heavier than he'd imagined, the rim fell nearly to his knees before his muscles stopped its descent. A thick layer of rust crumbled in his hands as he retraced his steps. With a grunt he raised the rim above his head and brought it down on the nearest board. The board broke in two. Corso stepped to his right, repeating the process as he moved along, breaking the wood into two-foot lengths. By the time he'd worked his way to the rear of the building and back, his head was reeling and he thought for a moment he might pass out. His nose had begun to bleed again, sending an intermittent drizzle of blood down onto his shoes.

He dropped the rim to the floor and was bent at the waist, waiting for his vision to clear, when he first heard the sound. An engine. The blat of a diesel maybe.

Carefully he picked his way across the maze of broken floor and made his way outside. Shading his eyes from the glare, he scanned the horizon. Nothing. He stood still and listened, but the sound did not repeat itself.

After several moments he heaved a sigh, stepped back inside the shed, and continued tearing up the shattered pieces of wood, throwing them outside onto the pile. While the far side of the floor had covered nothing but dirt, this side was lined with black plastic.

As he worked his way toward the front of the shed, he began to realize that the black plastic was

40

not a single sheet of material but instead a large folded package held together by long lengths of silver duct tape.

Curious now, he used the flat of his hand to press down on the upper layer. Beneath the black, something brittle shifted with a dry clack. Instinctively Corso pulled his hand back and peered into his rust-covered palm. Then he heard the noise again.

This time he was positive. The sound of a diesel engine at work sent him hurrying back outside. Out on the road, a bright yellow road grader sent a black plume into the sky as it moved along, pushing the snow before it.

Corso began to wave his arms, trying to catch the driver's attention. A full minute of frenzied waving sent Corso to his knees in the snow, where he hung his head and watched the snow turn red, drop by drop. And then the blat of the horn, and when he looked up, one of the side windows of the road grader was open and a hand was waving.

He stayed on his knees as the huge machine backed up, turned its front wheels, and started down the driveway toward him. Above the roar of the machine, he heard Dougherty's voice cry, 'Yahoo!' He looked to his right. She was standing in the open doorway. She opened her mouth to speak, but by then Corso was already back inside the shed, finding the end of the duct tape and peeling it off. The pieces of plastic began to separate on their own. Corso reached down and yanked the top of the plastic apart.

The sight sent him reeling backward, tripping over one of the floor joists and falling heavily to the dirt. The roar of the diesel was closer now. Dougherty was shouting something into the wind. He climbed to his feet. His head throbbed as he shuffled back across the floor. He peeked. Quickly. Out of the corner of his eye. As if he might turn to stone. There it was. The ivory grin. The tufts of brown hair still stuck to the skull. The empty eye sockets staring back at him. He brought a hand to his mouth and turned away as his stomach turned over.

He moved carefully, making his way outside. The machine was right in his face now, idling as the driver popped open the door and began to climb down. He was a round-faced little guy wearing orange thermal coveralls and a red plaid hat with earflaps. One look at Corso stopped his descent. His satchel face folded itself into a frown, and then, without a word, he climbed back into his seat. He stuck his head out the side window. 'You don't look so good, buddy,' he yelled. Corso nodded his agreement. 'I'll send an aid car right out,' the driver promised. 'You just take it easy till they get here.'

As Corso made his way over to the driver's window, he heard the lock click on the inside of the door. He looked up at the driver's gray stubbled face. 'Better send the cops too,' he shouted. 'There's something in the shed they ought to see.'

42

CHAPTER 5

P lace has been deserted for the better part of fifteen years,' the sheriff said. 'Ever since Eldred Holmes packed up his wife and kids and moved on.' She thought it over. 'Back in the mid-eighties sometime. I can't for the life of me remember where it was they were supposed to be moving to.' She looked back over her shoulder at the shed, which was now surrounded by yellow police tape and half a dozen deputies. 'Doesn't look like they got wherever they were going, though.'

'You think that's them in there?' Corso asked.

She shrugged. 'I peeked in and poked around a little before we sealed it off.' She looked down at Corso. 'We don't have our own lab or technicians. We've gotta wait for the state boys to show up. But the fake dental work looks a lot like Eldred Holmes to me.' Before Corso could ask the obvious question, she went on. 'When we were kids, he used to scare the heck out of all the other kids. Had this big old set of snaggle teeth stuck out from his lips. Then, later on, he got 'em fixed. Had 'em pulled and a bridge put in. I know because he pulled it out and showed it to me once. Right in the middle of Royals Drugstore.' She jerked a thumb back over her shoulder. 'Looked a lot like the one in the mouth of that skull in there.'

Thirty yards away, two teams of emergency medical technicians emerged from the house, carrying Dougherty on a gurney. Her hands were wrapped like a boxer's. The gurney's wheels were unable to negotiate the snow, so they had to carry her toward the rear of the waiting aid car. She waved a pillowed hand at Corso. He waved back, as they folded the aluminum legs and slid her into the ambulance.

A black Lincoln Town Car nosed into the far end of the driveway. A plume of exhaust settled over the back half of the car like a cloak. The door opened. A thickset man in a black overcoat stepped out of the car and began to make his way gingerly toward the house. The sheriff shaded her eyes with her hand.

Two-thirds of the way down the driveway, he spotted the sheriff and began to veer in her direction. She muttered something under her breath as he approached, but Corso couldn't catch the words.

He was a blunt-featured man somewhere in his sixties. His eyebrows were grown out and curly, while his mustache was neatly trimmed. The overall effect lent him a somewhat scholarly quality. 'Judge,' the sheriff said, without offering her hand.

44

'What do we have here, Sheriff?' he demanded.

'We've got some bones buried under the floor of the shed, Your Honor.'

Before he could ask another question, she said, 'That's all we know right now, Judge Powell. We're waiting on the state boys to get a forensics team here.'

The judge set his jaw like a bass and started for the shed. The sheriff barred the way with her arm. He looked down at her arm with a mixture of anger and disdain.

'Don't you dare—' he began.

She met his irate glare. 'We've got an active investigation going on here, Judge.' She motioned toward the yellow tape surrounding the general area of the shed. 'I've got it sealed off,' she said. 'State Patrol hates it when they get a contaminated crime scene. Gets 'em thinking we're a bunch of hicks.' She dropped her arm. 'I'm gonna need to keep everybody out until they get here.'

His lower lip quivered as he swallowed whatever he'd intended to say next. Instead he took a deep breath and expelled the air through his nose in a pair of locomotive plumes. 'You'll keep me posted,' he said. It wasn't a question.

'Of course,' she said.

He shot Corso a look and then went back to glaring at the sheriff.

'I'll be in my office,' the judge said. 'I'll expect to hear from you before the end of the day.'

45

'The timelines are not under my control, Your Honor,' she said. 'The state boys will—'

He cut her off. 'By the end of the day,' he repeated, before turning on his heel and marching off. She stood silently, watching him make his way back to the car. Followed the big black car with her eyes until it was out of sight. Sighed.

'Richardson,' she called.

Across the trampled expanse of snow, a tall guy in a matching brown uniform turned toward the voice. Instead of the warm flaps-down model the sheriff was wearing, Richardson wore one of those state trooper military model hats with the leather strap so tight around his chin it was a wonder he could speak. His ears were as red as signal flags.

'Yes, sir,' he barked.

She cupped her hands around her mouth. 'We gotta get these aid cars outta here. Clear the driveway.' She pointed to a white van with a satellite dish on the roof. 'Start with those media types. Get 'em outta here.'

'Public's got a right to know,' Richardson yelled.

'Which is why he called them?' she said under her breath.

She crooked a finger. Richardson marched over and stood stiffly at attention, staring out over the sheriff's head. She stepped in close, speaking to the point of his collar. 'First you get them the hell out of here. Then later we'll talk about you calling them.'

He stiffened. 'The right of the public to have free access—' he began to recite.

'Shut up,' she said through her teeth. 'The rights of those poor people in the barn are what concerns me. However it was they came to be there . . . they have a right to some respect. They have a right to be treated with dignity.' Richardson's thousand-yard stare never wavered as the sheriff continued. 'What if they were people you knew? What if they were members of your family?' She patted him heavily on the shoulder and said, 'Try to weigh that kind of thing against your great desire to be on television.' She patted him again, a little harder this time. 'Who knows . . . maybe your better side will emerge.' Before he could respond, she went on. 'Get the driveway clear. Remind the media types that there's no parking on Hawthorne Road . . . especially in a snow emergency like this. If they park that damn van there, call Bob Sowers and have them towed. Once the aid cars leave, we can bring the rest of the cruisers back in.'

'Yes, sir,' he barked again, before turning on his heel and marching off into the melee. The sheriff sighed heavily as she watched him go and then shifted her gaze down to Corso, who lay strapped to a gurney at the rear of an orange and white aid car. The top third of his head was bandaged like the Mummy. His nose was packed with gauze.

She shook her head sadly. 'The "sir" stuff is

Richardson's way of reminding me that he doesn't think sheriff is a job for a woman,' she said. 'He ran against me last November. I beat him by thirty-seven votes. He's gonna run again next year, so he's trying to get himself on TV as much as possible.' She sighed again. 'Probably gonna win too.' She grinned down at Corso. 'Gulf War hero, you know.'

She was middle-aged, black hair, brown at the roots, crammed up under her winter hat. She could have been fat or she could have been slim – at that moment she was wearing too many layers of clothing to tell. The crinkles at the corners of her blue eyes put her somewhere in her late forties.

She read Corso's mind. 'I didn't hire him, so I can't fire him,' she said. 'His father's the chairman of the City Council. Clint Richardson's the one who talked the council into making me take his kid on as deputy sheriff. Said I wasn't making a strong enough impression in the community. Needed some new blood.'

Corso watched as the doors on the other aid car were closed. One guy stayed inside. The other three started Corso's way. The last police cruiser was backing out of the driveway. 'Done nothing but fight me on everything,' she said. 'Won't even wear a proper hat, for pity's sake.'

'They're his ears,' Corso offered.

'Wanted to carry a forty-caliber, and when I wouldn't let him, he started loading his own thirty-eights with enough powder to either blow his hand off or kill somebody in the house next door.' She shook her head. 'He just don't get it.'

The sheriff put a hand on Corso's shoulder. He turned his head in her direction. 'Speaking of not getting it, Mr Corso . . . you want to tell me what a world-famous writer and his photographer friend were doing driving around on a night like last night?' Corso shrugged. She leaned in closer. 'Ole Swanson dead in his truck I can understand. Since his missus died last spring, Ole's been getting so drunk every night it was just a matter of time before he did something stupid and ended up dead. But you, Mr Corso, if you don't mind me saying . . . you really ought to know better.'

Because his eyes were incapable of keeping up with the movement of his head, Corso averted them slowly. He watched as one of the trio of EMTs slipped and fell heavily in the snow. Watched as his buddies helped him to his feet, dusted him off, and then pulled him Corso's way. Corso could feel her gaze on the side of his head.

'I guess I was looking for something,' he said.

'What was that?'

'A free lunch.'

The sheriff whistled under her breath. 'A costly commodity.'

'Apparently so,' he said.

The EMTs checked that his straps were tight and then lifted him into the back of the ambulance. The sheriff stood in the doorway as they buttoned the gurney down.

'You think the whole family's in there?' Corso asked.

'I didn't want to touch anything,' the sheriff said. 'But if you ask me, there was more than one set of remains in that bundle.'

'Yeah,' he said as the doors swung shut.

It's hard to know Jesus. No matter how I try to keep his picture in my mind, the face just leaks out my ears like sand. I think it's 'cause I've got all these other pictures in there. Things that happened to me . . . here in my life. Not to somebody else a way long time ago. I can stare at the picture of Jesus in Papa's Bible . . . the one with him standing on a cloud with all this white light coming out from him like he's the sun or something. I can look at it for an hour, and the minute I stop, all I can see are Billy Cameron's eyes, and that pink party dress Brittany Armstrong wore to the last day of school . . . and my hair . . . my hair . . . all scattered and lying there. Mama says that's why those nun ladies wear those black things and lock themselves all up together in musty buildings. So's they can keep their minds empty. So's they can make room for Jesus.

CHAPTER 6

The television image flickered, but Richardson's voice came through loud and clear. Beneath the talking head and the bank of microphones, they kept flashing the words *Deputy Sheriff Cole Richardson*. Live from downstairs in the hospital lobby. Back over his shoulder, the guy who showed up at the Holmes place – Judge Powell – stood shoulder to shoulder with a tall man who looked a lot like Deputy Richardson. His city councilman father, Corso guessed. Although Richardson didn't come right out and say it, the message was that if he had been sheriff for the past seventeen years, those poor people in the shed wouldn't have been lying around out there all this time.

Someone rapped on the door. Corso clicked off the TV and told whoever it was to come in. The kid's yellow nylon jacket was so bright it made Corso squint. HERTZ. Big black letters across the front. Cursive *Craig* embroidered up higher on his chest.

'Uh . . . Mr Corso,' he stammered as he pushed a clipboard toward the bed, 'if you wouldn't mind signing right here.'

Corso marked his place in his journal and used his pen to sign on the dotted line. The kid tore off the top copy of the rental agreement and handed it to Corso. From his right-hand jacket pocket he produced a set of keys. Corso nodded toward the end table. The kid took the hint, placing the keys next to the water pitcher.

He walked to the window and looked down into the parking lot. 'Hunter green Expedition. Right down there,' he said. 'Next to the white Buick.' He turned back toward Corso. 'Plate number's on the keys.'

Corso nodded his thanks and picked up his journal. The kid began to leave the room. From the rear, it was obvious he had something tucked beneath his arm.

'What's that you've got there?' Corso asked.

The kid stopped walking. Checked everywhere except under his arm.

'Under your arm,' Corso said.

The kid looked like he was surprised to find a book tucked away in his armpit.

'Oh,' he said. 'It's . . . ah . . .' He pulled the book out and glanced at the cover. 'I've read all your books, Mr Corso.' He held out a copy of *Missing Lync*, Corso's second book. '*Lync* is my favorite,' the kid blurted.

'And you want me to sign it?'

'If you . . . I mean . . . I brought it, but then it didn't seem . . .'

'No problem,' Corso said quickly. 'Give it here.'

Corso set the book on the bed and retrieved his pen from his journal. 'Can I personalize it?'

The kid looked bewildered. 'Excuse me?'

'You want me to put your name in it?' Corso asked.

The young face brightened up. 'If it wouldn't be too much—'

'That's Craig with a C?'

The kid covered the embroidered name with his hand. 'Oh, no,' he said. 'I'm Michael. I borrowed the jacket . . . from . . . mine had a . . .'

Corso scribbled in the book and held it out. 'Here you go, Michael.'

Michael used two hands to hold the book against his chest. 'Thank you,' he said, backing toward the door. 'If there's anything else we can . . . Hertz is always . . .'

'You've already gone beyond the call of duty,' Corso assured him.

The kid's expression said he thought so too. He nodded and smiled his way back into the hall. The door silently closed behind him. Then opened again. The kid stuck his spiky head back in the door. 'Er . . . Mr Corso, sir . . . my supervisor . . . Craig Mason . . . he wanted me to ask you if maybe you couldn't be' – he winced – 'you know . . . be a little . . . a little . . .'

'He wants me to try and not crash this one.'

'Something like that. Yes, sir.'

'Tell him I'll do the best I can.'

The door had only been closed for a moment

when the sheriff pushed her way into the room, followed by a pair of cowboys in matching beige suits. Each man held a dark brown stocking cap in one hand and a Stetson hat in the other. The sheriff made a rueful face. 'Mr Corso, these gentlemen are from the Dallas County Sheriff's Office. This is Officer Duckett,' she said, indicating the older of the two, a slitty-eyed specimen who looked like he'd spent a lot of time squinting out over the prairie. 'And Officer Caruth,' who was under thirty, wide-eyed, and looked like this was as far from home as he'd ever been. 'As soon as the doctors say it's all right for you to travel, these gentlemen are here to take you back to Texas. On a material-witness warrant.'

Corso went back to writing. Somebody cleared their throat. 'Well then . . .' the sheriff stammered. 'I'll let you gentlemen know when Mr Corso here's cleared for takeoff.' The cowboys issued a couple of thank-yous and reluctantly shuffled from the room. Once they were gone, Sheriff Trask stood for a moment, hands on hips, breathing deeply, looking around the walls. 'What's with them and those hats?' she asked finally. 'You'd think they'd leave the damn things back in the motel room instead of carrying them around with 'em all day.'

'It's a Texas thing,' Corso offered. 'You gotta spend some time there to understand.'

She shook her head and grinned. 'You want the bad news, the worse news, or the worst yet news?' she asked affably.

'You mean . . . other than the cavalry there.'

'Yeah.'

He finished writing a sentence and then looked up again. 'Let's start with the bad. That way I'll have something to look forward to.'

'You've drawn quite a crowd, Mr Corso. We got every damn news agency in the world down in the lobby, wanting to talk to you' – she waved a disgusted hand – '. . . or me, or anybody else they can get to say anything at all. It's taking every deputy I own just to keep them pinned downstairs.' She gestured toward the TV. 'Don't matter what channel. Turn it on and there's some old picture of you and they're running on about your troubles with the *New York Times* and all that. If it isn't you, it's me or the state boys tellin' 'em we got no comment. That's how the Dallas boys got a line on you.' She used her right hand to massage the back of her neck. 'Or worst of all, it's Richardson running his mouth about how Eldred and Sissy have been lying out there for all these years right under my nose and how I never even had a clue.'

'I watched a little of it earlier.'

'He's digging my grave, Mr Corso.'

'He's sure as hell setting you up to fail. All that stuff about having a dramatic announcement for the press in the next few days is just an invitation for a retraction, if you ask me.'

Corso watched as her eyes turned inward. She was silent for a moment. When she spoke it seemed as if her words had been rehearsed. 'I'm too damn

56

old to start over,' she said. 'Richardson beats me in November . . . I mean . . . what in hell am I gonna do? Apply down at the Burger King? See if maybe I can't get on with the Parks Department? Being sheriff is all I know. I just can't see myself—'

She caught herself. Stopped. Brought a hand to her mouth and walked around in a tight circle. 'I've also got a pair of Wisconsin state troopers who want to ask you a few questions about finding the bodies.'

Corso lifted his hands from the sheet and then let them fall.

'I've got nothing to hide,' he said.

She nodded. 'And then there's your friend Ms Dougherty.'

'What about her?'

'Seems she's got some pretty graphic images tattooed all over her.'

Corso's eyes narrowed. His tone was brittle. 'How's that a problem for *you*?'

'Nobody in these parts has ever seen anything like that before. The only way I could keep medical staff from making up reasons to go in her room for a peek was to post a guard on the door. That puts me an extra officer down.' She cast a glance Corso's way, started to say something, and then stopped. He read her thoughts.

'Somebody did it to her,' he said.

'You mean . . . she didn't—'

'An asshole ex-boyfriend drugged her up and put that shit all over her.'

'No kidding.'

'She almost died from it.'

She shook her head in amazement. 'And I thought *we* had problems.'

'Trust me, Sheriff, Hopalong Cassidy and Gabby Hayes there are gonna be a big problem for me.'

She looked surprised. 'All you gotta do is testify,' she said.

'There's a minor problem with that plan.'

'Such as?'

'Such as I don't have the information they think I do.'

She was momentarily taken aback. 'I was given to understand that you did.'

'Me too,' Corso said. 'But it didn't work out that way.'

She eyed him closely. 'Well now . . . as a guy who once got canned from the *New York Times* for making stuff up . . . that leaves you between a rock and a hard place, now doesn't it?'

'It means they can hold me indefinitely without charging me with anything. Lawyers or no lawyers. No bail. No nothing. Anywhere from six to nine months in the hoosgow,' he said.

'Grand juries have a lot of power,' she said.

'Don't suppose there's any way I could talk you into telling those Dallas cops to take a hike,' Corso said. 'As I understand extradition law, you don't necessarily have to turn me over.'

She nodded. 'Ordinarily I'd have quite a bit of

latitude in the matter. I'd be able to weight the value of co-operating with another department against the gravity of the crime and then make my own decision. Under regular circumstances I could make them fight for you in court. I could even let you walk, if I wanted.'

'But . . .'

'But . . . with the whole damn world watching on the six o'clock news, and my own deputy sheriff telling everybody this is just another example of me being out of touch with the community . . . I just don't see as I've got any choice but to hand you over.'

'A girl's gotta do what a girl's gotta do,' Corso said.

She cast him an annoyed look. 'Hold the guilt, Mr Corso. I don't need any help beating myself up.' She paced across the room to the window and stood staring out into the parking lot. 'Maybe my detractors are right,' she said after a moment. 'Maybe I have lost touch with the community.'

Something in her tone caught Corso's ear. He frowned and levered himself higher in the bed. 'What makes you say that?' he asked.

Her face said it was a stupid question. Her voice began to rise. 'I've had a local family rotting away under a shed floor. They been right under my nose for the past fifteen years.' She waved an arm. 'As the crow flies, it's no more than five miles from here and I've . . .' She went silent. Knotted muscles trembled along the edges of her jaw.

'Something personal here?' Corso asked.

Her mouth sprang open in denial, but nothing came out. 'You've got a good ear,' she said finally.

'It's what I do.'

She continued to stare silently out the window. 'So?' Corso pressed.

'Miss Sissy Warwick,' she said.

CHAPTER 7

Nineteen seventy-three. I was twenty-two and fresh out of college.' She rolled her eyes and made a face. 'I'd just figured out I was never going to be Shirley Temple. That *dainty* was never going to be the first thing anybody thought of when I came to mind. *Horsy* maybe . . . but not dainty.' She stifled a sigh. 'Anyway . . . I came back home to lick my wounds for the summer. A little R and R before figuring out what I wanted to do with the rest of my life.' She looked over at Corso. 'You ever live in a small town like this?' she asked.

Corso shook his head. 'Not since I was a little kid,' he said.

'Well then, you've got to understand . . . towns like this are pretty much closed societies. People come and go, but nothing really changes. Most of the kids we send up to the university at Madison stay gone for a while. They meet mates, have children, move someplace else. They come back to Avalon on the holidays to show off the grandkids. And then later on they start coming back to see how their parents are getting along. And then later on for good . . . get away from the hustle of the city . . . you know, the urban lifestyle and all.' Corso nodded that he understood. 'What I'm trying to say is that . . . up until a couple of years ago, we didn't even have a motel. All we had was a hundred-year-old rooming house.' She folded her arms. 'Which had the same people living in it for as long as anybody could remember. Because just about everybody who comes to town is related to somebody who already lives here and is staying out with them at the family farm. We really didn't need anyplace to house strangers, because we didn't have any strangers.' She sighed and scratched the back of her neck. 'We're not exactly a destination getaway . . . if you know what I mean.'

Corso chuckled.

'So when a young woman who isn't related to anybody here in town shows up and takes up residence, it's something people are going to notice. It's something that's going to get talked about over coffee and down at the barbershop.'

'And that's what happened?'

'Right after I got home from college, so it must have been the middle of June sometime. Hottest damn summer anybody could remember.' Her eyes moved inward. 'Sissy Warwick. Jet-black hair and those big blue eyes. Real exotic looking. Like nobody you ever saw before. Like she could have been from the Middle East or Turkey or someplace like that. Claimed to be twenty years old, but I always thought she was more like eighteen.' She caught herself rambling. 'Anyway, Sissy Warwick shows up in town one day. Gets herself a room at Harrison's. Next thing you know, she's got a job as a receptionist at the medical center, and it seems like you can't hardly walk down the street without running into her.'

Corso smiled. 'Town just wasn't big enough for the both of you, eh?'

The sheriff lifted her eyebrows in resignation. 'Maybe that was it. Maybe it *was* just a case of having two hens in the same barnyard,' she said. 'You could be right. Lord knows . . . everything she did that summer sure seemed sinister to me.' She listened to an inner voice for a moment and then said, 'Wasn't just me, though. Lotta people in town felt the same way. For a while there, all anybody could talk about was who was this girl and what was she doing here.'

'So?'

'So, right there in the middle of that sweltering summer' – she made an expansive gesture with her arms – 'it was like this girl was everywhere. No matter what sidewalk you walked down, she was there. No matter what tree you stopped under, she was there. If you went to the library, she was sitting over in the corner reading a book. If you—' She read Corso's expression. 'Okay, so maybe I'm exaggerating a little . . .'

'You make it sound like it was yesterday.'

She got serious. 'It's like it was. I didn't realize

how much she'd affected me until I looked into that barn Friday morning. How I'd practically forgotten about Eldred and Tommie and James. But how Sissy' – she waved a finger – 'how Sissy Warwick had never been far from my thoughts. How something about that woman was still grinding away at me, all these years later.'

'The damnedest things stick in our hearts, don't they?'

She thought it over. Decided she agreed. 'Something about her just didn't ring right for me,' she said finally. 'That was a really vulnerable time for me. I was trying to figure out who I was and didn't like some of the answers I was getting from the universe. I didn't believe in myself, and something about her made it impossible for me to believe in her either. It was like neither of us was for real.'

'Interesting.'

'It was like a voice inside of me said we couldn't both exist and have things be right with the world. Like I couldn't be the person I was and have her alive on the planet at the same time. It was that visceral. I felt like we were mutually exclusive or something.'

'What else?'

'She was just way too friendly. Remembered everybody's name. Had that smarmy, car salesman quality about her. Always asking questions. By the time she'd been here three months, she knew as much about the town and everybody's business as people who'd lived here all their lives.'

'And then?'

She swallowed hard. 'So, you know . . . she's been around for about six months when I start hearing the rumors, and—' She stopped herself again. '—I was probably the last to know. I was so busy driving back and forth to Madison, pretending to look for a job, I nearly missed the whole thing.'

'What rumors were those?'

Corso watched as her professionalism failed to defeat her obvious discomfort. Her hands made quotation marks in the air.

'She had a number of "things" going on with local men.'

'Affairs?'

She nodded. 'Prominent local men.'

'Such as?'

'Such as my predecessor, Sam Tate. Which is how I ended up being sheriff.' When Corso didn't speak, she pointed a finger at his chest and ambled his way as if to impale him on its blunt tip. 'You're like a snake on a rock,' she said. 'You just sit there sunning yourself until people blurt out what it is you want to know.'

Corso smiled. 'Way I see it, most everybody has an intense desire to tell their story. All you got to do is shut up and give them a chance to spit it out.'

Her eyes narrowed. 'As I recall, that was pretty much Sissy's MO too.'

Corso's face was stiff. 'You figure that means

I'm fated to develop an unquenchable yen for local law enforcement personnel?'

'I don't think Richardson would like that at all,' she deadpanned.

'You're probably right,' he said with a smile. 'So . . . it was this Sam Tate's sexual proclivities that got you elected.'

'Actually, it was his death proclivity.'

'Ah.'

'Two weeks before the election.'

'Good timing.'

'Better for me than Sam.'

'That's the way things generally work out.'

'Sam was gonna outpoll me twenty to one. I was only running for sheriff because I couldn't figure out what else to do with my life.' Her eyes clouded over. 'Just go back in town. Came home to look after my dad.' She met Corso's eyes. 'Alzheimer's,' she said. 'I had a degree in criminal justice and five years' experience as a Saint Paul County deputy.' She shrugged. 'So I ran for sheriff.'

'And then . . . that fateful night.'

'Sam took Sissy up to his family cabin on Hunter Lake. Came out later they'd been up there a bunch of times.' Her lips were pressed tight. 'He died of a massive cerebral hemorrhage. Dropped stone dead on top of her while flying united. She had to call search and rescue. Fire department don't service that far out in the boonies.'

'So they find Sam Tate dead.'

'They also find a Polaroid camera and a bunch

of snapshots of what she and Sam had been doing with each other. That's when the rumors started about the others. How she had a bunch of other lovers. How she'd taken pictures with all of them. I'm telling you, this town was humming.'

'Rumors from where?'

The sheriff shrugged. 'Who knows. It's a small town.'

'Full of *prominent* men,' Corso said with a sneer.

'And the shit hit the fan. Just about this time of year – a month or so before Christmas – the town is buzzing. Everybody's looking at everybody else and wondering. We've got our own version of *Peyton Place* going on. I'm figuring either one of her lovers is gonna kill her or the wives are gonna get together and ride her out of town on a rail, and either way, with Sam dead and only two weeks to go till the election, sooner or later I'm going to end up having to deal with it.'

'So you won the election.'

'Hell, no!' She laughed. 'He beat me from the grave!'

'Musta been the sympathy vote,' Corso said.

'Town charter says if a candidate dies, the other candidate gets the job.' She spread her hands in mock resignation. 'The rest is history.'

'What was the big attraction?' Corso asked.

'Whadda you mean?'

'What was the big sexual attraction to Sissy Warwick?'

'I wasn't aware men needed one,' she said.

Corso's lip curled. 'Work with me here, Sheriff. *Prominent* men don't risk their tranquillity and let people take pictures of them doing it unless there's something pretty special going on.' He watched as her neck began to redden, as the color began to work its way into her cheeks and finally all the way to the tops of her ears.

'Supposedly . . . she was just hell in bed.'

'That's it? She was a good roll? These guys risked life, limb, and community property just to . . .'

She winced at the gesture he made. 'The pictures of her and Sam made it plain that she was . . . you know . . .'

Corso kept silent.

'Kinky,' she finally blurted. 'She was quite . . .' Again she stopped. Regrouped. 'Of an alternative persuasion.'

'What alternative was that?'

She looked as if she'd just smelled something vile. 'Dressing up . . . spanking . . . that sort of thing.' She waved a hand in front of her face as if to brush the odor away. 'And whatever else it is those people do to each other.'

'Did the names of these prominent men ever come to light?'

'Not officially. But believe you me, Mr Corso, everybody in this town's got their own list of who they think it was.'

She took a deep breath and turned away. The set of her shoulders told Corso all he needed to know. 'What else?' he pushed.

She spun his way, embarrassment turned to anger. 'Else? What do you mean *else?* Isn't that enough? Jesus.'

She met his stony gaze with her own. Silence settled into the room like cigarette smoke. After an uncomfortable moment, she said, 'The talk in the barbershop was that she liked it up the ass.'

'So this Sissy Warwick is now the town "ho,"' Corso prodded. 'Givin' the good old boys a little something they can't get at home. Takin' pictures of it all. Causin' all kinds of chaos among the local gentry.'

'I can see you're an incurable romantic,' she said.

For the second time Corso laughed. 'Yeah . . . ask anybody.'

She went on. 'Everybody in town figures she'll do the right thing and either kill herself or disappear back to wherever it was she came from.'

'But no.'

She shook her head. 'Next thing you know, I'm hearing she's hot and heavy with Eldred Holmes.' She shook her head in remembered astonishment. 'First time I heard it, I laughed out loud.'

'Why's that?'

'It was crazy. They were just such an unlikely pair,' she said.

'Ah' was all Corso said.

'And Eldred . . . I mean there wasn't a less likely candidate for romance in the whole county. Eldred might have been our least prominent citizen. You want to talk backward and shy, I'm telling you,

Mr Corso, Eldred was the poster boy for awkward. Poor kid spent his whole life out on that eighty acres where you found him. His parents were deaf. They died the year before Sissy came to town. By the time I saw them together, he'd already had his teeth fixed. Bought himself some new clothes. Stopped cutting his own hair.'

'You think this Eldred knew about the *prominent* men?'

She frowned. 'Wouldn't have mattered. She had old Eldred firmly in hand.'

'And then?'

'And then, the next thing you know they're getting married, and everybody's picking up their jaws and waiting for the pictures to appear in the newspaper. They're all wondering what she wants from poor Eldred. Figuring she's gonna move in for a while and then screw him out of the farm, since that was pretty much all he owned.' She cast a glance at Corso.

'But no.'

'No.' She shook her head in disbelief. 'Next thing you know she's pregnant with Tommie. They're out there trying to scratch a living out of some real marginal acreage. Trying to be self-sufficient. Running a few cows. Growing some feed. Just doing what folks around here mostly do.'

'So what happened?'

'Nothing. That's where it gets really weird. They just sort of settled in. Had a second kid. James.' She stopped, as if listening to herself. 'They were

70

like hermits. Just stayed out there on the place. You maybe saw Eldred once, twice a year, if he needed something from the Grange, but that was it. Other than that, you never saw any of them in town . . . ever. Wasn't until the boys grew up that anybody remembered they were alive. Half the people who remembered what happened with Sissy were dead by then. And then one day about the time the boys got to be adolescents, she had to start coming into town to bail them out.'

'At-risk youth, eh?'

'Big time. It's not good for kids to be raised in isolation. They miss out on the whole social inter-action thing. The socialization process. Didn't do Eldred any good, and it wasn't good for his boys neither. Soon as they started to mature – just about the time puberty kicked in – they started to be a problem. Boosting cars. Starting fights on Saturday nights. A couple of B and Es.' Her lips rolled into a smile. 'They got drunk and drove Eldred's one-ton truck through the front wall of the Dairy Queen. One thing after another. I used to spend half my time cleaning up the messes the Holmes boys made.'

'So.'

'So that's just about the time the state starts building the freeway. Right up there on the side of Barnett Mountain by their farm. She came into town for the first time in years, blew a gasket at the Zoning Commission – had to be escorted out of the courthouse. Then, a couple of weeks later, I hear they're gonna move.'

"'Cause of the freeway?'

She turned toward Corso. 'That's what everybody thought.'

Another silence settled over the room. 'Interesting little mystery,' Corso commented. 'Somebody could make quite a name for themselves . . .' He let it hang.

'Probably get somebody re-elected,' she said.

'Several times.'

'Ten years anyway.'

A bright metallic click was followed by the whoosh of the door. Richardson held his hat in front of himself with two hands, like he was protecting his crotch. 'If you two are finished commiserating—' He paused. 'Folks are getting real restless out here.'

CHAPTER 8

Two cops. Wisconsin State Patrol. One in uniform. One in a gray suit. Sporting the last two Marine Corps flattop semper fi haircuts in America. All spit, polish, and reptile eyes. Five minutes of introductions and small talk about the weather before the shorter of the two motored his suit over to the wall and tried to push the bed out, so he could slip between it and the windowsill. Wanted to have Corso surrounded, if he could. Suit used his hip on the bed, but the locked wheels refused to roll.

'Leave the bed where it's at,' Corso said. 'You wouldn't want to affect my delicate medical condition, now would you?'

The two cops shared a look. Suit ambled back over to his partner. 'Seems like Mr Corso's a bit testy this morning,' suit commented.

'Must be that long Texas vacation he's got coming,' said his partner. His salt-and-pepper eyebrows were thick and had grown together into a single questioning line across the center of his forehead.

Suit moved in closer, rested his hand on the

edge of the bed. Guy had nostrils big enough to hide a quarter in. Kept flaring them, as if testing the air for carrion. With the other hand, he unbuttoned his jacket. 'What can you tell us about the bodies in the shed?' he asked.

'Same thing I told Sheriff Trask. I was ripping up floorboards when I saw a big plastic bundle. Thing was all taped together with duct tape. I was curious. Pulled off a piece of the tape, and next thing I knew I was staring at a skull. Guy came along in a road grader. I sent him for the cops.' He looked from one cop to the other. 'That's it.'

Suit leaned in so close Corso could smell his breath mints. 'So . . .' he began. 'You're telling us it was just the luck of the draw.' He sneaked a peek at his partner. 'Famous guy like you . . . makes a living making the police look stupid . . . and we're supposed to believe you just stumbled onto a pile of bones.'

Corso picked up his pen. Thumbed his journal open. 'You can believe whatever you want. I was just trying to keep from freezing to death. I've never been here before. Never even heard of this place before last night. You want to make some sort of conspiracy out of it . . . feel free.' He went back to writing.

'So . . .' Uniform began, 'you're saying you had no prior contact with the Holmes family whatsoever.' His eyebrows seemed to have a life of their own. Moving around on his brow like a hyperactive caterpillar.

'That's what I'm saying.'

'You're sure of that?'

Corso looked disgustedly out over the top of his journal. 'What's the alternative, fellas? You think I murdered that family and then waited fifteen years to come back to the scene of the crime? In the dead of night? In the middle of a blizzard?' A tight smile crossed his lips. ' 'Twas a dark and stormy night . . .' he intoned in an English accent.

They were not amused. 'Man with a pair of felony assault convictions really ought to be more helpful,' Uniform said. 'Kind of snotty attitude like that could lead a body to thinking somebody had something to hide.'

'Think whatever you want,' Corso said.

The door eased open. Sheriff Trask stepped into the room. She held a thick manila envelope in both hands. It hung down to her knees as she leaned back against the wall. Her knuckles were white. Her face was the color of oatmeal.

Corso closed the journal on his thumb. Smiled at the cops. 'The brass sent you down here, didn't they?' The cops did a Mt Rushmore impression. Corso emitted a dry laugh. 'They want to make sure I'm not writing a book, don't they? The idea that I might be mucking around in something that may make them look bad was just more than they could bear, wasn't it? So they sent you boys down here to make sure this whole mess isn't going to end up in print.'

The cops shifted gears. 'We ran your name through the computer,' Suit said.

'Got your rap sheet,' Uniform added.

'I've been rehabilitated,' Corso said with a smile.

'Got a couple of hits from Interpol.'

'I'm published in thirteen languages.'

'You come up as an associate of Anatol Kalisnakov.'

'I know Mr Kalisnakov.'

'In what capacity?'

'I hired him to teach me self-defense.'

'You hired a former KGB assassin to teach you self-defense?'

'His résumé was impeccable.'

The pair traded looks again, and then, out of the blue, Suit asked, 'What do you know about an organization named Melissa-D?'

Corso pretended to think it over. 'I know a woman named Melissa Duncan,' he offered. 'Lives in Sand Point, Idaho.'

'Not a person,' Suit snapped. 'An organization. Melissa-D.'

Corso used his right hand to pull an imaginary chain. Lightbulb on. He kept his voice steady and his expression flat. 'Melissa-D is an urban legend. It's something reporters talk about when they've had too much to drink, which is frequently. It's just a story. It doesn't exist. It's apocryphal.'

'Is that so?' Uniform looked over at his partner. 'Apocryphal, he says.'

'Big word.'

Corso spelled it for them. Neither bothered to write it down.

'Our information is that this Melissa-D is a worldwide information resource organization. Supersecret. Superexpensive. Only got a dozen clients.'

'One of which is you,' Suit added.

'I told you. It's a myth,' Corso said with a wave of the pen.

'Supposed to have hacked into virtually everything,' Suit went on. 'Police departments. Every government agency in the world. The State Department. The FBI. You name it, they're supposed to be on the inside.'

Uniform jumped in. 'Rumor is that for the right price, they can provide you with just about any kind of information or documentation you might need.'

'I told you,' Corso said, 'it's just a story. There's no such thing.'

'According to Interpol, there is,' Uniform said. 'And they list you as a regular customer. They say Mr Kalisnakov is probably the person who put you on-line with them. They think that's where you keep coming up with information that nobody else has access to. The stuff you put in those books you write.'

'What do you say to that?' Suit demanded.

Corso shrugged. 'Apparently stupidity doesn't honor international boundaries.'

'So they're just making it up. That what you're telling us here?'

Corso's voice began to rise. 'Maybe they're confused. Maybe the conversion to the euro has addled their minds. Maybe they lead rich fantasy lives. How the hell do I know?' Corso reached over, grabbed Suit by the wrist, and removed his hand from the bed.

'Why don't you two kiddies take a hike,' he said. 'If you've got any more questions, talk to my attorney.' Corso recited Barry Fine's address and phone number. They didn't write that down either.

Suit rolled his shoulders and smirked at Corso. 'You enjoy your little Texas vacation now, Mr Corso. Who knows, given enough time, maybe those southern folks can teach you a few manners.'

'A little antebellum gentility,' Uniform added.

Corso smirked back. 'Lordy be,' he drawled, 'now wouldn't that be somethin?'

They took their time leaving the room. Sort of sidled out in that 'we're in no hurry' cop way, nodding at Sheriff Trask and casting smug looks back Corso's way, until finally the door hissed and they were gone.

The sheriff bumped herself off the wall and walked over to the side of the bed. 'You're right,' she said. 'The big boys are terrified that you're going to write a book and make us all look like a bunch of hayseeds.' She took one hand off the envelope and ran it through her thick hair. 'All of a sudden I'm on everybody's speed dialer. I'm hearing from people who generally don't return my calls. Got a call from the commandant of the

78

State Patrol. Got a call from the lieutenant governor.' She smiled at Corso. 'Not to mention a number of *prominent* local men.' Corso smiled. She went on. 'Seems like everybody's got their panties in a wad over what we might've found out at the Holmes place and what you might be fixin' to write about it.'

'Only thing I'm fixin' to do is cool my heels in a Texas jail.'

Sheriff Trask brought the envelope up to eye level. 'Got something you can ponder while you're cooling your heels,' she said.

'What's that?' he asked.

'She's not in there,' the sheriff announced.

'Who's not in where?'

'We just got the preliminary report from the lab boys. Three skeletons. All males. Eldred and the two boys. No Sissy.'

'No shit.'

'They found this in the bundle with the bodies,' she said jiggling the manila envelope. 'Sealed up in its own Ziploc bag.'

Corso watched as she reached in and extracted a baby blue photo album. 'Family Album' was embossed on the cover in gold. Black smudges all over the cover. Fingerprint powder. Corso opened the book. As advertised. Family photos in more or less chronological order. Smudges all over everything. Eldred Holmes, looking mostly goofy and confused. The boys stopped Corso cold. They could have been Hawaiian. Could have been part

79

African-American. Could have been Heinz 57. Very interesting-looking kids. The sheriff read his mind.

'Kinda makes you wonder about Sissy's genetic makeup, now don't it?'

'Sure does,' Corso said.

'Caused a lotta talk in town. Had some folks thinking maybe she wasn't white at all.'

Corso turned the page. The house, inside and out. The farm. Pictures of the freeway project as it cut through the hillside above the house. Sissy Warwick was in about two-thirds of the pictures. At least that was the presumption. Somebody had carefully scissored out the face in every photo of Sissy, leaving only an anonymous, faceless form adrift amid the mundane images of everyday life. Corso leafed all the way to the back and then handed the album back to the sheriff. 'They get any usable prints?' he asked.

'Nary a one,' she said. 'It was completely clean. Photos and all.'

'Very meticulous,' Corso said. 'Almost psychotic.'

The sheriff closed the album and slid it back into the envelope. Her expression said she wished she didn't have to do whatever came next. 'Those Texas boys are getting impatient, Mr Corso. I don't think they like the weather.' She shrugged. 'I've held 'em off as long as I can. They're in a hurry to get back home, and the doctors say you're fit to travel, so I guess you better get dressed. It's too damn cold out there for a hospital gown. You'll freeze your butt off.' She stood for a moment staring down at Corso. 'If I had my druthers,' she began. 'I wish I could—'

'I know,' Corso said. He managed a small smile. 'Me too.'

She started for the door. Stopped. Turned around. 'Your friend Ms Dougherty wants to say good-bye before she goes. I'll wait a few minutes and then—'

Corso cut her off. 'Send her in,' he said. 'She's seen it all before.'

The sheriff had her hand on the door handle. 'I'll leave you a little time to visit and get packed before I come back with the Texas boys,' she said. 'Sorry it had to be this way.' She gave him a little two-fingered salute and then disappeared.

Corso sat back in the bed and waited for several minutes. When Dougherty failed to show, he swung his feet over the edge of the bed and set them on the floor. The cold tile sent a shiver up his legs as he slowly levered himself off the mattress. He felt weak and slightly off balance as he stood unsupported for the first time in nearly three days.

Half a dozen shuffling steps toward the closet and his legs began to come around. Before opening the door, he stretched and groaned and rolled his neck in a circle. He pulled open the door. His Gianni Versace overcoat lay huddled in the corner, wrinkled and streaked with dust. The rest of his clothes hung haphazardly from those hangers that don't come off the bar. His head swam as he bent to pick his suitcase up. He leaned against the doorjamb before continuing.

He rested the suitcase across the arms of the nearest chair, popped the brass latches, and began to poke around inside. A blurred picture of his mother flashed on a screen inside his head. A moment later, her voice filled his ears.

He listened, hoping to hear her again. Instead the voice was Meg Dougherty's.

'Your ass is hanging out, Corso.'

'Yeah' was all he said as he pulled on a change of socks and underwear.

He found a pair of jeans and then turned to face her. Her hands were no longer bandaged. They hung from the ends of her arms like boiled fish. She was wearing her brave face and her 'fit in' clothes. The face, smiling but rigid, was the one she put on when things got out of control and she didn't want Corso to know she was terrified. The clothes, a long-sleeved black-and-white flannel shirt over a pair of black jeans, were the ones she wore when they were working someplace where the vampire princess act just wasn't going to float.

'How're the hands?' he asked as he buttoned his jeans around his waist and then dragged the hospital gown over his head and dropped it to the floor.

She managed a wan smile. 'A little tender, but otherwise okay.' As if to prove her point, she held them up and flexed her fingers several times.

He rummaged around in the bag. Produced a black T-shirt. Wiggled in, one arm at a time, and then slipped it over his head, pulled it down, and tucked it into the jeans. Beneath the winged Harley-Davidson logo, big white letters, *Smoke em till the wheels fall off.* He hiked up his pant legs, stood on one foot at a time, and pulled on a pair of black cowboy boots. He stomped his feet until he was satisfied with the fit.

'That what they're wearing in jail these days?' she asked.

'I'm going for the ominous look.' He gave her a little grin. 'As I recall, about the time I get to Texas, my wardrobe choices are gonna be limited to something in the area of bright orange coveralls and flip-flops.'

'Be sure to tell them that orange is definitely not your color. You're a winter. Orange is definitely a fall color.'

'I'll keep that in mind.' He chuckled under his breath and then pointed toward the bed. 'The keys to the new rental car are on the nightstand there. It's that green Expedition down in the lot,' he said, nodding toward the window. 'Hertz says we should try not to total this one.'

She retrieved the key and dropped it into the right-hand pocket of her jeans. Her brave face was slipping. Her voice was tinged with concern. 'You sure there isn't something I can—'

'There's nothing to be done right now,' he said quickly. 'Barry's got a legion of associates working on it. In the meantime, I'm just gonna have to roll with the punches.'

'Maybe if I—' she began.

Corso pinned her with his gaze. 'Drive carefully,' he said. 'I'll give you a jingle whenever I get back to Seattle.'

'I could—'

He held up a hand. 'Listen. Do me a favor here, and don't make this any worse than it has to be. I'm sorry I dragged you into this. It was wrong. I damn near got you killed, and I've managed to get myself arrested and extradited to Texas. If I didn't know better, I'd ask the gods how things could possibly be worse. I'd—'

By the time he got that far, she'd crossed the room and put her arms around him. He stood rigid, his hands at his sides, as she locked him in her embrace. After a moment, his arms began to rise as if they had a will of their own, until they stood together in the gray light, holding each other in a mutual embrace.

Thirty seconds past the time limit on social hugs, they stepped back from each other and pretended to rearrange their clothes. She cleared her throat. 'I've gotta pack and get out of here if I'm gonna make my flight.'

He turned toward the window. 'See ya,' he said.

'Yeah.'

He stood gazing at the parking lot below and the town beyond until he heard the hiss of the door and silence filled the room. He walked to the bed, picked up his journal and his pen, and began to write.

CHAPTER 9

Missed the door entirely. Wasn't until he heard the scrape of a shoe that Corso looked up. By that time Sheriff Trask was standing in the center of the room, hands on hips, looking at Corso as if she were going to stare a hole in him. Corso clipped his pen over the pages, closed the journal, and slipped it into the outside pocket of his suitcase. He got to his feet.

'Where's our Texas friends?' he asked.

'Seems they got hungry and went to lunch over at Ruth's.' She took a quick survey of the room. 'Left me a note saying they'd be back to pick you up at one o'clock sharp.'

Corso checked the clock on the wall. Twelve-oh-nine. He was reaching down to retrieve his journal when her voice froze him.

'Guy like you'd probably be able to get quite a ways from here by one o'clock,' she said. 'With any luck at all, a guy like you might even be able to stay lost for the next week or so, until that grand jury's term expires, and then . . . you know . . . just maybe put this whole thing behind him.'

Corso took his time drawing himself up to his

85

full height. Her expression said she wasn't kidding. 'I think maybe I missed the beginning of this movie,' he said.

She gestured his way. 'What with the short hair and that big old knot across your forehead and that pair of shiners, you don't look a bit like any of the pictures they're showing on the TV. You're a whole different guy.'

Corso didn't speak. His face tingled from the tension in the room.

'What if I let you walk?' she asked finally. 'What if I let you grab your big black bag and walk right out of here?'

'I thought you were worried about your image.'

She made a rude noise with her lips. 'That Richardson boy's already got me bent over a barrel,' she said. 'Only way I'm gonna come out of this on top is if I come up with something splashy on this Holmes thing. Something nobody else's got. Something I can call a news conference about and blow him out of the water.'

'I wouldn't hold my breath,' Corso said. 'Case is cold as hell.'

Her eyes narrowed. 'That's where you come into it, big fella.'

'How's that?' He checked the clock again. Twelve thirteen.

'You've got five days to kill, right? Till that grand jury peters out.' She didn't wait for an answer. 'If I let you walk out of here . . . you agree to spend those five days finding out whatever you can about Miss Sissy Warwick.' Corso opened his mouth, but she kept talking. 'You ask those Melissa-D people of yours to find out where she came from. You—'

'There's no such thing,' Corso said quickly.

She waved his protest off. 'You do whatever it takes to get me something I can use.' She walked over and stood directly in front of him. 'You look me in the eye and tell me you'll give me five days of your best efforts, and I'll let you walk out of here.'

'Me escaping isn't going to do a thing for your image.'

'It's not an escape,' she said. 'You're not under arrest for anything. For all I know you merely tired of our hospitality and decided to seek warmer climes.'

'There'll still be a lot of heat.'

'I won't melt,' she said.

'No guarantees.'

She nodded and held out her hand. 'We got a deal?'

Corso took it. Her hand was callused and hard. He shook it.

'Deal,' he said. Twelve fourteen.

Corso looked toward the door. Trask read his mind. 'Your friend is still in the building. I told her I had something for her to sign before she could leave. You take the rental car. When the shouting dies down, I'll see to it she gets to the airport and makes a flight back to Seattle.'

By the time she finished talking, Corso had shouldered his way into his overcoat and picked up his suitcase. She motioned for him to follow. She crossed the room to the door. Eased it open and stuck her head out into the hall. She motioned Corso forward and then pointed to the right, down the long hall toward the flickering green EXIT sign at the far end. 'You friend Ms Dougherty is four doors down in four-eleven,' she said. 'You say your good-byes and then go down the back stairs there. Take you right out into the parking lot.'

Corso nodded. She caught his eyes. 'We've got a deal, right?'

'I'll do the best I can,' he said.

Her eyes lingered on his for a moment, before she pushed open the door and stepped out into the hall. She held the door open as she surveyed the area. A minute passed. Corso could hear the slide of feet. 'Go,' she said finally.

Corso hurried down the deserted hall without looking back, grabbed the door handle on room 411, and without knocking slipped inside. Meg Dougherty had her camera equipment spread out on the bed. She was using a white towel to wipe everything clean. She brought a hand to her throat. Swallowed twice. 'Oh. You scared the hell out of me. I thought you were—'

'Yeah, the sheriff . . . I know,' Corso said quickly. He held out his free hand. 'There's been a change in plans. I need the car.'

She recovered quickly. Reached into the pocket of her jeans, looking for the keys. 'What's the deal? I thought you were—'

'I'm getting out of here,' he said.

'Where?'

'Anyplace but Texas.'

She held the keys out in front of her. Corso hurried over, but at the last second, she folded them into her fist and put it behind her back. Corso slid to a stop on the cold white floor. 'No time to screw around here, honey,' he said. 'I've gotta hurry.'

'I'm coming,' she announced. 'And don't call me honey.' Corso's turn to do dumbfounded. 'What do you mean, you're coming?'

'Just what I said. I'm coming.'

Twelve seventeen. Corso dropped his voice to a hoarse whisper. As he spoke, he flailed the air with his arm. 'Coupla days ago you wanted no part of this thing. You were insulted as hell, big-time bitchy, and wanting to go back to Seattle as quick as possible. Now all of a sudden . . .' He stopped.

Dougherty wasn't listening. Instead she was packing her gear. Wincing occasionally as her big red hands packed each camera and lens into its proper bag and case. 'That was then . . . this is now,' she said as she zipped the Qantas flight bag. She grabbed both her bags and turned Corso's way. 'Don't just stand there with your mouth open, Frank. Get the door for me. I'll go downstairs and get the car started.'

Corso didn't move. She shook her head in exasperation. 'Don't try to figure it out, Frank. It's part of our charm. It's what makes women a mystery. Now open the damn door.' He grabbed the handle and pulled the door back against his chest. By the time he checked the hall and turned to urge her forward, she'd already shouldered her way by and was striding down the polished floor toward the elevators.

The smell of her lingered in the air above the bed as Corso dropped his bag on the sheet and slid the zipper open. In an inner compartment, he found his cell phone. Instinctively, he checked the room before using his thumb to dial the number.

He was prepared for the unusual number of brittle clicks and electronic exchanges before a human voice split the static. 'This is not a secured connection.'

'I know,' he said.

'No further messages will be accepted from this number.'

'I know.'

'The sending unit must be decommissioned.'

'Yes. I know.'

'Please enter your access code.'

He did so. 'Again,' said the voice. He complied. Three clicks and a new voice. Female this time. 'This is an unsecured connection.'

'I know.'

'No new business can be conducted on an unsecured connection.'

'It's old business,' Corso said.

He heard the clicking of a keyboard. 'Abrams, Arnold Jay. Any and all on a locate.' More clicking. 'Nothing.'

'Ten months and he has yet to generate a single scrap of paperwork?' Corso said.

'Yes, sir,' she replied. 'As that is your only current account, this communication is now—'

'Hey hey hey,' Corso chanted into the mouthpiece.

'—terminated.'

He expected to hear a dial tone. When he heard only silence, he went on. 'I know it's outside the protocol,' he began, 'but I've got a problem.' From the other end, nothing but silence. 'Sissy Warwick. She'd be somewhere in her middle forties about now. Lived in Avalon, Wisconsin, from nineteen seventy-three to nineteen eighty-seven. That's the last record anybody has of her.'

'This is an unsecured connection. I'll have to consult with my superior. Would you care to wait?'

'No,' he said. 'I've got to go.'

Click.

Corso walked into the bathroom, set the cell phone on the toilet lid, and used both hands to remove the white porcelain top to the tank. Old-fashioned ball-and-lever. The inside of the tank stained brown by the minerals in the water. He rested the top in the sink and then picked up his phone. Pushed two buttons. The light came on.

He dropped the phone into the tank and watched as it waffled its way to the bottom. Watched until the light went out, then replaced the top and headed for the door.

CHAPTER 10

Twelve twenty-one. Corso stood in the window and watched as the gray cloud of exhaust enveloped the back half of the Ford Expedition. The windows were blurred by beads of condensation, making Dougherty nothing more than a rumor of movement in the car's interior. A flash in his peripheral vision drew his eyes to the left. Two blocks down, Duckett and Caruth were crossing the street, on their way back to the hospital from lunch. Corso smiled. Trask had been right. Although they wore their matching stocking caps pulled down over their ears, each man also carried his cowboy hat. Just in case. You never knew.

Corso smiled as he counted in his head. Gave it another minute and a half and then headed for the door. Down the long hall, a pair of white-clad nurses stood together in the silver glare of the nurses' station. One gestured with an aluminum clipboard. Pulled a pen from her pocket and wrote something on it. The other nurse seemed to agree. He waited some more.

Twelve twenty-three. The nurses parted company,

one disappearing behind the desk, the other squeaking her way down the hall and into a room. Time to go.

Corso's cowboy boots clicked against the worn linoleum as he hurried toward the stairs. The stairwell smelled of disinfectant, acrid and twitchy to the nose. He stretched his long legs and began to take the stairs two at a time. Down one flight to the landing, using his free hand on the metal handrail to propel himself around the corner and down.

He was halfway to the ground when he heard it. Whistling and the *chick-chick* of feet on the stairs. He skidded to a halt. Stood still. Swallowed his breath and listened. No doubt about it. Somebody coming up the stairs at a trot. Whistling what? He listened again. The tune was disjointed and ragged, but familiar. A hymn maybe. 'Jesus Loves Me.' That's it. ''Cause the Bible tells me so . . . Jesus loves me.'

The tune moved closer now. Corso took a deep breath, put on his most nonchalant and friendly face, and started down. Just another guy carrying his bag down the back stairs. He was four steps above the second landing when the stranger came into view. Richardson. Red ears, funny hat and all. Their gazes met. The tall cop's jaw worked twice, but nothing came out. His eyes became slits. He smiled as much as the chin strap would allow and then reached for the gun on his hip.

He had the revolver halfway out of the holster

94

when Corso tossed him the bag. Not hard. Just a soft underhand lob. Just as Corso had hoped, Richardson forgot about his weapon and instinctively caught the bag in both hands. Guy thing. Somebody throws you something, you catch it. Period.

Corso launched himself from the step. Landed in Richardson's arms. Right on top of the bag. Nose-to-nose. The impact sent the cop staggering backward into the wall, driving the breath from his lungs, banging his head off the surface with a sound not unlike that of a ripe melon landing on concrete. Richardson's eyes rolled back in his head. His body went slack. Only then did Corso hear the sound of the gun clattering down the stairs, end over end. Corso ducked and winced, waiting for the bouncing weapon to discharge. Nothing. For a moment his head swam and he could see the reflection of flames on Sissy Warwick's ceiling. He gulped air and looked around. Silence.

Gathering his wits, Corso put two fingers on Richardson's throat. He felt the steady drum of blood. Satisfied, he rolled the unconscious cop over, pulled up the thick winter coat, and removed a pair of handcuffs from their black leather case. Took him a minute, but he eventually got the big man's hands manacled behind his back, then rolled him over again and removed his tie, which he wound around Richardson's ankles and then threaded through the hand-cuffs. Hog-tied. Feet pulled up behind him. Corso felt the man's throat again. Pulse still strong and steady. His scalp tingled from the adrenaline rush. He grabbed his suitcase and started down the stairs.

The gun lay wedged in a corner of the first-floor landing, pointing at the ceiling as if in surrender. Corso picked it up, jammed it in the pocket of his coat, and jerked open the door.

A blast of arctic air raked his face as he crossed the parking lot toward Dougherty and the idling car. He shuddered inside his coat. Looked around. From his hospital room above, it had appeared that the snow, which was piled up on the perimeter of the parking lot, was perhaps waist deep. From ground level, he could see how wrong he'd been. Here in the land where the temperature doesn't rise above freezing until May, the snowblowers had piled the stuff up fifteen feet in the air, creating the feeling of being inside a massive igloo. He pulled open the car door and threw himself into the seat.

'Let's get out of here,' he said.

She sat staring at him.

'Let's go,' he said.

'Are you okay?' she asked.

'Sure.'

'You look like you've seen a ghost.'

'Just get me out of here.'

She pushed the shift lever into Reverse and backed quickly out into the center of the lot. 'Where to?' she asked.

'Anyplace but hell or Texas,' Corso said.

CHAPTER 11

The moon's silver fingers poked and probed until Corso finally cracked an eye. He blinked several times and then squinted up at the night sky. Big old silver moon, hanging low like a dull nickel, standing sentinel above the frozen fields and skeletal trees that lined the narrow two-lane road. He pushed himself upright in the seat. Stretched and groaned. Ran his hands over his face.

'Where are we?' he asked.

'I'm not sure,' Dougherty said, without taking her eyes from the road. 'Somewhere in Iowa. I turned south on Iowa 76 about an hour ago. Last sign I saw said Cedar Rapids was a hundred ten miles.'

Ahead in the distance, a brightly lit sign hovered above the treetops. Diesel. 1.24. Above that in red neon: F O D

'I've gotta pee,' Dougherty said.

'Might as well fill 'er up while we're at it.'

She shook her head. 'First the bathroom.'

Frozen gravel popped and snapped beneath the Ford's tires as she wheeled the car across the lot and parked it between a pair of ancient pickup trucks. Half a dozen 18-wheelers lined the far end of the lot. EARLS the place was called. No apostrophe. Just EARLS. A diner. Thirty-foot Streamliner, built in the late fifties. All stainless steel. No porcelain. Sign on the roof said it all. EAT.

The yellow light from the diner's windows cast trapezoidal shadows across the frozen ground. Corso pulled open the door and let Dougherty precede him inside.

Twelve steel-rimmed stools on one side. Mostly full. Six Naugahyde booths on the other. Mostly empty. Pies in a mirrored case behind the counter. Atop the case a grainy black-and-white TV blared out the local news. A pair of ancient waitresses and a guy in a dirty apron behind the counter. Maybe ten customers. Truck drivers mainly. John Deere caps, jeans, and flannel shirts. Guys with that big-gut-and-no-ass look you get from eighteen hours a day behind the wheel. As they stood in the doorway, a guy with no discernible chin came limping past, bussing dishes in a red plastic pan.

'In or out, honey. We ain't heating the outside,' one of the waitresses called. Corso nudged Dougherty forward. He stepped inside and let the door swing closed behind him. The air reeked of cigarette smoke and primordial grease.

Corso put a hand on Dougherty's shoulder, guiding her left toward the rest rooms. Halfway down the aisle, Corso slipped into a booth. Back to the door, he watched as Dougherty walked through the archway and turned left. She stood with the open door in her hand. Said something to somebody, hesitated, and then stepped inside.

A waitress appeared at his elbow. She had a face like a satchel and a mouthful of brown teeth, spaced out like pickets on a fence. 'What'll it be?'

Corso ordered two coffees. Above the clink of silverware and the low-octave chatter, the TV speaker spasmed, '. . . in the valley, clear and cold, highs in the low twenties, lows near zero. The National Weather Service reports . . .'

Dougherty and the coffee arrived two minutes later. The look in her eyes told Corso something was amiss. 'Problem?'

She waited until the waitress was out of range and then leaned across the table. 'There's this woman in there. Absolutely shit-faced. Puking her guts up in the sink.' She waved a hand. 'And there's like no privacy, no nothing. I had to go so bad . . . and she's obviously not going anywhere . . . so I had to drop my drawers right in front of her.'

'I take it she was impressed with your artwork?'

'I think the sight of my ass may have sobered her up.'

She looked down at the cup of coffee in front of her. Frowned. Looked at Corso.

'I didn't think these guys could manage a double grande no-fat hazelnut latte, so I just ordered coffee,' Corso said.

She shrugged in resignation. Took a sip. Winced. 'I can't drink this,' she said.

The TV newscaster droned. 'President Bush has proposed a national campaign to promote abstinence among teens. The president said today . . .'

Whatever sobering effect the sight of Dougherty's tattoos may have had on the other woman had apparently been short-lived. She lurched out of the women's room like she was on ice and banged face-first into the far wall. Somewhere in her sixties, she'd teased her jet-black hair straight up. The tangled mane seemed to float above her head like smoke from an oil fire. She'd used that indoor tanning cream, which had dyed her pouchy face and neck the color of a ripe tangerine.

Using both walls for balance, she tightroped her way out through the archway into the diner, where she slid her large, veiny hands along the tops of the booths to keep herself upright as she shuffled forward. Her rheumy eyes rolled in her head as she moved slowly along. She was doing all right until she came abreast of Dougherty. Then she stopped.

She leaned closer and tried to focus. 'I seen you,' she slurred. 'You from the circus or somethin'?' She cackled, swayed on her feet, and then began to sing. 'Lydia, I'm Lydia, the ensephlopedia . . .'

Dougherty stared silently into her coffee. The woman leaned over and placed both elbows on the table. 'Never seen nothin' like that before. All them arrows and stuff, pointing right at—'

Dougherty stood up. She towered over the woman. 'Take a hike,' she said, 'before I kick your drunken ass all over this place.'

The woman started to speak but thought better of it and instead went tottering off, looking back toward Corso and Dougherty and muttering to herself. Dougherty stared off into space. At the far end of the diner, the drunken woman was getting loud. Shouting her outrage to the world. Nobody else in the place seemed to notice. Just another Saturday night at Earls.

Dougherty suddenly stiffened. Corso read her expression and looked back over his shoulder. A man in a red windbreaker was coming their way. His once-blond hair, turned the color of dirty brass, was slicked back. Even from a distance, he looked drunk.

He was breathing heavily through his mouth as he lurched to a stop at Dougherty's side. 'You the bitch threatened my Emily?' he demanded. His eyes were watery and bloodshot. His nose looked like a half pound of raw hamburger.

'Emily needs to sober up,' Dougherty said.

He reached out and grabbed her by the shoulder, then leaned over and put his face in hers. 'No fancy cunt like you got cause to say something—'

'No need for that kind of talk,' Corso said.

'Was I talkin' to you, fuckface?' the guy demanded. 'I wanna talk to an asshole like you, I'll—'

That was as far as he got. Corso grabbed him by the back of the hair and drove his face down into the table so hard the whole diner shook. The shattered nose left a trail of blood on the tabletop as the man slid slowly to the floor. Nobody moved. Except for the TV, the place was silent. All eyes were aimed their way.

'I could have handled it,' Dougherty said.

'The *c* word upsets me.'

She smiled, then slid her coffee away. 'Let's get out of here,' she said.

They rose together. Stepped over the unconscious guy, out into the aisle. Corso threw a five-dollar bill on the table. 'On the regional front,' the announcer droned, 'Wisconsin State Police authorities are investigating the murder of Avalon, Wisconsin, Deputy Sheriff Cole Richardson, who was found shot in the head early this afternoon. Unnamed sources have told KUMO News that the officer was apparently killed by his own gun. Although no formal charges have been brought, Wisconsin authorities are seeking reclusive author Frank Corso in connection with . . .' A five-year-old picture of Corso flashed on the screen. '. . . whose current true-crime book, *Death in Dallas*, has been on the bestseller lists for nearly thirty-three weeks. In the past Mr Corso has . . .' By the time Corso gathered his wits, Dougherty was already out the door. '. . . fired by the *New York Times* for fabricating a story . . .' Corso followed her out.

CHAPTER 12

She had a good arm. None of that awkward girlie throwing stuff. The keys came zipping through the night air on a line, hitting Corso square in the chest and falling to the ground. He made no move to pick them up. Just stood there staring at her.

'You want to tell me what in hell is going on here?'

Corso bent at the waist and picked up the keys. He slipped the chrome ring over his index finger. She walked over to the car, jerked the door, and found it locked.

'I need in,' she said.

Corso took his time, stopping to look back toward Earls and the faces dotting the window and then moving forward again. As he neared, she stepped back as if he were radioactive. Corso put a hand on her shoulder.

'I had to go through the cop to get out. He was—'

She waved him off. 'Why does everything always get more complicated with you, Corso? Five minutes with you and things have always gone from bad to worse.'

'I didn't kill him.' He held up two fingers. 'I swear.'

'I know that, you idiot,' she said disgustedly. 'I'm just pissed off is all. Open the fucking car.'

'He pulled a gun on me.'

'And you what?'

'I left him on the stairs. Handcuffed.'

She made a lunge for the keys. He put them behind his back, then reached into his overcoat pocket and came out with a gun. 'I took his gun with me.' He pushed the cylinder release and shook the cartridges out into his hand. 'Look,' he said.

She hesitated and then peered down into his palm. She frowned, looked up into Corso's face, and then used a fingernail to move the bullets around in his hand.

'They're all there,' she said.

He nodded twice and handed her the gun. 'Smell it,' he said.

Holding the revolver between her thumb and forefinger, she brought the barrel to her nose. Gave it two tentative sniffs.

'What's it smell like?' Corso asked.

She thought it over. Sniffed again. 'Oil.'

'Right. That's because it hasn't been fired since it was cleaned.'

He reached over and plucked the gun from her fingertips. One by one he inserted the shells back into the chambers and then swung the cylinder shut, before returning it to his coat pocket. She shifted her weight from one foot to the other and pointed his way.

'So . . . why's the TV saying—'

'Probably because his gun and I turned up missing at the same time. If I were in their position, I'd be thinking the same thing.'

'You've . . . we've gotta go back. Make sure they understand you didn't do this. You just show 'em the gun and then they'll . . .' She stopped. Looked at Corso.

'Right,' he said. 'That's what I was thinking too. That's why I kept it.'

'So let's—'

'Then it occurred to me that they've got no way of knowing I didn't kill him and then clean and reload the gun.' He shook his head. 'How can I prove that didn't happen?'

She massaged her temples. 'I don't know,' she said after a moment.

'Me neither,' said Corso. 'But I've got a feeling this whole thing's got something to do with that family we found in the shed.'

'Why's that?'

''Cause nothing else going on in that burg has enough passion attached to it to get somebody killed.' He slipped the key ring from his finger and opened the back door. 'I'll take you to an airport,' he said. 'Get you back home as soon as I can.'

'I'm going with you,' she said.

'Don't be an idiot. This isn't a joke anymore. We're not talking about some little contempt of court rap here. All of a sudden it's about murder. There's going to be some real serious folks looking for me now. I don't want you along for that.'

'I'm coming with you, Corso. Whether you like it or not. You got me into this, and I'm going to see it through to the end. Period.'

'Think about it—' he began.

'I have,' she said. 'And I'm coming along.'

Corso sighed. She had her muley look on. The one where there was no sense arguing with her. He looked back over her shoulder at the diner. The line of faces had left the window. A pair of truck drivers came down the stairs and started across the lot.

'Then we better get organized here,' he said to himself.

She watched in silence as he unzipped his bag and pulled everything out. The sound of an interior zipper came to her ears. Corso used both hands to fold one side of the bag's lining out over the top, and then another zip and his hands emerged holding a white plastic sack.

Corso set the sack on the rear bumper. He untied the handles, reached inside, and pulled out four inches of money. Dougherty's jaw dropped.

'Jesus,' she said. 'How much money is that?'

'Ten grand.' He removed the rubber band. Took about a quarter of the stack and slid it into his pants pocket. 'I brought it along in case we needed anything while we were hiding out from the Texas cops.' He replaced the rubber band, set the bundle of cash on the tailgate. From inside the sack, he produced a small brown paper bag. He shook it out onto the tailgate.

She looked down at the pile of paper and plastic. First thing she saw was her own picture on a Washington driver's license. She picked it up. 'What's this?'

'A little alternative ID,' he said with a wink. 'Just in case.'

She furrowed her brow and tapped the license with her fingernail. 'Margaret Dolan. What kind of name is that?'

'Irish,' Corso said. 'I was being sensitive to your cultural heritage.'

She tossed the license back into the pile. 'Things are bad enough already, Corso. I'm not handing anybody some piece of phony—'

'They're not phony,' Corso said.

'Of course they're phony,' she sputtered. 'I'm not this Dolan—'

'You can hand that ID to any cop in America and come out of it smelling like a rose.' He shushed her with a raised finger. 'Because what's on those IDs matches what's in everybody's databases.' He paused to let his message sink in. 'The ID is real. The credit cards work. From now on, you and I are Margaret, no middle name, Dolan and Francis A. Falco. The A stands for Albert.'

'As in Sinatra.'

He shot her a small smile. 'That cultural thing again.' He sorted their new documents into two piles, pulled out his wallet, and removed several items. 'Better stash your other ID. Don't want to be handing anybody anything by mistake.' She watched as he removed everything with his name on it and replaced it with the pile on the tailgate. Then she lifted her cape, found a red wallet in the small Mexican purse she wore slung over one shoulder, popped the snap. Started dropping things in a pile.

A minute later, the transfer was complete. Corso zipped the cash, the documents, and the gun into the interior pocket. He reattached the lining and then stuffed his clothes back inside. After zipping the bag, he closed the tailgate.

'You sure you want to do this?' he asked.

She glared at him. 'Where are we going?'

Corso watched as a pair of 18-wheelers roared to life and then eased out of the lot heading north. 'I don't know,' he said. 'You got your cell phone?'

'Where's yours?'

'It had an accident.'

Reluctantly she reached inside her cape and produced a red Nokia phone. In one motion, Corso plucked the phone from her fingers and dropped the keys into her outstretched hand. 'I need to make a call,' he said. 'Why don't you gas up the car?'

She closed her fingers on the keys. Turned and walked toward the front of the car.

Corso stood on the frozen gravel. Listened to the closing of the door. Heard the engine start and then the Ford pulling away.

She drove to the brightly lit gas pumps without turning her lights on. A kid in a pair of blue coveralls trotted out. Corso turned away. He thumbed the phone's ON button. The battery was good. The wireless service bad. He dialed. Waited for the electronic symphony to subside and then dialed his access code. Same voice as always.

'This is not a secured connection.'

'I know,' he said.

'No further messages will be accepted from this number.'

'I know.'

'The sending unit must be decommissioned.'

'Yes. I know.'

'Please reenter your access code.'

He did so. More clicks.

'No new business can be conducted on an unsecured connection.'

'Sissy Warwick,' he said.

He heard a keyboard. 'Two hundred seventy-three partial name matches. Seventy-six still living. One exact match.'

'What's the exact?'

'Sissy Marie Warwick. Born September fourth, nineteen fifty-seven. Died on the same date in nineteen seventy-two. Cause of death: leukemia. Buried in the Cemetery of the Sisters of the Sacred Heart, Allentown, Pennsylvania. Grave number one-one-two-six-seven. Survived by siblings Robert and Allen and parents Rose and Alfred.' He pondered the ignominy of dying on one's birthday as he listened to the sound of the keyboard. 'We have an anomaly,' she announced. 'Also in September of nineteen seventy-two, six days after the DOD, Sissy Marie Warwick requested and was granted an official copy of her birth certificate.'

'Six days after her death.'

'Yes sir.'

'Neat trick.'

'On September eleventh of that same year, she was issued a duplicate Social Security card.' More typing could be heard. 'A data gap follows,' the voice said.

'Being dead will do that,' Corso said.

'The name reappears. Nineteen seventy-three, Avalon, Wisconsin. A person of that same name and birth date marries one Eldred Holmes, together they produce—'

'That's enough,' Corso said. 'Anything after Avalon?'

'Nothing, sir.'

Before he could ask another question, she said, 'I have been instructed to inform you that recent events have created a situation where no further queries will be accepted from your access code.'

'I understand.'

'You will need to decommission your present sending unit.'

'Of course.'

Dial tone. He bounced the phone in the palm of his hand as he walked across the frozen gravel.

Dougherty was signing the credit card receipt when he arrived. The kid handed her a copy and then hurried back to the warmth of the station office. She waited until the kid closed the door. 'The credit card worked.'

'I told you. They're real.'

Her face said she wasn't convinced. 'You wanna drive?' she asked.

'Not particularly,' Corso said. 'You all right with it?'

'Sure. Where to?'

He thought it over. 'East,' he said finally. 'Pennsylvania.'

Dougherty climbed into the driver's seat. Corso walked around the front of the car. He stopped for a moment, bent at the waist, and placed something in front of the passenger-side tire. The Ford's engine roared to life. He got into the passenger seat and fastened his seat belt. Dougherty dropped the Ford into Drive. A loud snap cut through the night air.

'What was that?' she asked.

'What?'

'It felt like we ran over something.'

'We did.'

'What?'

'Your phone.'

I don't care what she says: I don't care what anybody says. Life is supposed to be fair. Things are supposed to work out right. Otherwise there'd be no reason for going on, would there? Might as well throw yourself in the ground if things were that out of hand. Problem is . . . most people just sit around and wait for good things to happen to them. Like life is something jumps on your back, insteada the other way around. It's always the dried-up ones like Mama May – they're the ones always telling little kids life isn't fair. 'Cause that's what they gotta believe, or else they gotta look at their own lives and blame somethin' other than bad luck for why they never in their whole lives got anyplace near their dreams. Gotta tell themselves that successful people they don't like just got lucky. All that talk of righteousness is hooey. People just do what's easiest. Then they repent. It's like the Nature Channel. Only the strong survive.

CHAPTER 13

hat kind of goddamn street name is that?' she groused. Corso read it out loud again. 'Mauch Chunk Road.'

'What in hell's a Mauch Chunk?'

Corso laughed. 'A small piece of a larger Mauch, I guess.'

Dougherty braked the Ford to a stop. Nothing but guardrail straight ahead. Perma Avenue angled off to the right. Girard Avenue to the left. The white Lincoln Continental that had been riding their rear bumper for the past five minutes honked twice and then swung out and accelerated around them in a cloud of fumes and frustration.

'Take Perma,' Corso said, pointing to the road on the right.

'That what the guy said?'

'Actually, our friend back at the gas station neglected to mention a fork in the road, but he did say the cemetery was on top of the hill, and Perma goes up and Girard goes down.' He tapped his temple. 'Not much gets by Francis Albert Falco.'

She checked the rearview mirror. Pushed the accelerator. 'Why do they always put graveyards on the tops of hills?' she asked. 'It's not like anybody's gonna be putting out lawn chairs and enjoying the view or anything.'

'Nearer my God to thee, and all that,' Corso said.

They rode to the top of the next incline in silence. Overhead, a slate gray sky flowed eastward, dark and sensuous, like cooling lava. A swirling wind lifted the last derelict leaves of fall and sent them aloft in dirty spirals. As they rounded a sharp corner near the summit, a ragged patchwork of shingled roofs appeared spread out over the valley floor. Here and there the spires of churches poked up through the social fabric, like slender white fingers pointing the way home.

'The place looks way better from up here,' Dougherty commented as she wheeled the Ford around the narrow corner. 'These rust belt cities have always given me the willies. Makes me feel like I need a shower.'

'Allentown used to run on iron and coke and chromium steel,' Corso said. 'When the coal ran out, all of a sudden it didn't run on anything at all.'

She wrinkled her nose at the acrid air. 'Why do people stay in places like this?'

'Because they were born here. It's all they know. And because they were promised that if they behaved themselves and worked hard, there was a life for them here. A place where they could raise kids and root for the Phillies and maybe retire to their front porches to watch the Fourth of July parade.'

She wheeled the car around another pair of corners, then sneaked a peek at Corso. 'That how you envision your golden years, Frank? Waving a little flag on the porch?'

Corso snorted. 'Not me,' he said. 'Not you either, honey bunny. We're not part of the scheduled programming. We're fringe people. Neither of us is ever gonna be the one bringing stringbean casserole to the Elks or the Eagles or the Eastern Star. We're always going to be on the outside looking in. That's what we do.'

He expected an argument, but instead she pointed out over the top of the steering wheel. 'There,' she said. 'That's gotta be it.'

It was a big old-fashioned cemetery. Maybe thirty acres of the dearly departed nestled beneath a towering grove of oaks and maples whose black branches spread like bony fingers across the sky. The burial ground was surrounded by a six-foot-tall wrought-iron fence. From where he sat, Corso's eye could follow the meandering, frost-heaved line of the barrier as it wandered drunkenly away from him toward the northern horizon. In other times and places the fence would have been worth more than the ground it guarded, but in an iron town like Allentown – a town where for sixty years the red glow of the steel cauldrons lit the edges of the night sky – for a town like this, half a mile of iron fence was nothing special. Just a rusting divider between what was . . . and what was yet to be.

Something was burning. Something oily and thick whose inky, airborne ash rained down from the skies like a misty morning in hell. The air was caustic and rough to the throat. As he paced back and forth in front of the grave, Corso felt the glands in his neck beginning to ache.

The headstone was simple. A rough-hewn block of local granite polished smooth on one side. Etched leaves as a border. 'Sissy Marie Warwick,' it read. 'September 4, 1957 – September 4, 1972. Beloved Daughter. May the Grace of God bring Eternal Peace.'

A violent shiver brought Corso to a halt, as a waking dream flickered before his eyes. As if looking through layers of gauze, he saw the thin, wavy shadow of a girl, hands clasped, hair blowing in the wind. Before he could move or speak, she turned her head his way, widened her hollow eyes, and then, as the wind gusted again, she was gone. He blinked twice, then turned away, embarrassed by his sudden flight of fancy.

Dougherty had her hood up. She rocked on her heels as she gazed toward the gathering sunset. He was relieved. She hadn't seen. Corso pulled his coat close around his body and hunched his shoulders.

'She stood right here,' he said.
'Who?'

'The new Sissy Warwick.' He made an expansive gesture with his hand.

'She stood right here somewhere. Saw this headstone and read those words and decided that Sissy Warwick was going to be her new name.'

Dougherty thought it over. 'You think maybe she even saw the burial?'

'That's an interesting thought, now isn't it,' he mused, looking around. 'Maybe from a distance,' he said. 'Maybe over there behind that oak thicket.' He walked in a slow circle. 'Yeah . . . I'll bet she did. That feels right to me.' He turned to Dougherty. 'This was a person with a plan already in place. Less than a week after the real Sissy Marie went in the ground, somebody was already using her identity to get a birth certificate and a Social Security card.'

'But how can we be sure she's the same Sissy Marie Warwick who shows up in Avalon, Wisconsin, a year later?'

'The woman in Avalon used the same birth certificate and Social Security number when she married Eldred Holmes a year or so later.'

She eyed him hard. 'How do you know that?'

'The sheriff told me,' he said quickly.

Her expression said she didn't believe him, but 'Weird' was all she said.

'What's weird is that it pretty much had to be a kid.'

She frowned.

'Think about it,' Corso said. 'The real Sissy

Warwick died on her fifteenth birthday. It stands to reason that whoever decided to take over her identity had to be somewhere in the vicinity of her age. Probably had to be a little older, rather than younger. You get much younger than fifteen, and I start to have doubts about your ability to put the thing together.'

'A kid, huh?'

'Don't see how it could be any other way,' he said.

Dougherty didn't argue. Instead she slipped her arm through his. 'Let's go,' she said, tugging gently on his elbow. 'Color me silly, but I don't want to be standing out in the middle of a graveyard when it gets dark.'

Arm in arm, they began to wind their way among the graves. No straight lines here. No military precision. The arrangement of the graves was haphazard, as if the stones and bones had been scooped into a giant hand and rolled out like dice.

This was the final resting place of the city builders. If they were Catholic, they ended up here. Rich and poor. Old and young. Slag skimmers and steel barons alike. Simple stone plaques covered with debris lay scant feet from ornate family mausoleums whose baroque marble angels, green and grimy with age, looked down upon the less fortunate with eternal disdain.

Fresh flowers decorated occasional graves, but most were grown over and ragged, as if the dead had been forgotten. On Corso's left, a fallen headstone lay in the grass, its uprooted base festooned with spidery roots and a weathered one-eyed Pooh Bear. Against the black of the upturned earth the remains of Mylar balloons gleamed slack and silver in the waning light.

The grass upon which they trod was a thick, spongy mat of leaves and dead, frozen grass. To the south, the hill fell away. Allentown now rested beneath the pall of blue smoke rising from its chimneys, spreading over the peaks and valleys of the rooftops like dirty cotton.

'What next?' Dougherty asked.

Corso thought it over as they walked. 'I guess we lay hands on the local phone book and see how many Warwicks we can find.'

She dropped his arm. 'That's all you've got? We beat the phone book?'

'That's it.'

'That's pretty damn desperate,' she said.

'You're telling me.'

To the north, a collection of buildings peeked from among a wall of trees. It wasn't until they'd walked another fifty yards that Corso looked that way again. When he did, he stopped. Pointed. 'The one in the middle,' he said. 'It's a church.'

'Sure is.'

The sharp slope of the steeple had been lost among the riot of branches. Four buildings, including the church. A pair of three-story blocks on the left. Dark and sharp-edged against the fading sky. A smaller building squatted on the right

119

of the church, its stone chimney adding a thin column of smoke to the gathering blanket of smog. Three dimly lighted windows cast shadows out onto the ground.

'Probably the Sisters of Whatever,' Dougherty said.

Corso nodded. 'Yeah.'

She turned and started away. 'Come on,' she said over her shoulder. When Corso didn't move, she wandered back to his side. 'Let's go,' she said. 'This place gives me the creeps.'

'Let's visit the Sisters,' he said.

'Nuns make me nervous,' Dougherty said. 'Something about them always makes me feel like I've done something wrong and should confess.'

'You can wait in the car if you want.'

She put her hands on her hips. 'Oh yeah, like I'm gonna sit in a graveyard waiting for . . .' Corso wasn't listening. His black overcoat was quickly blending into the night as he strode in the direction of the lights. Dougherty weighed her options. Looked around the graveyard. Then stretched her long legs and ran headlong after Corso.

CHAPTER 14

Somebody was inside. Corso could feel it. He pulled the iron handle again. Kept pulling until a full foot of rusty chain emerged from the bricks, then let it go. Inside the rectory, the dull clank of clapper on bell echoed in the darkness.

'Place looks deserted to me,' Dougherty said. 'I'm bettin' they just leave the lights on for security.'

'There's somebody in there,' Corso insisted. 'I can tell.'

'X-ray vision, huh?'

'I come from a long line of folks who don't answer their doors. Trust me, there's somebody inside.'

The wind was stronger here. Overhead, the trees circling Our Lady of Perpetual Sorrow's driveway swayed like ghostly dancers. The circular drive hadn't seen a car in ages. The bricks were littered with dead leaves, acorns, and small shards of broken branches. The untended flower beds, grown tall in the summer sun, were bent double now, their brown stalks cracked and frozen in place. The wind carried the fecund odor of mold and decay and death.

The rectory's ancient front door consisted of half a dozen maple planks held together by ornate wrought-iron hinges. The arched entrance had a little built-in sliding speakeasy window. Corso used his thumb, trying to slide the metal plate aside, but it wouldn't budge. As he tried again, the window suddenly slid open, pinching his thumb between the metal and the wood. Instinctively, he brought his thumb to his mouth.

His thumb was still in his mouth as he bent at the waist and peered through the opening. Whoever was on the other side was standing right up against the door. All he could see were a pair of rimless glasses and two sparkling blue eyes.

'We weren't expecting you until morning,' a woman's voice said.

'Excuse me?' Corso said.

'You're the movers, aren't you?'

'No, ma'am. We're not. I wanted to ask someone about the cemetery.'

He heard a sigh. 'We're no longer accepting internments,' the voice said.

'No, I wanted to ask about one of the graves that's already there.'

Corso thought he heard whispering but wasn't sure.

'Which grave was that?' the voice asked.

'Over on the east side of the cemetery. Sissy Marie Warwick.'

This time, he was positive. The whispering took

on a more urgent cadence, and then, without warning, the little window slid shut with a bang.

'Having your usual effect on women, I see,' Dougherty sneered.

As Corso raised his fist to the door, a series of metallic clicks and scrapes filled the air, and the door swung inward, until it stopped on a thick black chain. A nun. Hard to tell how old. Seventy-something at least. Wearing the basic nun's headdress over a plain gray dress and black stockings. A black metal cross hung from her neck like an albatross. She looked Corso up and down. Her eyes came to rest on his bruised brow. 'What happened to your head?' she wanted to know.

'Car accident,' he told her. 'Banged myself up pretty good.'

She was momentarily startled when Dougherty stepped into the light. 'Oh,' she stammered, 'I thought . . . I didn't realize . . . a young lady . . .'

The door closed for a moment. The sound of urgent voices seeped through the maple planks. Corso couldn't make out the words, but the rhythm of the phrases suggested a heated debate. The chain rattled, and then the door eased open again.

Corso was momentarily taken aback. Something was different. Same face, same glasses, same everything, except that this time she wore a black cardigan sweater over her dress.

'Won't you come in,' she said.

Corso stepped aside, but when Dougherty hesitated, he stepped in first. The air was thick and warm and smelled of brewing tea. Dougherty followed. The door swung shut on its own, leaving them standing in a narrow flagstone hallway.

There were two of them. Identical in every way except for the sweater.

'We're sisters,' Sweater said.

Before Corso could respond, the other one piped in, 'Really sisters. Not just Sisters in Christ.'

'Twins,' said the other.

'Ah,' Corso said.

'This is Sister Agnes. I'm Sister Veronica,' Sweater said.

Dougherty started to speak, but Corso cut her off. 'I'm Frank Falco. This is Meg Dolan.' Dougherty cast Corso a quick look that said she didn't require any help remembering her alias. She put on her canned smile and began to rub the warmth into her red hands.

'Can we get you some tea?' Sister Veronica inquired.

'That would be great,' Dougherty said.

Corso and Dougherty followed the women down the narrow hall to a small kitchen at the back of the building. A plain wooden table and four chairs held down the center of the room. Every other flat surface was covered with cardboard boxes, taped closed and marked in red. Plates. Utensils. Cookbooks.

Sister Veronica apologized for the clutter. 'Amazing what people collect over the years,' she said with a wan smile.

Her sister scowled and made a dismissive noise with her lips. 'Some people are entirely too worldly for their own good,' she said. Her mouth was pinched and wrinkled around the edges like a snare.

'My sister means Father Jonathan,' Veronica explained. Her hand swept around the room. 'He lived here in the rectory for thirty-seven years,' she said. Her eyes crinkled with a smile. 'Father *did* like his comforts.'

'Far too much,' Agnes added. 'His habits were the death of him.'

'He died back in February. Heart attack.'

'Sloth and gluttony,' said Agnes. 'The perils of the acquisitional life.'

Sister Veronica rolled her eyes. 'Please excuse my sister,' she said. 'Even after these many years in the service to our Lord, she's never become resigned to the foibles of human nature.'

'This world could use a little more righteous indignation,' Agnes said.

'Perhaps a little,' her sister chided. 'Just a little.'

The lines sounded rehearsed. As if they'd been playing the same parts for so long, they'd become bored with their own banter. Sister Veronica touched Dougherty on the elbow. 'We promised you some tea, now didn't we, dear?' She gave a laugh. 'What a space cadet I'm getting to be.'

She was still chuckling at her own forgetfulness as she crossed to the stove and dug a plain white mug out of one of the boxes. She looked at Corso with a question in her eyes. He shook his head. She set the cup in the sink and then filled it from a small porcelain teapot. She returned, holding the cup in both hands, like an offering, and handed the mug of steaming tea to Dougherty. 'I'm afraid we're out of cream and sugar,' she apologized. 'We're leaving in the morning.'

'Would have been a waste,' Agnes said quickly.

'Where are you moving to?' Dougherty asked, sipping from the mug.

'Muncie, Indiana,' Agnes said. 'Our order has a facility there.'

'The Archdiocese is closing the church,' Veronica said.

'Selling the property.' Agnes shook her head. 'After a hundred and twenty-five years. Like the house of God was a meat market or something.'

'Things change, sister,' Veronica said, her voice weary.

Corso could feel the moment slipping down the well of their personal disagreements. 'They sell the cemetery too?' he asked.

Veronica looked offended. 'Of course not,' she said. 'How could they—'

'If they could have, they would have,' Agnes snapped. 'It's all about money, these days. Nothing but the almighty dollar.'

Veronica sighed. Behind the rimless glasses, her eyes looked inward. 'When we first came here, there were forty-two Sisters. Now it's just us.'

'When was that?' Dougherty asked.

'Nineteen fifty-nine,' they said in unison.

'We were teachers,' Agnes explained.

'Mathematics and literature,' Veronica said, indicating first her sister and then herself. 'That was before the school closed, back in eighty-one.'

'You said—' Agnes began.

Her sister cut her off. 'We had eighty girls then. Twenty boarders and sixty town girls. We were the largest Catholic girls' school in . . .' As she spoke, her voice took on an artificial quality, theatrical and bright, as if she were talking to herself in the dark to keep from being afraid. As if her words, and only her words, could keep the darkness from sinking its claws into her back.

Sister Agnes was having none of it, though. Her face was a mask of determination. She stepped between Corso and Veronica. 'You said you were interested in the Warwick grave,' she said in a voice far too loud for polite conversation. While her statement was directed at Corso, her eyes never left Sister Veronica. They passed a long look, so full of avarice and recrimination it could only have been shared by people who'd spent far too much time in one another's company.

'I seem to have touched a nerve,' Corso said to nobody in particular. Dougherty hiccuped and spilled tea on her hands. Neither nun noticed. They stood, six feet apart, locked in silent combat.

'Sister, please . . .' Veronica said finally.

'It's an omen,' Agnes said. 'Don't you see?'

'Don't you blaspheme,' the other woman warned. 'Don't you dare.'

'Don't all things come from God?' Agnes demanded, gesturing at Corso and Dougherty. 'That's what you always tell me, isn't it?'

'Actually, we came from Wisconsin,' Corso said. Dougherty smiled and stepped on his foot.

Sister Veronica blinked first. She sighed and turned away. She walked to the sink. Poured the rest of the tea down the drain. Agnes stared at her sister's back for a moment and then turned toward Corso and Dougherty.

'Why are you interested in that particular grave, Mr . . .'

'Falco.'

'We have over three thousand souls in our cemetery. Why that one?'

'I think someone may have stolen Sissy Marie Warwick's identity.' He measured his words carefully. 'I think someone may have used her identity for criminal purposes.'

'What criminal purposes might that be?' Agnes asked. It was as if the oxygen had been sucked from the room and replaced with the electric, anticipatory air that precedes a thunderstorm. Corso looked from one sister to another.

'Maybe murder,' Dougherty said.

A crash sounded from across the room. Veronica had dropped the teapot into the sink, where it had shattered. 'Oh, look what I've done now,' she said. 'I can't believe how clumsy I've become.'

She used the tips of her fingers to pick the shards from the sink. She began to blather about the ravages of age, but nobody was listening. Agnes stepped over and stood directly in front of Corso. 'Perhaps you should tell me about it,' she said.

Corso laid it out for her. Everything he knew. Halfway through Corso's story, Sister Veronica stopped puttering at the sink. She stood facing them now, tight-lipped, her hands steepled before her. 'Had to be somebody just about the girl's age,' Corso said finally. 'That's the only way it works out.'

'What year was that?' asked Sister Agnes.

'She showed up in Wisconsin in the summer of nineteen seventy-three.'

Agnes turned to her sister. 'Well . . . that's the capper, now isn't it?' she said.

Veronica hesitated and then gave a grudging nod. 'You were right,' she said in a low voice. 'All of you were right.' She looked as if she was going to be sick.

Corso met Agnes's gaze. 'Sounds like *you're* the one with the story to tell now.'

'Finally,' Agnes said. She took a deep breath and began to speak. Seems that back when the Sacred Heart School was in its prime, the good Sisters used to occasionally take in girls from the community who had been orphaned or abused or both. That was the way things were handled in those days, before the government got involved and screwed everything up. At least that's how Sister

Agnes saw it. She indulged herself in half a minute of politics before she caught herself rambling. Got right to the point. Just before Christmas, 1970, a young girl showed up on their doorstep, claiming to be an orphan. The girl said her name was Mary Anne Moody. Claimed to be fourteen and without any other place to go.

'Said her whole family had been burned up in a fire,' Veronica added.

Agnes shot her sister an annoyed look and went on. The girl's arrival had created something of a tempest among the Sisters. Some had been inclined to turn her away. She was not, after all, a local girl. Nor was she even Catholic. Others had been more kindly disposed toward Miss Mary Anne Moody. After a rather spirited debate, it was decided to take the girl in.

'Charity cannot come with strings attached,' Veronica said. 'It was our Christian duty.'

Agnes ignored the interruption. Mary Anne Moody had stayed with the Sisters, attending school and living on the premises, for nearly two years. She turned out to be a difficult, headstrong girl, often in conflict with both the Sisters and her fellow students. Occasionally violent. Often subject to discipline. From Agnes's tone, it sounded as if many of the Sisters of the Sacred Heart had come to rue their decision to take the girl in.

'She was a constant problem,' Agnes said. 'The most headstrong and willful child I ever met.' Veronica averted her gaze and offered no rebuttal.

Not only was the girl troublesome, she was also possessed of a number of habits that gave the good Sisters cause to wonder about their charity. The first came to light when a number of drawings were found in her room. The clipped way Sister Agnes dismissed them as 'inappropriate' and the red spots that appeared on her cheeks spoke volumes.

'And that wasn't the worst of it.' Agnes paused. 'She had a positively morbid fascination with the graveyard. With death and dead people.'

Seemed that whenever Mary Anne Moody turned up missing, which was a fairly regular occurrence, all one had to do was take a walk out into the graveyard and there she'd be. Standing around. Talking to herself. Copying the information on the headstones into a small secretarial pad she carried.

'What for?' Dougherty asked.

The sisters shook their headpieces in wonder.

'What about the Warwick grave?' Corso prodded.

Veronica couldn't stand it anymore. 'Right before she left—'

'Disappeared,' Agnes corrected.

Seems that in the months immediately preceding her disappearance, Mary Anne Moody had become fixated on the grave of Sissy Warwick. Had been found standing by the graveside on at least a dozen occasions. Veronica and some of the Sisters believed that Mary Anne found the grave fascinating because she felt guilty, as survivors often do, about being the only member of her family to live through the tragedy and in some unhealthy way she identified with this girl of her own age who had found a peace that had to that point eluded her. That was the positive spin.

More worldly types, Agnes among them, had seen the girl's actions as the precursors of a troubled and ungodly life and had demanded that the young woman be exposed to mental health professionals. At the mere mention of one Dr William Harkens, a psychologist from County Mental Health, both sisters blushed.

'He was a young man and rather good-looking.' While Veronica said the words as if in apology, Agnes was shaking her head. 'What he was, sister' – she paused for effect – 'what he *was* . . . was without his trousers.'

Once again, the facts of the story depended almost entirely upon the disposition of the teller. Some believed that the young psychologist had attempted to sexually compromise the young woman. This theory was borne out by the fact that he had insisted on being alone with Mary Anne during their therapy sessions, and it was permanently compounded when Sister Ellen, hearing odd noises emanating from Father Jonathan's office, burst in to find both Mary Anne Moody and her therapist in a state of what she later described as 'a palpable sexual tension and partial undress.'

Dr Harkens claimed to have been the victim of

a determined sexual assault by the young woman, whom he reckoned to be both wickedly wanton and wise to the particulars of passion in a manner most unseemly for a girl her age. Needless to say, the doctor was summarily removed from his position and the therapy sessions brought to an abrupt end.

'And that was the end of it?' Dougherty asked.

'Events intervened,' Veronica said.

'Miss Mary Anne Moody was what intervened,' her sister corrected.

The way Sister Agnes told it, the story seemed cut-and-dried. Back in those days they used to hold Friday night Bingo over in the basement of the Parish House. Used to pack the place to the rafters and turn a substantial profit. The cash was entrusted to one Sister Alice Ignatius, who at that time was well into her eighties and prone to caching the cash in her room until the bank opened on Monday. On several occasions, owing to her advanced age, Sister Alice failed to recall exactly where it was she had stashed the cash. As her room was small and offered limited conceal-ment possibilities, a quick shuffle by younger Sisters always produced both the wayward bundle and tears of thanks from Sister Alice.

'I'm telling you all this,' Agnes said, 'because I want you to understand why some of our number were opposed to calling the authorities.'

'She means me,' Veronica added.

'We found her dead,' Agnes said, 'one Saturday

morning. At the bottom of the basement stairs.'
She swallowed heavily. 'She broke her neck.'

Corso stiffened. 'And the Bingo money?'

'Never found,' said Agnes.

'How much money are we talking about?'

'Fifty-three hundred dollars.'

The sisters passed a look.

'What else?' Corso asked.

Sister Agnes drew in a breath and steeled herself. 'Sister Alice Ignatius was found in a very compromising position,' she said finally.

'She could have just landed that way,' Veronica said.

'Never in a million years,' her sister said.

'What did the authorities think about how she was found?'

'Oh . . . we didn't leave her like that,' Agnes said. 'We couldn't. We—'

'And the girl?'

'Gone.'

Corso couldn't help himself. He looked at Veronica. She had removed her glasses and was wiping the lenses with a paper towel.

'Sister Alice was well along in years,' she said. 'We thought perhaps Mary Anne had found the body or perhaps had been present when Sister Alice fell. We thought' – she waved a hand – 'having lost her family and all . . . she may have been so traumatized by the event that she ran.'

'My sister looks at the world through rose-colored glasses,' Agnes said.

'Is a little compassion so wrong?' Veronica asked.

'When it's misplaced, it is . . . yes.'

Corso interrupted. 'So . . . because the Sister was so old. Because she had a history of misplacing the money.' He hesitated. 'Some of your number didn't believe there was necessarily a connection between Sister Alice's death, the missing cash, and the sudden disappearance of Mary Anne Moody.'

'Believe it or not,' Agnes said.

Sister Veronica settled the glasses back onto her face. 'Hindsight is always twenty-twenty, sister,' she said in a singsong voice. 'It may sound silly now, but . . .' She couldn't find the words.

'Did she leave anything behind?'

'Sister Alice?' Veronica asked.

Agnes rolled her eyes. 'He means the girl, sister.'

Veronica shook her head sadly. 'No,' she said.

'Yes,' said Agnes. 'As a matter of fact, she did.'

CHAPTER 15

Dougherty threw her bag onto the far bed. Looked around and sighed. 'Am I crazy, or do all these damn hotel rooms look exactly alike?'

Corso shrugged. 'I don't even see them anymore,' he said. He unfolded the luggage stand and set his bag on top. 'The Sisters sure were a trip,' he offered.

'No shit,' Dougherty said. 'Kinda makes you wonder why people choose a life like that.'

Corso unzipped his bag. 'I asked an old Shaker woman that once. Why she'd chosen a life of celibacy and religious devotion over a life in the regular world.'

'What'd she say?' Dougherty was stuffing clothes into the dresser drawers. Even if they were only staying for the night, she always unpacked and stowed her stuff. Corso, on the other hand, always lived out of his suitcase.

'She said she had the same desires as everybody else. Wanted kids and a family and all that happy horseshit.'

'Yeah?'

'Said she also had a desire to be closer to God. To live the life of the spirit rather than the life of the body. She told me she never really made up her mind. That all she was sure of was that she wouldn't be able to do a good job of both. And that even when I was talking to her, sixty years later, she still wasn't sure she'd made the right decision . . . only that she'd surely been forced to make the choice.'

'*Sophie's Choice*, huh?'

Corso chuckled. 'Something like that,' he said. From under his arm he retrieved a battered file folder. Legal sized, fastened by its own rubber tie. He tossed it on the bed before heading for the bathroom. 'Don't start without me,' he said. 'I'll be right back.'

Dougherty always got out of her outdoor clothes as soon as she arrived. Corso generally fell asleep wearing his boots. As she changed into a black sweatsuit, she heard the sound of water running in the bathroom and was reminded of how quickly Sister Veronica had begun to make busy work in the sink at the very mention of Mary Anne Moody's drawings, and how, after Sister Agnes's return from the basement, for the only time all evening the sisters had agreed on something, namely, that she and Corso should take the drawings with them, to better peruse at their leisure . . . *elsewhere*. Definitely elsewhere.

Corso emerged from the bathroom, wiping water from his face with a small white towel. He walked to Dougherty's side. 'Whatever's in there, sure seemed like the good Sisters didn't want to be around when we opened it,' he said.

'You want to do the honors?' Dougherty asked.

'Go ahead,' he said.

She moved slowly, sliding the rubber fastener off as if the folder might be wired to explode. Used only the tip of her finger to lift the lid. Corso peeked over her shoulder. Jammed inside were what appeared to be half a dozen sheets of rough paper, folded together in fourths. Dougherty slid them out, unfolded them, and smoothed the whole bundle out on the bedcover. Maybe two feet by two feet, the top drawing froze the breath in their throats. They stared open-mouthed until Dougherty broke the spell.

'This is too sick for words,' she said.

Some of it was very rudimentary, like the work of a much younger child. Stick figures. The lines dashed and violent. A house on fire. Engulfed in yellow and orange crayon. From one of the upstairs windows the letters read EEEEOOOOOW. In the foreground, a girl and a boy stick figure held hands, placidly watching the scene. Above them, a pair of angels rose into the sky.

The rest of the yard was taken up by graves and tombstones. Five of them. R.I.P. Their occupants lying atop the graves. Eyes x-ed out. Four men and a woman. It wasn't hard to tell which was which because that's where the drawings became much more realistically rendered, as even in death the male figures sported enormous red-tipped cocks, erect, rampant, and curving upward, their rendition so vibrant and alive they seemed nearly to tremble in their tumescence.

Dougherty peeled the top drawing from the pile. And then the next. And the next. Seven in all. Mostly the same as the first. Dead bodies, soaring angels, and huge cocks. Except for the last few. That's where it really got ugly, as the male figures rose from the dead and used their enormous appendages on the female figure in a startling number of ways. Corso reached over and flipped the pages. At the top of the third drawing she had written in red crayon: 'S'VILLE.' Along the right-hand margin of the final scene, a series of numbers were spaced out from top to bottom: 1 0 1 2 4.

Dougherty moved quickly now, refolding the pictures and fitting them back into the folder. Finished, she pulled her hands back as if the paper were hot to the touch.

'I don't ever want to see those things again,' she said. She wrapped her hands around her middle. 'That makes me sick to my stomach.'

'Hard to believe images like that didn't give anybody a hint that there might be a problem brewing with this girl. Mighta saved that poor therapist his job.'

Dougherty's tone sharpened. 'That's the Catholics for you,' she said. 'Sweep it under the rug. Never admit to anything. Buy your way out of it if you have to. Just transfer pedophile priests from parish to parish where they can just keep on preying on kids year after year because everybody's more worried about their damn image than they are about the kids.'

Corso checked the digital clock on the nightstand between the beds. Nine twenty-three. 'You hungry?' he asked.

'No,' she snapped. Then changed her mind. 'Yes,' she said.

Corso dialed twenty-two.

'Room service.'

Corso sat up with a start. For a long moment he had not the slightest inkling of where he was. Wasn't until he heard the rustle of linens and saw the outline of Meg Dougherty tossing in her sleep that he remembered. The Hilton. Allentown, Pennsylvania. He checked the clock: 1:01 A.M. He sat on the edge of the bed and whispered the time to himself as if reciting a litany. And then, out of the blue, he had it. A voice in his head asked: 'What if it's a zip code?' Confused for a moment, he lay back on the bed and closed his eyes. Next thing he knew, he was snapping on the light. Dougherty rolled over, scowling at the glare. He picked up the phone, dialed 0.

'Front desk.' Female voice. Under thirty. Slight accent.

'I need a favor.'

'What kind of favor, sir?'

'You guys have computers down there, right?'

'Yes, sir.'

'You on the Internet?'

'Yes, sir.'

'I have a zip code. I want to know what town it belongs to.'

He heard her sigh. 'Sir . . . I'm not sure . . . at this time of night . . .'

'What's your name?' Corso said.

He could feel her discomfort. 'Denise,' she said finally.

'Tell you what, Denise. You find out where this zip code belongs, and I'll give you a hundred bucks. How's that sound?'

'What's the number, sir?'

He told her. Took nine minutes before the knock on the door. Denise was a chubby little Hispanic woman in red hotel livery. She handed Corso a folded piece of paper; he handed her a crisp hundred-dollar bill. They managed a weak mutual smile before Corso moved his foot and the door swung shut.

Corso walked back into the room to find Dougherty awake, propped up on her elbow. 'Had one of your brainstorms, huh?'

Corso nodded. 'I was asleep. In my dream, I could hear the numbers being chanted by a bunch of kids. Like school. Like somebody was making them memorize the thing.' He shrugged. He knew better than to try to explain the Muse. People either thought he was losing his mind or expected

141

him to be able to call her to task at will. Never occurred to them there was a reason why the Muse was always a woman.

'So . . . what's the verdict?' Dougherty asked.

Corso unfolded the paper. Looked over at Dougherty. 'Smithville, New Jersey.'

'Never heard of it.'

'Me neither,' Corso said. 'Which is pretty weird, considering how much time I spent in the area. You asked me yesterday, I'd have said I'd heard of just about every place in Jersey. It's not all that damn big.'

'You think she capped the nun, don't you?' Dougherty said.

'Yeah,' Corso answered immediately. 'I'd bet a finger on it.'

Dougherty wrinkled her face. 'What kind of person kills a nun?' She scooted down in the bed and pulled the blanket over her shoulder. 'How do you go to sleep at night after you pushed an eighty-year-old nun down a flight of stairs?'

'You gotta really not give a shit' was all Corso could think to say.

Sarah Fulbrook straddled her bicycle and looked down at her younger sister. Emily knelt awkwardly in the gravel as she fumbled with the clothespin-and-playing-card apparatus she was using to make her new bike sound like it had a motor.

'Will you come on,' Sarah said. 'You're such a spaz.'

'A minute,' the younger girl said, trying to adjust the wooden pin she'd taped to the frame of her bike. The tape had loosened during the three-mile ride from the house and no longer held the playing card in the spokes properly.

'We got to get to Mama May's before it gets dark,' the older girl said. 'Hurry up.'

'I got a light,' the little girl said proudly. She flattened her lips and pulled with all her might. The wad of tape did not move.

'Swear to god, I'll leave you out here,' Sarah said.

'You leave me out here, Mama will kill you.'

'I'm not afraid of her.'

The little girl stopped what she was doing and looked around. 'You better watch out,' she said, scanning the surrounding trees for movement. 'She'll hear.'

'What's your problem?' Sarah demanded.

'Mama hears everything,' Emily said.

'Bullshit.'

'I'm gonna tell.'

'You tell . . . I'll make you wish you didn't.'

Again the little girl checked the area. This time looking for an ally rather than a spy. Her threat to tattle was hollow, and they both knew it. Tattling on Sarah was not a good idea. You only had to cross Sarah once to find out why.

'What's with you?' Sarah demanded. 'Mama's back at the house. She's not a witch or nothing. She don't see all and know all. She just says that so's we'll do what she says. She does it to Papa too.'

Emily was unconvinced. 'You're just mad 'cause she cut off your hair,' she said.

Sarah dismounted her bike and threw it to the ground. Emily tried to scoot off on her butt. The older girl was too quick for her, landing on her knees first, driving the air from her body. Emily hiccuped for breath and watched helplessly as her older sister jerked the playing card from her hand and tore it to pieces, then held it above her quivering head and let it fall into her hair like paper rain.

'You get on that bike, you hear me?'

Sarah got to her feet, picked the little girl up by her pigtails, and set her on her feet.

'Get on the damn bike,' she said.

CHAPTER 16

Dougherty put on her turn signal and wheeled the Ford Expedition into the far-left lane. The small green and white sign said Ramapo Valley College. She concentrated as she negotiated the long sweeping turn of the cloverleaf, turning them east on Ramapo Valley Road. As they rolled away from the highway and under a thick canopy of overhanging trees, Dougherty's eyes flicked up to the rearview mirror just in time to see a Bergen County Police cruiser flip on its lights bar.

'Shit,' she said, and looked over at Corso. 'We've got company.'

'Be cool,' he said. 'We're as legal as can be.'

He reached into his pocket and pulled out a thick wad of hundred-dollar bills. 'Here,' he said. 'Stash this. Anything goes wrong, this'll get you back home in style.'

She didn't argue. Just snatched the money and jammed it into the pocket of her jeans, then clapped her hand back onto the wheel.

Quarter mile up the road, she pulled into a paved turnoff. The cop left his lights blazing as he made his way to the driver's side. Dougherty rolled down the window. Gave him her best smile. 'Something wrong, Officer?' she asked.

'Could I see your license and registration, please?'

She dug around in her purse and pulled out her license. Corso found the rental agreement in the glove box and gave it to her. She handed both to the cop.

The cop was still studying the paperwork when another cruiser pulled in behind his own. The second cop got out, walked around to the passenger side, and stood three yards behind the passenger door with his hand resting on the butt of his gun.

The first cop leaned down and peered into the car. 'You'd be Mr Falco,' he said to Corso, who said he was indeed Mr Falco.

'I see some ID?'

Corso produced a driver's license and handed it over. 'Is there some problem?' Corso asked.

'Stay in the car,' the cop said. 'I'll be right back.'

Corso counted thirty and then looked back over his shoulder. Cop number one was holding on to the paperwork and speaking into his radio. Cop number two left the passenger door open as he joined his buddy in the front seat.

'What's he doing?' Dougherty wanted to know.

'His cop thing.'

'I wasn't speeding or anything,' she protested.

'I know.'

'If he—' she started.

'Just stay cool,' Corso said. 'You're not wanted for anything. Even in the worst-case scenario, you walk out and go home.'

Another minute and the cops were back. Cop number two stood at the rear of the car while number one came up to the window. 'You folks mind if we have a look through the car?' he asked.

Before Dougherty could open her mouth, Corso said, 'Yes, we do.'

'Excuse me?' the cop said.

'Yes, we mind if you search the car,' Corso repeated.

The cop made eye contact with Corso and held it. Then straightened up and walked to the back of the car, where he conferred with the other officer before returning to the driver's side window. He bent down again. 'So you're refusing us permission to search the car?'

'Yes, I am.'

'Why would that be, sir?'

'Because it's my right to refuse,' Corso answered.

The second cop was at the window now. 'That kind of attitude might look like you've got something to hide,' he commented.

'How you decide to interpret things is none of my concern,' Corso said. 'If we've committed some traffic violation, we'd like to hear about it. Otherwise we'd like to be on our way.'

Again the cops stepped to the rear of the vehicle and talked it over, this time for the better part of five minutes, before cop number one wandered back to the window.

'Can't say I think much of your spirit of co-operation,' he said.

'Duly noted,' Corso replied, stone-faced, his eyes locked on the cop's.

Nobody blinked. Their eyes were still boring into one another when the officer handed the paper-work back to Dougherty. 'You folks drive carefully now,' he said.

They sat still. Watched as the two officers returned to their cars and drove off, one east, one west. Dougherty breathed for what seemed like the first time in an hour.

'You are such an asshole,' she said. 'You could have gotten us—'

'Gimme my money back,' Corso said.

She pulled the wad out and dropped it in his lap. 'God damn you.'

'Let's go find this Rosen guy,' he said.

'We went to the post office,' Corso said. 'They said they don't deliver mail to Smithville anymore. As far as they're concerned, the zip code no longer exists.'

'Postmaster in' – she looked at Corso – 'what town was that?'

'Suffern, New York,' Corso said.

'Said we ought to come over to the community college and ask you about it. They said you were the local expert on the area.'

His name was Randy Rosen. Assistant professor

of history at the Ramapo Valley College of New Jersey. Fifty-something, with uneven skin and a nose that belonged on a much larger face. He'd mastered the needy academic look. Thick salt-and-pepper hair in need of a barber. Threadbare herringbone sports coat in need of dry cleaning. Cramped little office in need of a fire. 'We're not a community college anymore. We've outgrown our populist beginnings. We're a' – he used his fingers to make imaginary quotation marks – 'a full-fledged, full-service college these days.' His voice carried the tinge of bitterness and disappointment common to failed academics, people whose modest appointments and offices represented their final rung on the academic ladder, a station above which they were not destined to rise.

Rosen leaned back in his chair and looked them over. 'If you're talking Smithville, you're talking Jackson Whites.'

'What's that?' Dougherty asked. She looked at Corso. *Jackson Whites* was the same phrase the postmaster had used.

'Depends on who you ask,' Rosen said. 'There are a number of myths and legends as to the origin of the people.' He took them in again, as if trying out a new pair of eyes. 'You mind if I ask what your interest is?'

Corso told him. As the story unfolded, Rosen's expression moved from detached amusement to rapt attention. 'And you think this girl—' He stopped himself. 'Of course, by now she's a middle-aged woman . . . You think she may have come from Smithville?'

'I think it's possible,' Corso said.

Rosen leaned back in his chair and laced his fingers over his stomach. Corso watched the professor process the information. Didn't take a lot of imagination to figure out what he was thinking. Might be a monograph here. Maybe even a full-blown paper. Something that might get him out of academic purgatory, one last booster rocket for a fizzling career. Maybe even get him a chair somewhere.

'What year are we talking about here?' Rosen asked.

Corso thought it over. 'I'm thinkin' late sixties, early seventies,' he said. Rosen tried to hide it, but something about the dates added fuel to his inner fire.

'Where to start?' he asked.

'What's a Jackson White?' Corso asked.

'Mostly it's a polite way to say *nigger*.'

'I didn't know there was a polite way,' Dougherty said.

'Actually, *Jackson Whites* is a bastardization of *Jacks and whites*,' Rosen said. '*Jacks* is what they called coloreds back in the sixteenth century.'

'So Jackson Whites aren't white,' Corso said.

'They're our local hill people. And most definitely racially mixed.'

Corso and Dougherty exchanged glances. Rosen smiled.

'I know what you're thinking. Is this guy crazy? This is New Jersey. More people per square mile than any other state in the Union. What's this talk of hill people living in isolation up in the mountains?'

They didn't argue. 'What they are,' Rosen continued, 'is an extended clan of closely interrelated families living up in the mountains around here.' He paused for effect. 'They've been up there since the Revolutionary War.'

'You mean . . . like hillbillies?' Dougherty asked.

'More or less,' Rosen said. 'If anything, they're more isolated than their southern counterparts and a whole lot more clannish.'

'What mountains are we talking about here?' Corso asked.

'The Ramapos.' Rosen got to his feet and started across the room toward the door. He gestured for Corso and Dougherty to follow.

They crossed the empty hallway and entered an unoccupied classroom. Rosen walked past the rostrum and pulled down a map. Corso and Dougherty stepped in closer. Northern New Jersey, southern New York. Rosen grabbed an old-fashioned pointer from the chalk tray and drew an imaginary circle around the area. 'Right here,' he said. 'Hard to believe, isn't it? Less than thirty miles from Manhattan, and it's one of the most culturally isolated areas of the whole country.' He tapped the map with the end of the pointer. 'A sixty-mile stretch of mountains wedged between the Hudson River and northern Bergen County, and almost nobody knows anything about it.'

'How'd that much property stay wild in a place like this?' Corso asked. 'You'd figure some land developer would have screwed it up by now.'

'Way back when, it was too rocky and remote to farm,' Rosen said. 'By the time anybody else wanted the property, the Jackson Whites'd been up there for a hundred years and weren't about to be moving out.'

'How'd they get up there to begin with?' Corso asked.

'There's a couple of stories,' Rosen said. 'The basic legend tells how the area was first inhabited by the Tuscarora Indians, who'd moved from North Carolina to join up with their allies, the Iroquois, in about 1713. Seems they'd had enough of getting their butts kicked by the British in the French and Indian Wars and were looking for a place to hide. About the time they got settled, the sons of black freedmen from the plantations in the Hudson River Valley heard about the place and began to run away and join them. They inter-married with the Tuscarora and some of the local Lenni-Lenape Indians as well. That's about the time their neighbors began to refer to them as "Jacks and whites."'

'What's the other story?' Corso asked.

Rosen leaned on the rostrum and went into his canned spiel on the subject.

According to the second part of the legend,

during the Revolutionary War, the British Army command at New York contracted with a Colonial sea captain and trader named Jackson to bring thirty-five hundred prostitutes, recruited in the cities of England, to New York to service the garrison. Unable to recruit that many English working girls, the industrious Jackson sailed to the West Indies and picked up an additional four hundred black women to supplement his English recruits.

Upon their arrival in New York, the black prostitutes, known as 'Jackson Blacks,' were separated from the rest of the women and billeted in a cow pasture in Greenwich Village called Lispenard's Meadows. When the British were driven out of New York during the War of Independence, the women, fearing reprisals, fled Manhattan and wandered northward into the Hudson Valley where they heard, possibly from Hessian deserters, that the Ramapos were a haven for Tory refugees, Dutch adventurers, and every other kind of villain imaginable.

They were, of course, despised by their respectable lowland neighbors either for being Hessians or Tory sympathizers, or for their mixed blood, or for being black or Indian or outlaw, or any or all of the above.

'And you're telling me these people are still up there,' Corso said when Rosen had finished. 'Living in isolation . . . thirty miles from Manhattan.'

'Maybe five hundred people. All interrelated,'

Rosen said. 'Mostly with Dutch surnames like de Fries, van der Donk, and Mann. That kind of thing.'

'When you say interrelated,' Dougherty began, 'you mean . . .'

Rosen nodded. 'Genetics have not always been kind to the Jackson Whites,' he said. 'Their isolation has produced some interesting genetic anomalies. Syndactyly and polydactyly were particularly common.' He used one hand to point at the other. 'Webbed fingers or toes, or extra fingers and toes.' He counted on his fingers. 'Also a lot of piebaldness, albinism, mental retardation . . . you name it, they've produced it.'

'How'd you become an expert on the subject?' Corso asked.

'Back in sixty-three, the state started making them send their kids to regular public school. I was a junior at Mahwah High School.' His face took on a look of longing. 'There was this girl. Justine de Vries.' He shook his shaggy head. 'The most exotic creature I'd ever laid eyes on. I started spending a lot of time up in the hills.' He showed his palms. 'Years later, when I needed a dissertation topic . . .' He spread his hands. 'The rest, as they say, is history.'

'Where's she now?' Dougherty asked.

Rosen's face took on a somber caste. 'Still up there somewhere, I guess.' He seemed to feel a need to explain. 'I heard she married a guy named van Dykan. After that summer, we lost track of each other,' he said. 'In those days it just wasn't possible, you know, a Jewish lowlander and a Jackson White. It wasn't . . . my parents were liberal and all, but I mean . . .' He swallowed hard. 'I haven't seen her in nearly thirty years,' he said. He made a face. 'Probably for the best.'

The ensuing silence was finally broken by the sound of feet and voices in the hall as students began passing between classes. Rosen checked the clock on the wall: 10:30 A.M. 'I've got a class to teach,' he said. For a second, he looked as if he wanted to say something, but then changed his mind.

Corso and Dougherty shook his hand and thanked him for his time. Rosen began to leave the room. He stopped. 'I haven't been up there in ten years,' he said absentmindedly. 'Not since Arlene died . . .' He stopped. 'She was my wife. She . . .'

They were about to get the story of Arlene's death and how happy they'd been together. Corso could feel it. 'How do we get up there?' he asked.

Rosen thought it over. Checked the clock again.

'You want to go up there, huh? To where Smithville used to be?'

Corso nodded. Dougherty agreed.

'Be in my office at noon,' Rosen said.

CHAPTER 17

From overhead the road would have been invisible. Nothing more than an occasional black line among a maze of oaks and pines and Atlantic cedars whose gnarly branches soared above the road like ancient vaulted arches. Intermittent spots of sunshine created a stroboscopic effect on the eyes as the Ford rolled along.

Rosen was using the sound of his own voice for comfort as Corso wheeled the big Ford around yet another switchback. 'We might as well start at the store. It's more or less the center of the Ramapo universe.'

'There's a store up here?' Dougherty said from the backseat.

Rosen threw his hands in the air. 'A store and a firehouse . . . a church, a post office . . . even a liquor store. All the necessities of life. The store started out back in the 1830s as Van Dynes Dry Goods,' he said. 'Went through so many owners the locals gave up on the proper name and just started calling it 'the store.' You hear one of them saying he's going to the store . . . that's, where he's headed.'

Corso dropped the Ford into low gear as the incline steepened. What had started as a two-lane blacktop road had, in the space of five miles, morphed into a well-worn goat track winding around the contours of the hill like a cracked asphalt bezel.

'These days the kids are much more worldly. They've been going to public school for three generations. The local demographic's gotten a lot more diverse. They don't stick out like they used to, so most of them leave and live down in the lowlands.'

'Where was Smithville in relation to the store?' Dougherty asked.

'Up north in New York State.' He pointed out the passenger window. 'Maybe ten miles that way, up by the Rockland County line.' Rosen shifted in the seat so he could face Dougherty. 'Even by Jackson White standards, Smithville was out in the boonies,' Rosen said. 'Smithville was the extreme northern end of the area. Their kids went to school in Mahwah. I've heard it said that the whole town was one big extended family. Maybe forty, fifty people all with the same last name. Real clannish. Everybody said they were hostile to outsiders, maybe even dangerous, so she . . . Justine . . .' He appeared confused for a moment. 'Justine . . .' He looked around the cab. 'She was . . .'

'The exotic girl from high school,' Dougherty said.

The words seemed to snap Rosen from his reverie. 'Yes. I was hot for going to Smithville. Would have been like discovering a lost Amazon tribe or something. But she never would take me up there. It was like her clan and the Smithville clan had a feud or something. She told me that all her life her family had told her to keep away from those people, like there was something wrong with them or something, but that nobody would ever tell her exactly what the deal was.'

As they crested a steep rise, the trees peeled back and the windshield suddenly filled with hazy blue sky. Instinctively both Dougherty and Rosen reached for the overhead handles as the front wheels briefly left the ground. And then they were bouncing, level again, a trio of bobbleheads staring in disbelief at the town before them in the clearing.

At first sight, Fredrikstown appeared smaller than it was. First thing you saw were the Sunoco gas pumps, the big green and red sign reading 'Ramapo Variety,' and then the post office and the liquor store and, at the far end, the firehouse and the flagpole. Wasn't until your eye finished taking them in that you noticed the six or eight clapboard houses set back from the road, fanning out on either side of the commercial buildings. Roofs green with moss, sides streaked gray and white by weather, the houses, with their neat little fences and yards, played counterpoint to the prevailing rural squalor, thus providing an

158

air of respectability, which the scene otherwise lacked.

Wasn't until Corso had gotten out of the car and had a chance to look around that he began to notice the other dwellings tucked back into the edges of the clearing. A three-sixty perusal revealed maybe a dozen houses and about half that many trailer homes wedged in among the trees. Allowing for houses he couldn't see, Corso estimated that something like a hundred and fifty people lived in greater Fredrikstown. Nearly a third of the entire Jackson White community, if Rosen's figures were to be believed.

'This is amazing,' Dougherty said from the backseat. 'It's like the Waltons.' Corso snickered as he stretched.

Rosen winced. 'Make sure you don't say anything like that to them, okay? Not only do these people not like to be thought of as quaint, but over the years, their dealings with outsiders have been something less than positive . . . so they tend to be a bit touchy.'

A trio of dusty pickup trucks were angle-parked in front of the post office. Ramapo Variety occupied the center of the block. The concrete stairs had been built wide, as if offering equal entrance to any of the five or six separate roads leading into the clearing.

They followed Rosen across the patched asphalt and into the store. Floor-to-ceiling shelves. Rolling ladders along each wall. Couple of those wooden

159

arm extensions whose metal fingers plucked cans from overhead shelves and then dropped them down into waiting aprons. Kind of general store you only see in the movies these days. Friction tape and first aid. Butter pecan and barrel staves. Shotguns and shortbread. You name it, they had it.

Must have been a slow day. Except for a couple in their mid-sixties, the place was empty. Gospel music seeped from a white plastic radio. Behind the counter, the man and woman were stocking the shelves. The man caught sight of them first.

He'd lost most of his hair. Apparently the deprivation had encouraged him to maximize what he had left, as he'd grown his remaining halo of hair about a foot long. The fringe hung down to his collar like Spanish moss from a bayou tree.

'Ilta,' he said.

She finished fitting a can of condensed milk onto the shelf before she turned toward the sounds behind her. She looked from Corso to Dougherty to Rosen, where her eyes flickered for an instant. She was as gaunt as the old man was chubby. Long gray hair piled up on top of her head. Her hawklike nose pointed unwaveringly at Rosen.

'I remember you,' she said. 'You're the one was doggin' after that girl from up by Hewlitt.' When Rosen didn't deny it, she searched her memory banks. 'Come back after that too, several times as I recall,' she said. 'Studyin' us.'

160

'He the one writes about us?' the old man asked.

'That's the one,' she said.

'Randy Rosen.' He offered a hand to the old man, who turned away. Rosen swallowed once and made introductions. Ilta and Hiram Woolfe.

'What you up here for?' the old man asked. 'You gonna study us like bugs again? That what you're doing here?'

'No, sir, I'm not,' Rosen said affably.

'What you want, then?' the old guy demanded.

'Trying to get a little information about a Smithville girl,' Rosen said.

The answer seemed to relax them both. 'It's gone,' Ilta Woolfe said. 'Been gone for thirty years or so. Nothing to tell.'

'One day it was there. Next it was gone,' the old man said. When he turned their way, his black eyes were defiant. 'They was good people. Minded their own damn business. Didn't talk about nothin' wasn't their own damn business.'

Rosen seemed momentarily flustered. Corso jumped in. 'So how did this closemouthed little community go from something to nothing virtually overnight?' he wanted to know.

'Kinda started with the Parker fella,' the woman said. 'As I recall, that was pretty much the beginning of the end for Smithville.'

Rosen turned to Corso and Dougherty. 'You remember Richard Leon Parker?' he asked. Dougherty shook her head. Corso nodded.

'The serial murderer.'

'Killed a bunch of girls from this area,' Ilta Woolfe said. 'All up and down the northern part of the state. Took a girl from Smithville. Velma de Groot was her name. Poor unfortunate thing, she was.' She swirled a finger at the side of her head. 'Not all there, if you know what I mean. That Parker fella snatched her right offa the bus stop . . . so a lot of her kin blamed the government for what happened to her. Stopped sending their kids down to school.'

Corso remembered the name well. Richard Leon Parker had been the primary suspect in a series of grisly rapes and murders. Schoolgirls. Nearly thirty, as Corso recalled. Hung himself in his jail cell before they ever got him to trial, either in shame, so nobody could be sure about what he had and hadn't done, or as a final act of cruelty, leaving the victims' loved ones without even the cold comfort of closure.

'Never woulda happened if'n the state had left us the hell alone,' her husband added. 'We was doin' just fine without them and their damn laws and their damn schools.'

His wife rolled her eyes. 'Soon as they stopped sending their young ones, the social workers arrived, and then they brought in the cops—'

'Same cops shoulda been lookin' for whoever killed the poor little de Groot girl. That's what they shoulda been doin' instead of pokin' their noses into what wasn't none of their damn business anyway.'

Rosen wagged a finger at the couple. 'That's right,' he said. 'Her name was de Groot. That was the big name in Smithville . . . de Groot.'

'That was the *only* damn name in Smithville,' the old man spat.

Rosen furrowed his brow. 'When was that?' he asked.

Ilta Woolfe stuck out her lower lip and thought about it. ''Sixty-eight, '69, someplace in there somewhere.'

'The old woman's right,' the man said. 'I remember 'cause that's just about the time some of them lowland hippies decided they was gonna join us up here in the hills.' His mouth broke into a grin. 'Found out damn quick,' he cackled. 'Found out they was better off back where they came from.' He slapped his rounded side. 'They surely did.'

'And there's nothing left up there at all?' Rosen asked.

They both shook their heads. 'Piles of trash,' she said. 'Old broke-down fences.'

'That'n dead de Groots,' the old man said with a twisted smile.

'Graveyard's about all that's left. It was a shame,' his wife agreed.

'It was a damn mess is what it was,' said the old man. 'Buncha people not doin' nothin' but mindin' their own business, when all of a sudden they got cops all over the place tellin' them what they gotta do, and the next thing you know they's people going off to jail and the whole damn town is just gone.' He swept his arm in a circle. 'Nowadays you can't hardly find a de Groot nowhere in the Ramapo hills. Used to be one of the names you heard most, and now, 'cept for old Rodney, you can't find hardly a one anywhere around here.'

His wife took the lead. 'You want to know about Smithville, you go see Rodney de Groot. He's about the last of them I know. Lives up next to Sterling Lake now. Right there on the south shore. If anybody's gonna know anything about what happened in Smithville back then, he'd be the one. He was there when the whole thing come undone. He's the one to know.'

'You sure he's still up there?' Rosen asked.

The old man scoffed. ''Course he's still up there. Where the hell else would he be?' He cackled again and went back to stocking the shelves.

'He was in a couple of weeks back,' the old woman said. 'Cashed his check and bought a twenty-pound bag of rice. He's up there all right.'

'Could you maybe draw us a map?' Rosen asked.

She jabbed a thumb toward the old man. 'Hiram will help you out. I'm no good at directions. Been here all my life and I got no more direction sense than a lowlander.'

Hiram didn't much like being volunteered but, after a bit of grumbling, led Rosen all the way across the store to a black-and-white Bureau of Land Management map that was tacked on the far wall. He pointed with a bony finger. 'Now pay attention here, damn it,' he said, ' 'cause I'm only gonna show you this once.'

The old woman had turned back to her work. Dougherty stepped in close.

'You remember that girl Mr Rosen was chasing?' she asked the woman's back. The only sign that the woman had heard was that her hands stopped moving. She shot a quick glance across the room, where her husband was running a finger along the map while Rosen scribbled notes. She looked back over her shoulder. 'Maybe I do.' She said it as if the mere acknowledgment of a person's existence violated some unwritten mountain code.

'You know where to find her?' Dougherty asked.

The old woman's eyes moved across the room and back twice and then stopped on Dougherty. 'He still carrying that torch, is he? After all these years?'

'I believe so.'

She stared up into Dougherty's eyes for a long moment. 'Women can tell that kind of thing, now can't they?' she said.

Dougherty agreed. Across the room, Rosen was pocketing his notebook and trying to thank the old man, who was having none of it. 'Don't be blaming me you get lost out there.' Hiram chopped the air with the edge of his hand. 'Folks come up from down below . . . next thing you know . . .'

The old woman beckoned for Dougherty to bend over, then whispered in her ear.

'She died back in '88. Cervical cancer.' She flicked her eyes toward the returning Rosen. 'You gonna tell him?' she asked.

Dougherty shook her head. 'Not me,' she said.

CHAPTER 18

Rodney de Groot's house sat on an unpaved road that ran along the southern edge of Sterling Lake, a mile-long ribbon of oily black water that had begun to see recent gentrification along its northern shore but that at Rodney's end remained firmly mired in the early nineteenth century. Although the property extended to the waterline, a thick stand of cedars shielded the house from the lake, as if any desire Rodney de Groot may have had for a lake view had been summarily sacrificed for the sake of privacy.

The cabin itself was two stories high. The exterior was covered with tar paper, which, in places, had peeled away, revealing the house's original white cedar shingles. The overgrown yard was decorated with seven cars. One up on blocks. Two on their sides. The newest, which looked like it probably ran, was a piebald twenty-year-old Chevy Impala parked over by the front door. Apparently Rodney saw fit to keep his collection of personal memorabilia nestled outside among the autos, as a couple of old refrigerators, a hand-wringer washing machine, a vacuum cleaner, and what appeared to be the remains of a pinball machine lay scattered about the grass. Despite the sensory overload, what caught Corso's eye was the central incongruity: the red hand pump standing on a small wooden platform in the yard and the satellite dish atop the ten-foot steel pole right there next to it.

Corso braked the Ford to a halt behind a restored red and black Studebaker pickup. Through the oval rear window, he could see a high-powered rifle with a scope, hanging from a gun rack. Corso got out, looked over at the pump again, and smirked.

To the left of the front door, a thick plank spanned a pair of five-gallon cans. A man with long tangled hair sat on the plank hand-rolling a cigarette.

Rosen did not approach. Instead he cupped a hand around his mouth.

'You Rodney de Groot?' he shouted.

The man on the porch gave a nearly imperceptible shake of his head and then looked down at the partially rolled smoke in his hand.

'Hey,' Rosen tried again. The guy brought the smoke to his mouth and licked the paper. His body language said the head shake was all they were going to get.

A white-haired African-American man appeared in the doorway. He was muscular and well built and moved with an economy of motion belying his advanced years. He wore a faded red T-shirt that had long ago had its pocket torn free and a pair of grimy white boxer shorts. When he spoke, the warm air in his lungs became a thick white plume in the cold air. 'Don't just stand out there shoutin',' he hollered. 'Come the hell in.' With that pronouncement, he turned and quickly disappeared inside. The wispy trails of his floating breath were all that remained.

Single file, they picked their way along an uneven bark path to the front steps. The man on the porch didn't move a muscle until Rosen stepped up onto the porch. His head seemed abnormally small for his body. He had a thin, pointed face and bright blue eyes. From close range, he was younger than he'd appeared from the car. He wore a visored leather cap that had become dark with age. His shirt was coarse-woven and had eyelets down the front through which he had woven a leather thong. Below the waist he wore canvas trousers and a battered pair of Red Wing work boots.

As the trio stepped up onto the porch, he turned his undersized head away, refusing to acknowledge their presence. 'Nice day,' Corso ventured on his way past. The man looked up, pinning Corso with a pair of defiant eyes. 'If you say so.' His mustache and fingers were stained yellow by nicotine. In a much practiced move, he flipped the cigarette in the air, caught it in the corner of his mouth, and simultaneously used his thumb to fire a kitchen match and light it. Pleased with his little trick, he took a big pull, expelling the smoke through his nose. Still holding Corso's gaze, he spat a thick brown stream onto the ground and then, with a narrow smile, turned his back to the doorway. Corso followed the others inside. He reached to close the door.

'Leave it open,' Rodney de Groot called. 'I favor the air.'

The cabin was L-shaped. Straight ahead was the kitchen, where Rodney sat at a yellow linoleum table chomping a pork chop, fried potatoes, and white bread. At the center of the space was a huge coal stove, from whose stout black body shimmers of heat radiated in all directions. The room to the right was lined with threadbare but comfortable-looking couches and chairs of all sorts. At the far end, a thirty-six-inch Toshiba flat-screen TV squatted in the corner like a shiny silver elephant. CNN. Close-captioned. Yasir Arafat making a speech.

De Groot asked each of them in turn if he could cook them a pork chop. Said they could have as much bread as they wanted, but seemed a little relieved when nobody took him up on, it. 'Don't believe in eatin' till I'm hungry,' Rodney declared. 'Hope you don't mind if I finish up here.' He shoveled another forkful of potatoes into his mouth and then swallowed and made a circular gesture with the fork. 'Find your-selves a seat,' he said. 'Don't get many visitors. Especially not people lookin' for me. Get some lost lowlanders . . . maybe some of those new folk from up-lake . . . but nobody lookin' for Rodney de Groot.'

As bidden, Corso, Rosen, and Dougherty found themselves a place to sit. For the next five minutes they watched in silence as Rodney methodically made his way through his meal. On two occasions he stopped eating long enough to refill his glass from the gallon jug of water on the table and then went back to his repast. When the plate was empty, he pushed it away and leaned back in his chair until the front legs came off the floor. 'Well,' he said, lacing his fingers over his middle, 'you folks came a long way off the beaten path. What can I help you with?'

'We were hoping you could tell us a few things about Smithville,' Rosen said. Rodney de Groot's eyes widened. He slowly set the front legs back on the floor and got to his feet. His deeply lined face was hard and blank.

'Dead and gone,' he said. 'Nothin' at all left there anymore.'

His tone carried a finality devoid of hope. As if Smithville had somehow reached a state of nonexistence where its mere mention was moot. He put his hands on his hips and stared out through the open doorway until Corso cut into his remembrance.

'That's what we want to talk about,' he said. 'Back at the end of the sixties when that Parker guy killed the girl and Smithville came undone.'

'May of '68,' Rodney said. 'We were comin' off

a drought winter. Wasn't even summer yet and the woods were burning,' he mused.

He went on for twenty minutes. Seemed like he talked about every person in Smithville, their kids, their kin. All of it. How it was that spring of '68. He picked at his teeth with a yellow twist-tie and gabbed right up to May 1968, when all of a sudden his conviction seemed to waver. He began to look as if he were suddenly hearing other voices from other rooms. He squared his shoulders and bowed his neck. 'Just a bunch of people living life the way they'd always lived it before. The way their folks and *their* folks . . . all the way back . . . the way they all lived it.' He said it with emphasis, as if his pronouncement were the end of the matter. And then his eyes wavered. He seemed embarrassed now, as if his prior recitation had somehow been in bad taste and he now regretted having said anything at all.

Rodney took a deep breath. Worked up some bluster. 'Then all of a sudden they couldn't do anything right. Wasn't nothing to be done, neither. Those that didn't move off . . . ended up dead or ended up in jail.' He was doing indignant, but his words carried no conviction. Corso picked up on it immediately. Dougherty also. She scooted forward on the couch and met Rodney's gaze.

'Jail for what?' she asked.

Rodney fanned the air in front of his face as if shooing a fly. 'Whole raft of stuff,' he said. 'Things got out of hand.' He said it again as if a simple repetition would eliminate the need for further explanation.

'Out of hand how?' Dougherty pressed.

'People turning on each other. Kin comin' down against kin. Kids turning on parents . . . social workers callin' in the law.' He shook his head in disgust. 'Whole thing just come apart.' He snapped his strong-looking fingers. 'Just like that.'

'During that time,' Corso began, 'was there a fire up there in Smithville? Something like where maybe a whole family burned up in a house?'

Rodney frowned hard and brought a finger to his lips. The room fell silent as he tiptoed over, took the door in hand as if to close it, and then, on second thought, peeked out. His relief was palpable. Leaving the door ajar, he turned back to his guests. 'Boy up and left,' he said. 'He's like that. One minute he's here, next minute he's off in the woods someplace.' Rodney walked to the table. He turned the back of his chair toward the visitors and sat down with his arms atop the seat back. 'That's Tommie de Groot,' he explained. 'My cousin Jeannine's boy. He's the only one left, 'cause he was down on the flats in the hospital when it all happened.'

Rodney looked from one confused face to the next. 'Food poisoning,' he said. 'Damn thing saved his life.' When his words again failed to produce a glimmer of recognition, he sighed. 'Right about that time' – he waved a hand – 'when the whole town was coming apart' – he stopped to make

173

sure they were with him – 'his entire damn family burned up. My cousin Jeannine and her husband, Paul. Three of the four kids too.' He used his fingers to count them. 'The boys, James and Christopher, and the little girl, Leslie Louise.' He snapped his fingers again. 'All of 'em gone . . . just like that.'

'How old was the little girl?' Dougherty asked.

Rodney acted as if he hadn't heard the question. 'I always told myself it was maybe for the best.' He looked at his guests for validation but didn't find any. 'They was right in the middle of the whole mess.' He made a pained face. 'Wasn't nothing good gonna come of it anyway. Might have been better that none of them was there for the end . . . the way it panned out and all.' His eyes took on a distant look. 'Might be better off up there in the graveyard, with the family,' he said.

'Better than what?' Corso prodded.

Again Rodney de Groot ignored the question. 'Only one still alive when it was over was poor Tommie there. By the time the dust settled, I was the only kin he had left around here. The welfare folks had him for a coupla years. After that, it was me. I raised him up since he was six.' Rodney cast a defiant eye at his visitors. 'Wasn't nothin' else I could do. I was the only family he had. Couldn't very well be turning a blind eye to the boy, could I?' He pointed out over Rosen's head. 'Got him a little cabin over on the other side of the rise there, but he spends most of his time over here

174

with me.' He made a sad face. 'Can't blame him for wanting a little company, can ya? After what happened to him and all. It's just natural.'

This time Rodney got the agreement he'd been looking for. Thus validated, he seemed to feel a need to explain. 'Tommie was in the Marine Corps for a while. Been around some, he has. He's a hell of a woodsman, though, that boy. Best damn shot you ever seen too! Knows every squirrel hole in the whole damn mountains,' he enthused. 'Takes that fancy old truck of his every summer and goes out to visit friends in Idaho. Kids he went to school with. Gets him a regular haircut and a shave and all.' His eyes traveled inward for a moment. 'He ain't like the others. They get away from these mountains, and they *stay* gone . . .' He wandered toward the door and looked out. Tommie's absence seemed to trouble him. 'Yeah . . . Tommy gets around some now and then, but he comes back. Coupla weeks later. He always comes back.'

Corso jumped in. 'I'm still a little unclear about—'

Rodney waved him off and then stepped out onto the porch. He'd had enough of talking. 'I'm gettin' old,' he said. 'Sittin' here blabbering like an old woman. Talkin' about the dead instead of getting on with my business.' He walked over and stood by the door. He was too polite to ask them to leave, but the interview was over.

He thanked each of them for the visit. As the others started back to the car, Corso walked to the pump. A blue metal cup hung from the well by a rusted piece of chain. A coffee can full of water rested next to the handle. Corso used the coffee can to prime the pump, then refilled the can before pumping himself a cup of water. He drank deeply, allowing some of the cold liquid to run down over his chin.

He replaced the cup, nodded at Rodney de Groot, and started for the car. 'Thanks for the drink,' Corso said on his way by.

The old man laughed. 'Ain't my water,' he said. 'It's the Lord's water is what it is. You want to be thankin' anybody for the drink . . . you be thankin' Him.'

CHAPTER 19

The Studebaker pickup was gone. Looked like it left in a hurry. A pair of angry black ruts showed where Tommie de Groot had swung the truck off the driveway and spun his tires getting around the Explorer.

Dougherty buckled her seat belt. 'Maybe Rodney's right,' she said as she settled in. 'Maybe the dead ought to be left alone.'

Rosen seemed to agree. He checked his watch. 'Gonna be dark in an hour or so,' he announced. 'And if you two don't mind, I'd rather not be up here in the dark.'

'How far's Smithville from here?' Corso asked.

'Over the next hill,' Rosen said.

'We got time to go there before it gets dark?'

Rosen looked weary and maybe a little scared. 'I guess,' he sighed.

Corso turned the key; the engine rumbled to life. 'Which way?' he asked.

'Left out of the driveway,' Rosen said.

Rosen talked as they drove. He was one of those people who felt a need to fill silence with his voice, as if he found something in the void sufficiently

177

frightening to require a constant stream of chatter to keep it at bay.

Halfway up a steep incline, Corso caught a silver flash in the rearview mirror. He braked the Ford to a halt and turned in the seat, staring back down the road.

'What?' Dougherty said.

'Thought I saw somebody behind us.'

Everybody took a turn staring out the back window, but whatever had caught Corso's attention did not reappear. He lifted his foot from the brake and urged the car up the hill. Rosen resumed his chatter. As they neared the top of a rise, he was retelling how he'd always wanted to come up here but how Justine just wouldn't hear about it. He caught himself. 'I've told you this before, haven't I?' he asked.

'You ever think about maybe finding out what Justine's doing these days?' Corso asked. Dougherty held her breath and turned her face to the window.

Rosen seemed surprised by the question. 'No. I mean . . . I'm sure she . . .'

'Maybe she's been thinking about you, all these years,' Corso suggested. 'With women, you never know.'

In the backseat, Dougherty bit her lip and tried not to listen. Rosen said something about roads not taken. She wanted to put her fingers in her ears and yell so loud she couldn't hear what was being said.

Corso brought the car to a halt at a T in the road. Rosen consulted his notepad.

'Go right,' he said. 'Smithville should be down the end of this road.'

Corso did as he was told. The Ford settled into the well-worn ruts, following the road like they were on rails. For a mile and a half, Rosen talked about the choices one makes in life. How seemingly meaningless decisions, made in moments of haste, nonetheless color the entire fabric of our lives. He'd been lecturing undergraduates for so long, it never occurred to him he didn't have much to add to the subject. Seemed to him that if he was talking, it must be interesting. Corso turned on the radio, couldn't find anything but static, and disgustedly snapped it off again.

A makeshift wooden fence appeared on the right. Made of cedar branches wired together into a primitive but sturdy version of a picket fence. Seventy yards later, a wide turnout led to a narrow walkway into the cemetery. Corso stopped the car. No mausoleums here. No disapproving stone angels. Mostly simple wooden headstones and crosses. Some leaning at crazy angles. Others ramrod straight, their carved faces weathered bone white by the summer sun. The graveyard of the de Groots.

Ahead the road was mostly grown over. Whoever came out to the graveyard never ventured farther. Ahead the grass was bumper high. Thick bushes encroached on the roadway from either side. Spindly limbs hovered above the roadway.

Rosen looked nervous. 'Whadda you think?' he

asked. What he was asking was what Corso thought about turning around and going back.

Corso had other ideas, however. 'I think Hertz is gonna be pissed off again,' he said, pushing the accelerator. As the big Ford plowed through the debris, it sounded like a thousand fingernails being drawn along the paint and undercarriage.

Half a mile later, the brush began to thin. A final dip in the road bounced them up and down just as the Ford burst out into a clearing. A cul-de-sac really, for this naked spot in the wilderness was both Smithville and the end of the road. The Woolfes and Rodney de Groot had been right. There was nothing left. Six feet of moss-covered stone foundation straight ahead. Three former fence posts standing like gaunt sentinels in the gathering gloom. Corso jammed the car in Park and got out, leaving the motor running. Rosen stayed put. Dougherty sat in the car for a minute and then climbed out.

It had begun to drizzle. She walked over and hooked her arm through Corso's, then moved with him as he slowly walked around the five-acre clearing. Overgrown patches of ground here and there spoke of long-ago dwellings. 'It's just over thirty years ago,' Dougherty said. 'You'd think there'd be more junk.' She gestured with her hand. 'You know, falling-down buildings and such.'

Corso stopped. Looked down at her and smiled. 'Yeah . . . you would, wouldn't you?' he said. He took her by the hand and led her over to the nearest of the homesites. He pulled her down with him as he squatted and began to dig in the dirt with his free hand. Beneath a thin frosted crust, the ground was mostly decayed organic matter and digging was easy. Six inches down, he stopped, lifted a handful of dirt to his nose, and sniffed. He tossed the soil aside and dug some more. A foot down, the dirt was streaked with black. Again he sampled the odor. This time, he smiled.

He opened his palm and lifted it toward her face. 'What do you smell?' he asked.

She took a tentative whiff and then another. 'Fire,' she said. 'I smell fire.'

He pulled her back the way they'd come. All the way back to the front of the car and the small piece of stone foundation. Inside the SUV, Rosen turned on the windshield wipers and leaned forward in the seat, watching them intently. The slap of the wipers filled the air.

Corso dug along the side of the little stone wall, pushed his finger deep into the dirt, and then pulled it back out. He drew his sooty finger along the tops of the rocks. A wavy black line appeared.

'Something happened up here,' he said. 'Something nobody wants to talk about. Something worth burning a whole town down over.'

Dr Rosen tooted the horn. Gestured that it was getting late. Dougherty grabbed Corso's arm and pulled him close. 'You better cut the nostalgiafest with Rosen,' she whispered. 'His mountain dream girl's been dead for years.'

Corso turned away from the car and made a pained expression. 'Damn,' he said, shaking his head. 'That's what I get for being optimistic.'

'Proves your ongoing theory that virtue is its own revenge.'

He put a hand on her back and guided her toward the car. 'Next time I get to acting all silly and sentimental, you be sure to remind me of that,' he said.

The interior of the Ford was warm on the face and hands. Rosen seemed relieved as Corso pulled the SUV in a wide circle and started back. His relief lasted only as long as it took Corso to get back to the entrance to the Smithville cemetery and pull to a stop. Corso looked over at the professor. 'I'll leave it running for you,' he said.

Rosen was all right with the idea of waiting in the car until he heard Dougherty open her door and step out. After that, it took him about five seconds to join them.

'Might as well see it while I've got the chance,' he said.

Corso reached in and turned off the engine. He used the electronic gizmo on the key chain to lock the doors, gestured 'after you' to Dougherty and Rosen, and followed them up the short path to the burial ground.

The graveyard was tiny. It would have fit in an unnoticed corner of the Allentown cemetery.

Maybe sixty graves in all. The earliest they found was from 1784. Guy named Wilhelm Van Dunk. Died when he was fifty-seven years old.

As they walked among the graves, they kept a respectful distance from the markers, stepping awkwardly here and there to avoid any possibility of treading on the dead. Of course, Rosen talked, his endless words echoing among the trees like musket fire.

Seemed the trip up into the mountains had actually been a journey into his past and, as such, had produced a moment of epiphany for Dr Randy Rosen. As they walked, he resolved to re-engage his research into what he now called the Ramapo people and, most emphatically of all, to see if he couldn't find out what had happened to the long-ago object of his desire, Justine de Vries. His newfound enthusiasm prevented him from noticing the strained looks on his companions' faces as they shuffled among the dead. Corso and Dougherty were grateful for his blindness.

Had they started their search at the other end of the graveyard, they would have immediately found what they were looking for. As it was, they came upon it last, and maybe it was better that way because the sight squeezed the air from their lungs and stood every hair of their bodies on end. Five graves, all in a row . . . like pretty maids.

Five identical wooden markers, lined up, it seemed, in order of rank. On the left, the carved letters read 'Paul de Groot Husband-Father

183

1924–1968.' Then 'Jeannine de Groot Wife-Mother 1926–1968.' 'James de Groot 1949–1968.' 'Christopher de Groot 1950–1968.' And finally, down at the end, 'Leslie Louise 1951–1968.'

The first four headstones had been vandalized. Each letter and number of the inscription had been individually x-ed out in black, almost as if somebody had been keeping score. Then the names and dates had been crossed out again horizontally, as if the black streaks themselves were part of an act of denial. The graves themselves were untended and ran to weeds. Except for Leslie Louise's down at the end.

Her marker bore none of the vandalism. The area around her final resting place had been smoothed and picked clean of debris. A rusted can of water had been dug into the earth, so it couldn't tip over. The can held a thick array of pussy willows, whose soft silver buttons quivered slightly in the evening breeze.

Dougherty broke the stunned silence. 'Somebody's very angry here,' she said. Nobody argued with her. Finally Corso coughed into his hand. 'They were both de Groots.' He pointed. 'Right? Didn't Rodney de Groot say Jeannine here was his cousin?' Dougherty acknowledged the fact. 'Paul here was a de Groot too.'

Rosen found his voice. 'They were probably cousins too,' he said. 'It was quite common for—'

Dougherty stepped in front of Rosen and walked along in front of the markers. 'How old did you think that Tommie de Groot guy on Rodney's porch was?'

'There was a gene pool that needed a lifeguard,' Corso said.

'Thirty, thirty-five,' Rosen offered. Corso nodded his agreement.

'Big gap between the last two kids,' she commented.

'Mama was nearly forty when he was born,' Corso said.

'Lotta birth defects with mothers that age,' Rosen said. 'Maybe that explains—'

A noise from the woods brought the conversation to a halt. They hunched their shoulders and froze. Everyone ceased breathing and turned their attention toward the surrounding thicket. Waiting. Scanning the maze of twisted branches for any sign of movement. Another crack. This time farther away. And then another.

'Let's get out of here,' Corso said, taking Dougherty by the elbow and hurrying toward the path. They hustled along the fence line in silence. Wasn't till the car came into view that anybody exhaled. Once inside, they got giddy. Making fun of their own imaginations as Corso backed out into the road. The kidding stopped when they saw the red and black Studebaker pickup truck blocking the road. Silence.

'Uh-oh,' Rosen said.

When Tommie de Groot stepped out of the truck holding his rifle in both hands, Corso thrust himself out from under the steering wheel and began to crawl over the seats toward the luggage in the rear. He was lying across the tops of the seats, shaking the clothes from his bag, when he heard the door swing open. He turned just in time to see Rosen step from the car and raise his open hand. 'Young man,' the professor began, 'I assure you that we—'

De Groot never removed the cigarette from the corner of his mouth as he raised the rifle to his shoulder and fired. Before the sound of the report, before the eye could register the muzzle flash, the back of Dr Rosen's head came off in a high-pressure spray of blood and bone and brain matter. The impact drove him one staggering step backward before he crumpled onto the road, his legs twisted up under him, like a discarded doll.

With one hand Corso reached for the door latch, with the other he groped for the zipper at the bottom of his suitcase. 'Come on!' he screamed at Dougherty. 'Get your ass back here!' She didn't need to be told twice. By the time he'd opened the rear hatch she was there, hurling herself out onto the ground just at the moment when Tommie de Groot let loose with another high-powered round. The bullet shattered the windshield and passed so close to Corso's head the shock caused his ear to go numb.

De Groot had covered half the distance between his truck and the Ford and was raising his rifle again when Corso put his hand on Deputy Sheriff

186

Cole Richardson's gun and then somersaulted out into the road. As he thumbed off the safety, another round rocked the car and then went whining out over their heads.

Corso took a single belly roll out to the left of the rear tire and fired a quick shot de Groot's way. In the instant before he rolled back to cover, he heard the sound of metal slamming into metal and the unmistakable tinkle of broken glass. He put his chin on the ground and, from beneath the car, looked up the road. As he'd hoped, the feet were retreating. He reached over and pulled Dougherty to his side.

'I think he's leaving,' he whispered.

Corso jacked himself to his knees and peered around the corner of the car just in time to see the red and black Studebaker throwing rooster tails of black earth into the air as it roared in a circle and disappeared from view.

Dougherty grabbed his belt. 'Dr. Rosen,' she said. Corso looked deep into her eyes and shook his head slowly. 'No way,' he said, dropping to her side and taking her in his arms. They lay on the wet earth and listened to the sound of the truck as it slowly faded to silence. Only then could they hear the ticking of the Ford's engine and the pecking of the drizzle on last season's leaves.

CHAPTER 20

Handcuffed, a person pretty much has to either lean forward or lie down on the seat, which was exactly what Corso had been doing for the better part of three hours when the cop jerked open the door and instructed him to sit up and turn, so his handcuffs could be removed.

'It's about fucking time,' Corso groused.

The cop admonished Corso for both his language and his attitude as he removed the steel bracelets and stowed them in his pocket.

Corso was still barking at the cop and rubbing his wrists when the other door opened and Dougherty slid into the backseat beside him. She started to speak, but Corso darted his eyes around the car's interior and shook his head.

She got the message. 'Ah . . .' she said. 'How about a little fresh air?'

They got out on opposite sides of the car. 'All right if I stretch my legs?' Corso asked the nearest Bergen County deputy.

The deputy looked to his partner, who shrugged. 'Hollister said to let 'em loose,' the second guy said. 'Why not?'

'Just don't get lost,' the first guy said. 'The brass is gonna want to talk to you guys again.'

Corso and Dougherty walked side by side. Slowly. Silently. Working out the kinks all the way to the far end of Fredrikstown. Other than the town's trio of streetlights, the place was completely dark. The town had closed its eyes and turned its face aside, as if to say these weren't their people and therefore it wasn't their problem. Mindin' their own business appeared to be what the locals did best.

Dougherty turned her back to the assortment of county and state police cruisers that littered the parking area. 'I think we're gonna ride,' she said in a low voice.

'What makes you think so?' Corso asked.

'They checked us out every which way but up,' she whispered.

'They called people I supposedly listed as references on a bank loan I never even took out.' She paused for effect. 'We checked out, Corso. Top to bottom. It was un-fucking-believable. Every damn person they called gave us a clean bill of health.' She reached out and bopped him playfully on the shoulder. 'I don't know where you got that ID from, man, but it was killer . . . absolutely killer.'

Corso grunted and rubbed at his wrists.

'You see the ambulance come by?' she asked.

He nodded. It had taken Bergen County Rescue nearly three hours to bring Randy Rosen's body down from the mountain. Corso's guess was that the forensics team wouldn't let the medics touch anything until they'd finished their business.

About an hour ago, the orange and white lights bouncing off the cruiser's headliner had brought Corso upright in the seat long enough to watch the aid car lead a grim procession down to the world below.

The way Dougherty's eyes turned down at the corners told him where this conversation was heading. 'I was thinking,' she began in a small voice.

'Don't beat yourself up,' he interrupted. 'No way we could've—'

'Shut up, Corso,' she snapped. 'I need to talk this out. So just listen to me and shut the fuck up.' Corso stopped rubbing his wrists and stuffed his hands in his pockets. She took a deep breath. 'I can't help feeling that man is dead because of us,' she said. She waved a hand in the air. 'I know what you're gonna say. How we're all responsible for ourselves. How he was old enough . . .' She looked over at Corso. Her eyes were beginning to fill. 'What is it you always say? After a certain age a man becomes responsible for his face.' Corso turned away. She was starting to lose it. 'He didn't have a face, Corso. It was all gone. It was . . .' The image left her momentarily speechless. He reached out and put a hand on her shoulder. She walked out from under it. 'You're gonna have to explain to me' – she began to sob – 'how it is we're not responsible for that poor man's death . . . how that's possible . . . how he would be alive right now if we hadn't come into his life this morning.' Her voice filled with anger. 'Come on, man, tell me. Make it all better for me. That's what you do, isn't it. You make it all better?' She caught herself yelling. Looked back over her shoulder at the cops, who'd stopped bull-shitting and were now staring in her direction. She shuddered in the night air. Hugged herself. 'Sorry,' she said.

He waved her off. 'No, you're right. If it weren't for us, Dr Rosen would be sitting in his living room, eating take-out Chinese or something.' He ran both hands over his face. 'I don't know if we were responsible, at least not in the way I use the word, but we sure as hell were players. That much is for damn sure.'

'That's not what you were supposed to say,' she whined.

'I thought you hated it when I try to fix things.'

'I do,' she said. 'Except now. Now I wish—'

'I should have picked up on it,' Corso said.

'What was that?'

'Rodney de Groot was scared. I thought maybe he was worried about Tommie . . . like maybe in a paternal way or something like that. But he wasn't. He was scared of what Tommie might do if he knew we were looking into the death of his family. That's why he got so uncomfortable so quickly and wanted us out of there. He was scared for all of us, himself included.'

191

The front door to the post office opened, spilling a jumble of voices out into the night. A pair of New York State policemen stepped onto the porch.

'What've they been doing in there all this time?' Corso asked.

'Checking us out and arguing over jurisdiction,' she said. 'This place is in New Jersey. Rosen was . . .' She brought a hand to her throat. 'The shooting happened in New York.'

'Who won?'

'Jersey,' she said. 'They got the college president out of bed. Rosen's got a mother in a nursing home down in south Jersey. The state cops are sending somebody from the college down there to tell her in person.'

'Hey . . . you two,' someone shouted. Back at the cop car jamboree, the Bergen County deputies had been joined by a phalanx of multicolored state and county policemen who'd emerged en masse from the post office, where they'd been holed up for the past hour and a half. Corso and Dougherty began to wander that way.

'The one in the tuxedo and the long coat is a New Jersey State Police lieutenant named Hollister. Everybody kisses his ass like it was candy,' Dougherty whispered. 'He's the one threw his weight around and made sure Jersey got the case.'

Lieutenant Hollister's sartorial splendor suggested that he'd been socially engaged when he'd received the call. The pained expression suggested that there was a Mrs Hollister somewhere, that she hadn't been amused by the interruption, and that her husband had a pretty good idea who was going to pay for the indignity.

The Rockland County Police and the New York staties said their good-byes and started for their cars. When Hollister began to walk toward Corso and Dougherty, the New Jersey contingent followed along in his wake.

He introduced himself to Corso. He offered a hand, which Corso ignored. Half a dozen engines sprang to life. The misty air was crisscrossed with streaks of halogen. They stood and watched as the New York cops rolled out of the parking lot and back down the hill.

'Sorry things took so long,' Hollister said. 'You get something like this, something right along state lines, and all of a sudden a situation that ought to be simple turns out to be ticklish.' When he looked at the red-faced sergeant on his right, the entire New Jersey delegation began to study their shoes. 'You combine the jurisdictional mix-up and the fact that the locals aren't exactly forthcoming, and you end up with first-class cluster fuck.' He nodded deferentially at Dougherty. 'Excuse my French, Miss Dolan,' he said. 'I'm a little off my feed tonight. I was at the theater when the emergency call came through.'

His eyes again lingered on the sergeant and then moved to Corso and Dougherty. 'Okay, here's how it's going to be,' he said. 'Preliminary reports from the lab say the scene played out pretty much the way you two say it did.' He stepped closer to Corso, put a hand on his elbow. 'Only thing I'm still a little unclear on, Mr Falco, is you moving the body from one place to another. You want to clear that up for me?'

'He went down in the road,' Corso said.

The bullet had taken Randy Rosen just under the right eye, busting out the socket and removing most of the back of the skull on its way out. Corso had carried the corpse in his arms like a sleeping child. His hands shook as he set the body among the damp weeds along the side of the road before getting back behind the wheel.

Hollister twisted his head and eyed the Ford, which was parked in front of the store with the pair of bullet holes in the windshield. 'That baby's got a hell of a lot of clearance,' Hollister said. 'You coulda—'

'I wasn't driving over him,' Corso interrupted. 'Clearance or no clearance, the man deserved better than being driven over.'

Hollister set his jaw and reluctantly nodded. 'Yeah,' he said. 'I know what you mean.' He sighed and began again. 'From preliminary reports, seems Mr de Groot has a history of psychiatric problems dating back to childhood. We've got an armed-and-dangerous out for Mr de Groot and an APB on his truck. Something as exotic as a Studebaker truck we ought to be able to turn in a hurry. In the meantime, I'm going to send you two down

194

to the barracks in Ramsey to make your formal statements. I've got a very unhappy stenographer on her way in right now.' He looked to his left. 'I'm going to send Trooper Paris here with you, to make sure you don't get lost on the way. You make your statements, you leave us information so we can find you when we need you, and you can go on your way. That sound okay to you?'

They said it was. Dougherty was still shaking Hollister's hand when they first heard the sound and everybody started doing the Chicken Little thing up at the sky. First the roar of the engine and then the *whop-whop* of the rotor blades slapping the air. Then the bright lights from above and the downdraft as the chopper began its descent. By that time, everybody had turned away from the hail of airborne debris and covered their faces with whatever was handy. The black bird landed among the remaining cars, the whine of its turbo deepening as it came to rest, the blades turning slower and slower until finally they came to a stop and the door swung open.

Three suits emerged at a lope. By the time they hit the ground, lights had begun to show all over Fredrikstown. Curtains parted, people stepped out front of their houses as reticence was overcome by curiosity.

The lead guy was about Hollister's age, shorter and thicker, with a thick black helmet of hair that had to be dyed. He pulled a small leather case from his inside jacket pocket and let it flop open right in front of Hollister's nose. 'Special Agent in Charge Angelo Molina,' the guy said. 'Federal Bureau of Investigation.'

Hollister gave the ID a quick perusal and then pushed the hand out of his face. 'What the hell is this?' he demanded. 'I just got the goddamn jurisdiction settled with the New York boys. What interest could the Bureau possibly have in this?'

'You called in for an ID on the weapon?' Molina asked.

Hollister looked over at the sergeant, who nodded vigorously.

'So?' Hollister said.

Molina looked to one of his minions, who produced a piece of paper and handed it to Hollister, who turned his body so he could read it in the streetlight. As his eyes traveled down the page, his scowl deepened. When he looked up again, his jaw was set like a bass. He dropped his hand to his side and then pinned Corso with a look that would have burned a hole in a brick. 'Damn good thing you boys got here when you did,' he said to Agent Molina. 'I was just about to let this cop-killing son of a bitch go.'

CHAPTER 21

I already told you.'

'Tell me again.'

Corso stared straight ahead. He winked at the indistinct shadows huddled behind the black glass. 'I bought the documents from a street peddler in Karachi,' Corso said. 'Guy named Abdul.'

'Abdul, huh?'

'Garcia.' Corso spelled it. 'Abdul Garcia.'

'And you figured that was his real name?'

'Guy looked honest to me.'

Special Agent Fullmer was about thirty. Despite elocution lessons, his southern drawl kept leaking into his sentences. Despite careful combing, the back of his head was beginning to show the tell-tale signs of baldness. So was his patience. He flung a handful of documents at Corso. They floated to the floor like plastic leaves. 'And you've never heard of an organization named Melissa-D. That's what you're telling me?'

'I didn't say that,' Corso said. 'Everybody in the news business has heard the stories. But that's all they are . . . stories. There's no such thing. I know a woman in Sandpoint, Idaho, named—'

'Shut up!' Fullmer screamed. He walked over and stood behind Corso. 'I'd like to wipe that smirk off your face, Mr Corso. I truly would,' he growled.

'I'm right here, Special Agent Fullmer,' Corso said. He rattled his manacles. 'What say you get me out of this belly chain and give it a try?'

His partner, Special Agent Dean, was pushing retirement. The bags beneath his eyes said that all-nighters like this were getting too hard for him. Probably why he got to play the good-cop role. Lot less energy expenditure that way.

'Don't worry about it, Gene,' he said. 'Wisconsin gets him up to that supermax at Boscobe, somebody'll wipe that smirk off his mouth with a shitty dick.' The older man levered himself to his feet. 'Besides which, his girlfriend's already given us everything we need. We can't hardly get her to stop talking.'

Corso laughed out loud. Fullmer leaned into his face. 'You think that's funny, do you?' he screamed. 'Funny, huh, do you?'

'She wouldn't piss on you if you were on fire,' Corso said. 'So why don't you just hold the bull-shit and do whatever you're gonna do. Far as I'm concerned, the party's over. You guys are getting to be a pain in the ass. My attorney's meeting me in Wisconsin. Until that time, I don't have anything more to say to anybody.'

Fullmer's face was so close Corso heard the earpiece squawk. He watched as the agent straightened up and listened to the voice in his ear. Fullmer looked toward the black rectangle, frowned, and then listened again. 'Let's go,' he said to his partner. Dean headed straight for the door. Fullmer detoured over to Corso. He reached over and jiggled the chain that ran from Corso's manacles down through a steel eyebolt in the floor. 'Stick around, Mr Corso,' he said with a grin. 'We'll be right back.'

Right back took twenty minutes. And even then it wasn't Fullmer and Dean. It was Special Agent in Charge Angelo Molina.

'You two are quite a piece of work. You and your friend Dougherty there.' He paced along the other side of the table with his hands thrust deep in his pockets. 'I've gotten more information out of suicide bombers than I've gotten out of you two.' His face spoke of grudging admiration. Corso wasn't buying it.

'You must have missed the last part of my chat with Fullmer and Dean,' Corso said. 'I no longer wish to talk without my attorney present. As Mr Fine also represents Miss Dougherty, she likewise no longer has anything to say.'

'You know, Mr Corso, keeping one's mouth shut until one's lawyer arrives is generally a good idea. In this case however . . .'

Something in Molina's tone caught Corso's attention. 'I was straight with you,' Corso said. 'I didn't clam up. I told you the truth. I didn't kill the cop. Only thing he was gonna have from his encounter with me was a hell of a headache. That's

199

how it went down. Just like I told you. You don't believe me, there's nothing left to say.'

With almost ceremonial deliberation, Molina pulled out the green metal chair and sat down opposite Corso, his back to the one-way window. 'Just for the sake of argument . . .' He waved a well-manicured hand. 'Let's assume for a moment that I believe you.'

'Just for the sake of argument,' Corso said.

'Hypothetically.'

'Okay, so you believe me. Can I go now?'

Molina smiled. 'Perhaps,' he said. 'But there's a minor hitch.'

'Why am I sooo not surprised?'

'Because I *did* hear you say you didn't wish to answer any further questions without your attorney present . . . which is, of course, your constitutional right . . . the very sort of right which the Bureau is charged with defending.'

Corso winced. 'Gimme a break,' he said.

Molina held up a finger. 'If, however, you would consent to answering a few straightforward questions from me . . .' He shrugged. 'Who knows?'

Corso thought it over. 'Such as?'

'You say in your statement that you fired Officer Richardson's weapon at Mr de Groot . . . who then fled.'

'Yes.'

'How many times did you fire?'

'Nice try. I told you. Once.'

'And you thought you hit something.'

'The truck, not him. Sounded like I broke a window or something.'

'But you're not sure?'

'Man had a high-powered rifle with a scope. I just stuck my arm out there and cranked one off. I wasn't looking.'

'Probably a wise move,' Molina conceded.

Corso tried to lean out over the table but was stopped by the chain. 'What's any of this got to do with a dead cop in Wisconsin?' he asked.

Molina reached into his pants pocket and brought out a fist. He held his balled hand above the table, thumb up, and slowly relaxed his grip. Six bullets dropped onto the scarred surface with a clatter. Five live rounds and one empty shell casing. 'These,' he said, 'have everything to do with a dead officer in Wisconsin.'

'How's that?'

'They're hand loads,' he said. 'All of them. Got an extra fifteen grains of powder packed in them.' He looked down contemptuously at the cartridges. 'Officer Richardson was lucky he didn't blow his hand off with these stupid things. I'd fire one of my men in a heartbeat for pulling a cowboy stunt like that.'

'Where are we headed here?' Corso demanded.

'Newark Airport, I believe.'

'What's at Newark Airport?'

'Mr de Groot's pickup truck. In the long-term lot.'

'Ah.'

'With one of its headlights broken out.' He gave Corso a moment to process the information. 'Newark forensics says it took a round. My own people found broken glass where you said Mr de Groot had the truck blocking the road. The glass matches samples from a company that specializes in after-market truck restoration.' He spread his hands and then dropped them on the table. 'On the surface, that would seem to account for the expended round we found in Officer Richardson's piece.'

'That's what I've been telling you. No way I offed a cop over a material-witness beef. That's insane. I don't even know anybody that stupid.'

'So then somebody drops your sheet in front of me, and right away I can see you're a dangerous man who has trouble controlling his temper. But' – he gently tapped the table – 'but I've accounted for the only spent shell in the gun you're supposed to have used in the crime.' He took a deep breath. 'Of course . . . I'm a cynical man, in a cynical job,' he said. 'So right away I start to stew about how you might have gotten hold of some more of those hand loads. I'm thinking maybe you left town with a whole handful of ammo we don't know about. I'm thinking maybe, at one time, you had the officer's whole equipment package in your possession. Maybe you threw it out the window somewhere along the line. Who knows?'

'So you called Wisconsin.'

Molina nodded.

'And?'

'And the rest of Officer Richardson's equipment was found intact. Two speed loaders . . . full of the same hand loads. Nothing missing.' He laced his fingers behind his head and leaned back in the chair. 'Except for his tie. I believe you mentioned his tie in your statement, didn't you?'

'I used it to truss him up. Around his ankles and then up through the cuffs so he couldn't get to his feet. He wasn't the kind of guy I wanted in my rearview mirror.'

'Of course, you could have taken the tie yourself in hopes of being able to use it later to muddy the water.' He wrinkled his forehead, then waggled a hand. 'But now we're getting into TV territory.' Molina looked to Corso for agreement but got nothing in return. 'So . . . I get back on the phone. I'm thinking maybe Officer Richardson wasn't wearing a tie that day. Maybe he was off duty. Who knows?'

'What did they say?' Corso asked.

'Actually, the jury was split on the matter. His boss, the sheriff, couldn't remember whether he'd been wearing a tie or not. His fellow officers seemed pretty sure he had been.'

'So?'

'So I recalled that you said in your statement that Deputy Sheriff Richardson had a flair for the media. That he liked to be in the news.'

'So you asked Wisconsin for some pictures,' Corso said.

'And guess what?'

'What?'

'With the exception of a shot where the vic and his father are shown ice fishing for Muskie' – his nostrils flared in revulsion – 'Officer Richardson was wearing the same regulation brown tie in every picture.'

'Can I go now?'

Molina made an apologetic face. 'I'm sure you understand what a dilemma I find myself faced with. On the one hand, I have an obligation to honor the Wisconsin warrant. On the other, I'm fairly sure you aren't the perp. At least not the way Wisconsin imagines it coming down.' Again he spread his hands in resignation. 'I don't need to be spending resources on something this old. I've got my own fish to fry. What to do?'

Molina pushed the chair back and got to his feet. 'What I did is what I always do. I backed up. Got simple instead of complicated. You show me crop circles, I think stoned kids, not Martians. It's just how I am. So anyway . . . I called Wisconsin. Wanted to talk to the ME who did the workup.' He shook his head in disgust. 'Turned out they don't really have an ME out there. They find a guy with a bullet in his head, they assume he died of a gunshot wound. What can I say? So it turns out the guy I talked to was an undertaker. Anyway . . . seemed to me if it came down the way you said it did, the deceased should have had some sort of contusion on the back of his head.

Assuming, of course, he still had a back of his head.' He waved a hand in the air. 'The want just said he'd been shot in the head with his own gun. I mean anything was possible.'

'And?'

'And sure enough, our friend the undertaker found a knot on the back of the vic's head the size of a tennis ball. A full-blown hematoma. He figured it happened when the vic hit the floor after being shot.' Molina rubbed his hands together. 'They faxed us out some pictures. I had a forensic pathologist from Quantico take a look.'

'And?'

'Couple of things. First off, the angle of the bullet was strange. The bullet entered beneath the chin and rattled around inside the skull. Quantico says it's consistent with the kind of wound somebody gets if they're struggling for the gun and it goes off. But the hematoma . . . now that's something else.' He began to pace. 'See . . . Quantico says there had to be a time lapse between when the victim hit his head and when somebody blew his brains out and stole his tie. Twenty minutes minimum. Probably more like thirty. Because if the heart had stopped pumping blood, the body couldn't have raised a knot of that size on the back of the man's head. You follow me here?'

Corso said he did. 'So,' Molina went on, 'now I've really got a problem. I pretty much know you're not the perp, but I can't think of a single good reason why I ought to help you out here. I mean sure . . . you gave us your version of the story in fifty words or less. Then you spent the next six hours toying with my agents, while your girlfriend in the next room won't even admit that Dougherty's her real name. With that kind of co-operation, I mean why in hell should I go out of my way to help you out of the soup?'

'You use a lot of food metaphors,' Corso said. 'You ever notice that?'

'I'm Italian,' Molina said with a shrug.

'What do you want?' Corso asked.

Molina bent over and picked up his briefcase from the floor. He set it on the table and opened the lid. He made sure he was looking at Corso when the bundle landed. Mary Anne Moody's drawings. 'You want to tell me about these?' he said.

'Now I'm wondering why it is I should help you out,' Corso said.

Molina smiled. 'Because, Mr Corso, you have pissed off a lot of people around here. We find you with a suitcase full of false documentation – documentation that has compromised the integrity of every known database including our own – and you run your silly-ass song and dance about somebody named Abdul Garcia. Our technical people would like to take you down to the basement. Get medieval on you. See maybe what they couldn't get out of you with your feet in a bucket of cold water and your privates wired up to a field telephone. If you know what I'm saying.'

Molina reached to unfold the pictures. 'Don't,' Corso said. 'I've seen them.'

'Not the kind of images that fade away, are they?'

'I want quid pro quo,' Corso said.

'You're in no position to—'

'Quid pro quo and I'll tell you everything I know.'

'Such as?'

'I want to know what came down in Smithville, New York, in the spring of 1968. It's going to involve people going to jail, people leaving the area in a hurry. Social workers calling the cops. It's gonna involve public school records and it's gonna involve kids, which means a lot of it is going to be sealed, and I want to see it anyway.' He rattled his belly chain. 'I want out of these goddamn manacles, and I want my own clothes back. After that, maybe we can talk.'

'And for this you'll give me what?' Molina asked.

Corso thought it over. 'I don't think it's got a name.'

'Try me.'

'Serial killers kill people they don't know, right?'

'Usually they start close to home, but once they get rolling it's mostly stranger to stranger. Why?'

''Cause I think maybe we've got a whole new category of killer here.'

CHAPTER 22

What am I going to tell a judge?' Molina demanded. 'That some famous author has a hunch some kid who's supposed to have been buried up in the mountains has actually been traveling around killing people for the past thirty years? Killing her own husband and kids. Killing *nuns*, for pity's sake. All this from a guy who's been fired by the *New York Times* for fabricating a story. Who's currently under indictment in Texas over some information he said he had when he didn't. Who's got a pair of felony assault beefs in his jacket. Come on, help me out here, Corso. We're gonna be digging up graves, we're gonna have to do a whole lot better than that.'

Corso threw his hand out over the array of files and folders that littered the table in front of him. 'It's all in there,' he said. 'The state of New York made Smithville send their kids to public school in March of '68. Eight boys, six girls.

'Ten seconds after the girls from Smithville hit the public school system they started telling anybody who'd listen they were being sexually

208

abused at home. It's no damn wonder the parents didn't want to send their kids to school. They knew what was going to happen.' He picked up a red folder marked 'Confidential.' 'There's a hundred seventy pages' – he shook the folder – 'a hundred seventy pages of conversations between counselors and social workers and five of the Smithville girls. Rape, sodomy, beatings' – he dropped the folder on the table – 'being passed around from house to house like trade goods. I'm less than halfway through this pile and there's stuff in there that would make a mechanic blush, for Christ's sake.' He grabbed the red folder again. Leafed through it until he found what he was looking for.

'Listen to this. It's dated April fourth, 1968. It's an interagency report on Leslie Louise de Groot. Generated by the Rockland County Department of Child Protective Services at the request of Hillburn, New York, School District Thirty-Two.' He rattled the papers. 'Here goes:

'Pursuant to your request for a psychological profile on the minor Leslie Louise de Groot, I met with the young woman in my office for a period of three hours on March twenty-seventh, 1968. Before beginning, I wish to stipulate as to the diagnostic difficulty inherent in reaching conclusions from such a short contact with the patient, for whom no prior medical records appear to exist.

That said: Miss de Groot appears to be an average fifteen-year-old girl. Five feet eight, somewhere in the vicinity of a hundred and twenty pounds. She has wavy black hair and blue eyes. While she claims to be what she describes as 'a Ramapo Indian,' in the absence of prior medical data, I would be unwilling to hazard a guess as to her actual ethnic or racial background.

'Paragraph,' Corso said.

'In the course of our conversations, Miss de Groot described the same horrific pattern of sexual abuse at the hands of her extended family as she related to your staff. I have absolutely no doubt as to her veracity in reporting these events. Nor do I, for a moment, doubt the debilitating effect of her experiences on her developing psyche.

'Miss de Groot is extremely disturbed. The bizarre nature of her experiences has forced her to cope in ways not normally demanded of human beings, and most certainly not of children. She harbors homicidal fantasies involving her abusers and yet, as is often the case, is unable to imagine herself in any other milieu. What we have is the classic approach-avoidance syndrome at its most extreme: a victim who is inexorably, and in all probability permanently, bonded to her abusers. Miss de Groot copes with her situation by attempting to control everything in her immediate environment. Variables that are not under her control are seen as threats and treated accordingly.

'Without further data, I am, at this time, unable to expand upon the above opinion.

'Now listen to this,' Corso said.

'The scope of possible behaviors emanating from the experiences which Leslie has suffered range from violence either to herself or to others, a wide array of compulsive behavioral disorders, extreme sexual aggression (which in Leslie's case could be manifested toward both women and men), and, as is often the case, could include extreme clinical depression and schizophrenia.

'The prognosis for this young woman is not encouraging.

'It's signed Phoebe Hill, M.D., Ph.D. Yadda-yadda.' Corso dropped the paper on the table. 'That's sick as hell,' Corso said.

Molina hooded his eyes. 'It's also thirty years old.'

'Nine adults did serious prison time for aggravated child abuse. The rest of the kids ended up in foster homes. Permanently. Somebody showed up one night and burned down whatever was left of the town. What the hell else do we need?'

Molina put both hands on the table. Leaned toward Corso. 'What?' he demanded. 'You think this is lost on me or something? I've got two daughters, man. Twelve and fifteen. Takes every bit of restraint I've got not to follow them around when they leave the house. Every day I see what human beings are capable of doing to one another for a blow job or a bottle of wine or maybe just for the hell of it. And every time my kids leave the house, I start seeing all the pictures that twenty years in the Bureau's stored inside my head. So don't be lecturing at me like you've cornered the market on outrage, okay. You're not the only person in the world who gives a shit.'

'Sorry,' Corso said.

'We need something that connects it to right now. Something that makes it important that we disturb the dead. Something timely that connects this Leslie Louise de Groot girl to this Mary Anne Moody and this . . .' He looked to Corso for help.

'Sissy Marie Warwick,' Corso said.

'Some connection other than *your* gut feeling that they're all the same person. I need something tangible.'

'Show the judge the drawings,' Corso said.

Molina winced. 'Edith Wells is a grandmother three times over. She and her husband, Grant, spend a couple of months every summer up at their little retreat in the Poconos. They're big with the Rockland County Opera and the ballet. You understand what I'm saying to you here? I show her those drawings, I'll be assigned to South Dakota within forty-eight hours. I don't think my family would like that. Matter of fact, I don't think they'd come along.' He shook his head. 'No way. Not gonna happen.'

'Then ask her what she figures the de Groot girl is doing now.'

'What do you mean *now*?'

'I mean like as we speak. She was in her mid-thirties when she left Avalon, Wisconsin. By now, if I'm right, and she's somehow still alive, she's in her midforties. Maybe had time to work up a whole new family. Who knows?'

Molina pulled at his lower lip. 'What do you think the weather's like in South Dakota this time of year?'

'Cold as a grave,' Corso said.

CHAPTER 23

S orry I punked out on you last night,'
Dougherty said. 'I just couldn't look at that
stuff anymore.' She waved the Coke bottle.
'Not that it helped any. I didn't sleep worth a
damn.'

'Me neither,' Corso said.

'Are we still under arrest?'

'I don't think so.'

'Where does that leave you with Wisconsin?'

'No clue.'

'Any word on what they found?'

'Nope.'

'Not even on whether they found anything at
all?'

'Uh-uh.'

The Newark, New Jersey, Regional Offices of
the FBI occupied the entire seventh floor of the
Ethan Dombrowski Building on East Third Street.
Once you got past the receptionist and the big
gold seal on the wall, and if you forgot about the
trio of interrogation rooms down the hall, the
place looked more or less like any other suite of
corporate offices. On the left, two conference

214

rooms, one big, one small, and then the day room where the agents mustered in the morning, followed by three adjoining interrogation rooms and then the johns behind that.

On the right, private offices. Special agents shared space with their partners and used the johns down the hall. Special agents in charge got nice rooms overlooking the street, with private facilities to boot.

Angelo Molina stepped out into the hall, motioned with his head for Corso and Dougherty to follow him, and then disappeared back into his office, leaving the door open.

Molina's stone-faced secretary sat with her hands folded as they marched past, through the outer area and into Molina's office. He had the whole ball of wax. The colorful flags with the gold braid. The big seal on the wall. The deep red leather club chairs, all of which were about six inches below his perch behind the big mahogany desk, from whence he could look down at the rabble below.

His face looked like somebody'd shot the family dog. He moved his hair again. 'Close the door.' Corso eased it shut and then stepped into the room.

'Results are still sketchy,' Molina said. 'The body had been badly burned to begin with, and after thirty plus years in the ground, there wasn't a hell of a lot left of it.' He pointed to his computer screen. 'What they can tell us at this point is that the remains are those of a female between the ages of thirteen and eighteen, who was probably about four months pregnant at the time of her death. Her teeth were intact. They're checking dental records right now.' His eyes traveled down the screen. 'At some point in her life she'd seen a doctor. She had three stainless steel screws holding her left shin together. Which may or may not be a help, because so far we haven't been able to turn up a single medical or dental record on any of these kids.' He looked up at Corso and spread his hands. 'Looks to me like it's the end of the trail. We crapped out on this one. Leslie Louise de Groot is exactly where she's supposed to be.'

'What now?' Corso asked.

'I spoke to Sheriff Trask this morning. Explained why there was no chance you were the perp and that you were no longer in FBI custody.' Something flickered in his dark eyes. Amusement maybe. Or disapproval. It was hard to tell.

'What'd she say?' Corso asked.

'She was pretty much flabbergasted. I got the impression she'd hung her hat on you as the perp. Maybe didn't follow up on the rest of her leads like the protocol demands.' He shrugged. 'I'm sure something like this isn't the kind of thing she deals with all the time . . . little place like that . . . in Wisconsin.'

He looked like the excuse tasted bad in his mouth and turned away.

'So . . . he's off the hook?' Dougherty asked.

'Yes.' Molina chuckled. 'Except for the pair of Dallas County deputies who showed up here bright and early this morning wanting me to hand him over on a material-witness warrant.' His eyes narrowed. 'You're lucky I didn't know the girl was in her grave at that point, Corso. I'd known that, I'd have let them have you.'

'What did you tell them?' she asked.

'I said that for the foreseeable future you were both going to be the property of the Bureau and otherwise unavailable for extradition.'

'And they said?'

'They wanted to wait in the lobby.'

Corso couldn't help himself; he laughed. 'Those old boys are tried-and-true, now aren't they? Never give up.'

'The Rangers always get their man,' Molina said.

'Speaking of that . . . you find Tommie de Groot yet?'

Molina seemed annoyed by the question. 'The car at the airport was a dodge. De Groot didn't fly anywhere. Didn't rent a car or a limo or charter a plane or even get on a bus. He hasn't cashed a check, used an ATM, or charged anything. If he had, we'd have turned him by now. We're completing a sweep of the area around the airport and investigating other channels of inquiry.'

'Maybe he knew Abdul Garcia too,' Corso said.

Molina colored slightly. 'You know, Mr Corso, I just may have had enough of your company for one week. For your information, Mr de Groot's spent half his life in mental institutions. He was granted a psychological discharge from the Marine Corps after beating another recruit damn near to death with a trenching tool. I'm starting to think you're not funny at all, and I'm willing to bet Randy Rosen's ninety-year-old mother doesn't find you very amusing either.'

The air in the room was electric with rancor and recrimination. Dougherty swallowed hard. 'So we can go, then?'

'By all means,' Molina muttered. 'Go.'

Dougherty grabbed Corso by the elbow and began to pull him toward the door. Corso had just given in and turned to leave, when Molina's voice stopped him.

'Few things before you go,' Molina said. He used his fingers to count. 'First off, you can see my secretary about where to retrieve your gear. Two, you're gonna need a new rental car. The Ford is evidence in a murder case. Three, you probably want to try somebody other than Hertz. They're not real happy with you guys. Four, I'd keep my eyes out for those Dallas boys if I were you. They seemed pretty damned determined to me. And five, next time you dream up some half-assed theory about teenagers rising from the grave, you take it to somebody else.' He cut the air with his hand. 'Now get out of here.'

They didn't quite make it to the door.

'Whoa,' Molina said. 'No way.'

His attention was welded to his computer screen.

He tapped the keyboard twice. Held up a 'don't move' hand to Corso and Dougherty and then used the keyboard again.

'I think I owe you an apology,' Molina said.

'How's that?' Corso wanted to know.

'Pathology was inputting the data on the girl's body. They got a kick-out from the computer on the steel screws in her shin.'

'I thought you couldn't find her medical records.'

'We can't. The kick-out was on a thirty-year-old missing person. Named *Velma* de Groot.' He looked up at Corso. 'The body was never found. She was supposed to be one of Richard Leon Parker's victims.' He tapped the computer screen. 'Compound fracture of her leg when she was nine.'

He spun the screen Corso's way. While Corso and Dougherty crossed the room to peer at the flickering monitor, Molina pushed one of the buttons on his phone. 'Dean,' he said, 'get whoever you used to exhume the girl. Get the rest of the family down here to the morgue as quick as you can.' Molina listened for a moment before losing his patience. 'You let me worry about the paper-work. You just dig those people up and get them down here. ASAP.'

W hat's your brother doing here this time of year?' he wanted to know. 'He don't usually come till summer.'

'What's the time of year matter?'

'Summers, at least I can take the girls camping and get away from him and that goddamn cigarette smoke of his.'

She looked away. 'He had a little free time. He wanted to see me.'

'The girls don't like him. They say he's always putting his hands on them. They tell you that?'

'That's that damn Sarah,' she said. 'Girl's an out-and-out liar.'

'That why you cut her hair off?'

'I cut her hair so's she'd stop spending all her damn time fooling with it.'

She turned to face him now. 'Why don't you just let me worry about the ladies' fashions around here. I'm thinking maybe somebody with as goddamn little hair as you got ought to keep his nose out of such things.'

'Coupla more days and then I want him out of here.'

'It's my house too.'

'It's my mother's house,' he corrected.

'And don't neither of you ever let anybody forget it, now do you?'

'Coupla more days,' he said again.

She walked across the room to the stove. 'Maybe if you'd spend more time getting this new stove installed and less time worrying about my brother, I wouldn't have to be cooking off a hot plate.'

He walked her way. She held her ground. Made him reach around her to grab the piece of pipe leaning against the wall. He pointed at one end. 'Needs another reducing bushing right here. Ajax was out of them. Be a coupla days till they get one in. Soon as that happens, I'll put it together.'

She walked away. Turned on the water in the sink. 'None too damn soon either.'

'Coupla days and I want him gone,' he said.

221

CHAPTER 24

W e're pursuing a number of other leads,' Sheriff Trask insisted. She went on about all the people who were in the hospital at the time of Officer Richardson's murder. All the local and national media types, not to mention curiosity seekers and the hospital staff, each of whom had to be questioned and systematically eliminated as suspects. She nodded at Corso and Dougherty. 'These two caused quite a stir around here,' she said finally. 'We had a hell of a circus going on that morning.'

Molina nodded in all the right places, as if affirming his complete confidence in the integrity of her investigation. Truth was, she didn't have a clue, and even if she did, she had neither the staff, the budget, nor the expertise to properly pursue the matter. Everybody in the room knew the investigation was going nowhere, but nobody was willing to say it out loud. Professional courtesy, you know.

'You get the slug?' Molina asked.

'Sure did,' the sheriff said. 'Thirty-eight caliber. Lab says it came from a Smith and Wesson Model

Ten with a four-inch barrel. Which just happens to be the same make and model as everybody in this department carries. The state police test-fired every piece from every officer in the department, including mine. No matches.' She shot Corso a look. 'That's why I figured it had to be Mr Corso here.'

'Makes perfect sense to me,' Molina said. 'S and W Model Ten's real common. Must be millions and millions of them around.'

The sheriff took a deep breath and finally made eye contact with Special Agent in Charge Molina. 'So,' she began, 'how do I rate a visit from the FBI? Especially a visit from the faraway New Jersey FBI.' She threw Molina a thin, insincere smile. 'As you can probably tell, I'm stretched pretty thin around here.'

She sat behind her desk with her hands steepled in front of her. The three available chairs were occupied by Dougherty and Special Agents Fullmer and Dean. Molina and Corso had refused an offer to have more chairs brought in and instead stood along the wall, whose surface was covered with plaques, commendations, public service awards, and pictures of Sheriff Trask in the company of an assortment of local dignitaries.

Molina was all professional goodwill. 'We're pursuing an interstate matter, which we believe may have started in our jurisdiction and later lapped over into yours.'

'And what matter might that be?'

Hard to tell what she expected for an answer. Not what she got, though.

'Your old friend Sissy Warwick,' Corso said.

The sheriff rolled her eyes, as if to say she didn't need to be reminded of another open case. 'I'm focusing my limited resources on the present tense,' she said. 'We've lost a brother officer, and until that matter is successfully resolved, I'm afraid I don't have the staff or the inclination to spare on anything quite that old.' She held up a restraining hand. 'We're certainly not forgetting about it. Matter of fact, we're expecting the final forensics reports from the state crime lab any day now. But like I said, for the time being anyway, I've got to husband my resources.'

'As well you should,' Molina agreed. 'The death of any peace officer is an affront to the entire law enforcement community.'

Corso watched as the sheriff's professional demeanor did battle with her personal curiosity. After an uncomfortable silence, the cat won. 'And how would Sissy Warwick Holmes have lapped over into your jurisdiction?' she asked.

Molina told her. Chapter and verse. Took ten minutes. Maria Trask listened in silence as Molina related what they knew for sure. 'You need to understand,' he said, 'that the condition of the bodies precludes most of the normal avenues for ascertaining cause of death.' He held up a finger. 'But as I'm sure you are aware, certain chemical compounds do not deteriorate over time. They remain in the body until the very end.'

'Word *has* reached us,' she said with a smile.

Molina went on. 'Preliminary forensic analysis of the other four members of the Paul de Groot family reveals a substantial residue of an arsenic-based substance still present in the hair and nails of the remains. The residue is consistent with what used to be sold as rat poison, back in the sixties.' He spread his hands. 'Of course, that type of product is no longer sold over the counter due to health and environmental concerns, but back then it was quite common.'

The sheriff laced her fingers together and leaned forward in her chair. 'So . . . you're saying this girl – what was she, fourteen or fifteen at the time? – poisoned her entire family, somehow or other managed to drag another girl into her bed, and then set the house on fire.'

'Except for her younger brother,' Corso amended. 'He was in the hospital with food poisoning on the night of the fire.'

'That's what it looks like at this time,' Molina said.

'You don't mind me saying, it sounds pretty far-fetched to me,' the sheriff said. 'You're assuming she killed this other girl?'

'We don't know for sure,' Molina said. 'The other girl went missing two days before the fire. They rode the same school bus together. Louise was questioned by state and local authorities. She claimed the other girl . . .' Molina looked to Fullmer for help.

'Velma,' Fullmer said.

'She claimed Velma said she'd be right back and walked off as they were waiting for the bus out in front of Mahwah High School. That's the last she saw of her. Turned out later that Richard Leon Parker had kidnapped another girl from that same parking lot.' Molina shrugged. 'The natural assumption was that the de Groot girl was one of his victims.'

'Until she turned up in another girl's grave.'

Molina shot a quick look over at Corso. 'Yes,' he said. 'The advanced stage of decomposition precludes determining a cause of death. She wasn't poisoned like the others, we know that for sure.'

'Also, we've got a few gaps,' Corso said. 'We've got about two and a half years between when her house burns and when she shows up in Allentown, Pennsylvania, and the better part of a year between the time she leaves Allentown and when she shows up here. What she was doing during those time periods, we don't know.'

'We're working on that right now,' Molina assured her.

'What about the brother? The one who shot this Professor Rosen.'

'Mr. de Groot took a taxi from Newark Airport to the nearby town of Elizabeth, New Jersey, where he purchased an '88 Chevy Cavalier for cash on the day after the murder. The plates registered to that vehicle were recovered during a routine traffic stop in Elgin, Illinois, yesterday morning. An elderly couple. Folks never even noticed they didn't have Illinois tags anymore. It appears de Groot's swapping off license plates as he goes along. Quite frankly, if he keeps it up, we'll have to get real lucky to catch him.'

'What do you need from me?'

'We're here mostly as a matter of courtesy,' Molina said. 'We've been in contact with the Wisconsin State Patrol, and we have the full resources of the Bureau office in Madison at our disposal. One of their forensics teams will be going through the house this afternoon.' Molina looked to his left. 'Mr Corso tells me that a family album was found with the bodies.'

The sheriff nodded. 'Yes, it was.'

'We'd like to borrow that, if we may.' Before she could respond, he went on. 'Also, I understand that the Holmes boys had an accident in the family truck.'

'Drove it through the front window of the Dairy Queen,' she said.

'Well then, somewhere in your records you must have the license plate number and the VIN number. It would be a great help if we had those as well.'

'You're going to try to find the truck? Fifteen years later?'

Molina gave her a thin smile. 'We're pursuing a number of other leads.'

If the sheriff got the joke, she didn't let on. Instead she sighed and pushed the red button on her phone. 'Barbara,' she said.

'Yes, Sheriff Trask' crackled over the speaker. The office door was open. Both the sheriff and her secretary could be heard in stereo, as both their real and electronic voices filled the air.

Fullmer opened his mouth for the first time. 'And . . . uh . . . Sheriff . . . while you're at it, could you get us the serial number of Officer Richardson's revolver? We handed the weapon over to your state police' – he looked embarrassed – 'and it seems we neglected to record the serial number.'

'For our records,' Molina added. 'I've got to get back to New Jersey. I just want to make sure everything's kosher before I leave.'

She almost smiled. 'I didn't think you boys made mistakes like that.'

Fullmer shrugged. 'Everybody's human,' he said. 'Long as we catch it now, we'll have all our i's dotted and our t's crossed.'

'I'll be right back,' said the sheriff. The rubber soles of her shoes squeaked with every step. She stopped halfway to the door. 'Anything else you boys forgot I can help you out with?' she asked. This time she managed a grin. 'Always glad to help you boys out with your kosher record keeping, I am.'

They assured her that was it. She gave a curt little wave and went squeaking out into the hall.

Molina grabbed his briefcase from the floor. Set it on the table in front of him. 'Which one of you is taking me to the airport?' he asked Fullmer and Dean.

Dean said he'd be doing the driving. Molina opened his briefcase and pulled out a laundry list of things he wanted the forensics team to check. Fullmer took notes. Then another list of investigative avenues for Fullmer and Dean. They both took notes.

Molina turned to Corso and Dougherty. 'This is where you came in,' he said. 'From here on, the Leslie de Groot–Sissy Warwick story is the property of the Madison field office. I'm leaving Special Agents Dean and Fullmer here for a couple of days for liaison. You two can stick around for that, if you want. After Madison takes over, you're history as far as the investigation is concerned. I went to the Academy with Paul Waymer. He's the SAIC in Madison, and there's no way in hell he's gonna let you two look over his shoulder while he investigates.' He snapped his case closed and spun the combination dials.

The sound of the sheriff's shoes preceded her into the room. She carried the Holmes family album and two file folders, one yellow, one green. She was still smiling. 'Color coded and all,' she said, dropping the album and the files on the table in front of Molina. 'We may be rural, but we've got our stuff together, we surely do.'

Molina slid the album and folders over to

Fullmer and Dean. They were busy jotting away as Molina and the sheriff shook hands and said their good-byes. Corso lingered, letting the FBI and Dougherty precede him out the door. When Dougherty looked back over her shoulder to see if he was there, he motioned for her to keep going and then held up an 'I'll just be a minute' finger. He turned back to the sheriff.

She gave him her stoniest gaze. 'Yes, Mr Corso?'

'That little deal you and I had.'

'I'm afraid I don't know what you're talking about,' she said.

He ignored her. 'Our arrangement was personal, and it's going to stay that way.'

She got to her feet. 'If you'll excuse me, I'm really swamped.' Again the black rubber soles of her shoes squeaked at every step as she crossed the room and disappeared.

Ten seconds later, she was back in the doorway. In the harsh overhead light she looked haggard and drawn. She checked the hall in both directions. 'Sorry,' she said. 'I'm under a lot of pressure here. I didn't know what in heck I was going to do if you started telling people I let you go. I've got all the aggravation I can handle right now. Clint Richardson spends more time in my office than he does in his own.' She shook her head. 'Two weeks ago I was worried about what I was going to do if I lost the election, and now I'd give you the damn job for a dollar.' She scooped the folders from the table. 'Time for my morning media flogging,' she said with a wry smile. 'You gonna be around for a while?' she asked.

'Coupla days maybe.'

'I'm asking because Clint Richardson's taking his son's death pretty hard. He's got a wild hair that no matter what anybody says, you were responsible. He figures you just found some legal loop-hole. Clint's a good man, but he's not real rational right now. I was you, I'd keep an eye out for him.'

'Thanks,' Corso said. 'We won't be around very long. My guess is the Madison Bureau's not going to put a whole lot of energy into something this cold. They'll look for anything obvious. Something that points to where she might have gone from here. They find something right away, they'll pursue it. The minute it looks like it's going nowhere, they'll kick it right back to the state, who'll kick it right back to you, who'll end up as the one who failed to solve the murders.'

'I see you've worked with the Bureau before.'

'Coupla times,' Corso said.

She ran a hand through her hair. 'You really think all these girls – Sissy and . . . what were the little girls' names?'

'Leslie Louise de Groot and Mary Anne Moody.'

'You really think they're all the same person?' she asked.

'Yeah. I do.'

She shook her head. 'This is like something out of science fiction.' She lifted her hands and then let them flop back against her sides. 'All I wanted from you was some little tidbit I could feed to the press. I wasn't looking for another mystery.'

'You need to be careful what you wish for,' Corso said.

She allowed as how that was true and then stepped back out into the hall. 'Come on,' she said. 'We don't want to keep our federal friends waiting, now do we?'

They left the conference room together. Said 'So long' at her office door.

In the lobby, Molina, Dean, and Fullmer stood in a tight circle. Dougherty was over by the door, squinting as she gazed out at the mounds of snow.

Molina stuck out his hand. Fullmer tore a page from his notebook and slapped it into Molina's palm; Molina then separated himself from the others and walked Corso's way. Molina handed the page to Corso. 'Here's what you wanted,' he said. His black eyes were as hard as rivets. 'You think you know something, don't you?'

Corso pocketed the piece of paper. 'Maybe,' Corso said.

CHAPTER 25

The snow around the Holmes farmhouse had been trampled to slush. Yellow police tape rippled in the late-afternoon breeze. Four unmarked FBI vans dotted the driveway. Half a dozen orange power cables ran from the Honda generator chugging away on the porch through the front door into the parlor, where the FBI team had set up shop.

'Looks a lot bigger in the daylight,' Dougherty said.

'All I remember from that night was this tiny purple light in the distance. So small it was like a match in deep space.'

'You know what I remember?' She paused and looked to her right. They'd removed the front of the shed and torn up the rest of the floor. All that remained was a hollow depression. A dozen little white flags, whose red numbers marked precisely where this piece or that piece of evidence had been found. 'I remember how hard you were to move,' she said. 'How it felt like I was trying to carry a car or something.' She looked over at the house and back. 'Gets me to wondering how she lugged the three of them out here and then wrapped them up in a nice little package and all. I can maybe see the boys. But the husband? I could barely move you thirty feet, with you trying to help.'

'It's the truck that bothers *me*,' Corso said.

'What about it?'

'I keep trying to get a picture of what the scene looked like. So . . . what? She kills the family, hides the bodies in the shed, then goes back inside, packs up everything in the house, loads it on a one-ton truck all by herself, then gets behind the wheel and drives off into the sunset?' He shook his head. 'No way, José.'

Dougherty folded her arms across her chest and thought about it. 'Maybe she had Eldred and the boys load the truck before she offed them,' she said finally.

'Possible,' he conceded. 'Or maybe she had help.'

Dougherty laughed. 'Probably invited the neighbors over. Mind helping me move old Eldred here? He's a mite heavy.' She giggled and hid her face with her hands. 'Sorry,' she said. 'I seem to be getting a little silly here.'

A movement in Dougherty's peripheral vision pulled her eyes toward the house, where one of the forensic technicians had taken a break from detecting and was making his way in their direction. He was a short little guy with Coke-bottle glasses, wearing the standard black windbreaker with 'FBI' in big white letters across the back. He moved carefully, navigating around piles of slush, trying to keep the stuff out of his shoes.

'You Margaret Dougherty?'

'That's me,' she said.

'We need you to come inside for a minute.'

'What for?'

'We need to take your fingerprints,' he said. He cast a quick glance at Corso. 'We've got plenty of his,' he said. 'And Avalon's got prints from both the boys. So once we get yours, anything we can't identify pretty much has to be either the mommy or the daddy.' He smiled. 'I hear they weren't big on entertaining.'

'You can still get fingerprints after fifteen years?' Corso asked.

'Depends on what they're on,' the little guy said. 'On most things, the oil would have dried out by now and blown away. On other surfaces, if they're not exposed to the elements' – he spread his hands – 'anything's possible.'

Corso looked to Dougherty. 'You've never been fingerprinted?'

'Nope,' she said.

The little guy took her by the elbow and began to move her toward the house. 'Won't hurt a bit,' he assured her. She looked back over her shoulder at Corso.

'I'm gonna take a little more air,' Corso said. 'I'll be back in a minute.'

They stepped carefully across the field of frozen ruts as they made their way to the porch. 'I'm

Warren,' the little guy said, offering a hand, as they mounted the stairs.

She stopped in the doorway as a river of images began to flow in her head. For a long moment, she could once again hear the roar of the wind and feel the bite of the cold on her skin. The memory caused her to shudder.

The FBI had moved in. On the left, against the far wall, a series of tables had been set up for use as desks. A trio of agents sat in front of laptop computers, pecking away at their keyboards. Special Agents Fullmer and Dean were seated side by side, each with a cell phone glued to his ear, talking and taking notes at the same time. Half a dozen technicians crawled over the place like ants. Power cables grew off in all directions like orange tendrils.

They stepped over the cables as they made their way to the kitchen, where Warren handed her over to a middle-aged woman named Claire and then disappeared.

Dougherty was still wiping the last of the ink from her fingers when Warren came back through the kitchen door. 'We can wait for an official comparison,' Claire said, 'but I can tell you right now she's not a match for what we got from the contact paper.' She picked up the white card upon which she'd rolled Dougherty's fingerprints, held it by the edge, and handed it to Warren. He brought the card up close to his face and squinted at the impressions. 'The exemplars on the paper were all archs and tent archs,' Claire said. 'These are all whorls and double loops.'

Warren nodded his agreement. 'Have Billy take some pictures of what we got from the contact paper and shoot them off to Washington. Let's see what the computer has to say on the subject.'

Claire fanned herself with the card as she walked out onto the back porch, only to return a minute later with what must have been Billy, a balding character with a face that spoke of perpetual aggravation. Dougherty watched as the man attached a Nikon digital camera to a short stand, slid the prints under the lens one at a time, and took shots.

Finished, he stowed the gear back in his bag, popped the flash card from the camera, and headed for the computers in the front room. 'We're almost done here,' Warren said. 'We got a heck of a good right hand from some contact paper we found out by the fireplace. The glue had dried out, but the impressions were plain as day. Just like they'd been made yesterday.'

'That was what I used to start a fire,' Dougherty said. 'It was lining the kitchen drawers.'

'That's what we figured,' the little guy said. 'If they're not yours – which Claire is right about, they're not – then they pretty much gotta belong to whoever lined the drawers in the first place, which I'm figuring is most likely the missing mommy.'

He turned to Claire. 'I think that's a wrap,' he

said. 'Everything we turned is consistent with the lab findings, so why don't we get everybody packed up and head for the motel.'

Claire rolled her eyes. 'Another night at the Timber Inn,' she said. 'Be still, my beating heart.'

Warren tried to cheer her up. 'We'll be back home in Madison by noon,' he said.

'If the food doesn't kill us first,' Claire said, and headed for the porch.

Warren squinted out through the open back door to the snow-covered yard beyond. 'They were laid out right there in the backyard someplace,' he said.

'Laid out?'

'The lab estimated they were dead for at least seventy-two hours prior to being wrapped up in plastic. Left outside, probably naked.' He looked myopically around the room. 'Everything we've found supports that thesis.'

'How'd they figure that?' Dougherty asked.

'The maggots,' he said. 'They found a bunch of third instars in the rectal cavities.'

'Third what?'

'Third instars. It's a stage in maggot development.' The putrid look on her face seemed to encourage him. 'Okay now, this isn't strictly my field. This would be what a forensic entomologist does, so . . . you know . . . I'm just kind of winging it here.' He grinned. 'If you'll forgive me the phrase.' And winked. 'So if you take a body and you put it outside, the first things that are going to find it are the flies. Most likely the blowflies and the common house flies are gonna come upon it first. Now as soon as they get there they're gonna lay masses of eggs in any natural body openings they can get to or in any wounds they find.'

'Eggs?'

'Millions,' he said. 'This is where it gets interesting. Depending on the temperature and the species of fly involved, the eggs take anywhere from fifteen to thirty hours to hatch. Most cases somewhere right around twenty hours. So anyway, the eggs hatch into the first-stage maggot.'

'A first instar.'

'Exactly. Okay, so after hatching, they immediately begin to feed on the tissues, and of course they start to grow. Real quick they get too big for the cuticle.' He stopped. 'That's like this little flexible case the maggot lives inside of. They call it a cuticle. Anyway, soon as it grows too big for its cuticle, it makes a new cuticle and then sheds the old one. Most maggots do this three times in their life cycle.'

'First, second, and third instars.'

'Precisely. The first instar usually takes the shortest time. Averages about sixteen hours. The second goes about twenty-three and the third-stage about thirty hours. All in all, you average it out, you find third stage instars, the body's been there about three days. You find them in the rectal cavity, the body was probably found naked. There's easier ways to get into a body than crawling up under somebody's shorts.' He offered her a shy

239

smile. 'Did I mention that the bodies had been set on fire? Postmortem. Then probably hosed off before they were packaged.'

'Why would anybody do that?'

He made a 'who knows' face. 'If I had to guess, I'd say the stiffs were all covered with creepy crawlies, and whoever did it wanted to get rid of them before they moved the bodies. Or . . . maybe they just liked to burn things. You put the family album in the grave with your family, and the way I see it, that makes you pretty much unpredictable. Either way, the fire didn't harm the bodies much, but it killed the maggots before they got a chance to do their thing. The plastic kept subsequent generations of flies from laying eggs on the bodies, so they just sat out there in the shed and more or less mummified.'

'Any word on what killed them?'

He looked insulted. 'Didn't exactly take a rocket scientist,' he said. 'Head trauma. Nonblunt. Something like a hatchet or a small ax.' He pointed to the stairway. 'They got it in their beds. The father first and then the kids.'

She pulled back. 'You're messing with me here.'

'Swear to God,' he said. 'It's all right there.'

'You mean to tell me . . . all these years later, you can come in here – with the place completely deserted and all – and figure out how these people died and what happened to them after that, and in just a few hours?'

'You want to see?'

240

'Yeah, sure,' she said. 'That'd be great.'

He walked over to the pile of cop equipment against the front wall, dug around for a moment, and came out with a black fanny pack, which he buckled around his waist. He reached into the heap again and produced a yellow flashlight. He flicked it on with his thumb, made sure it was working, and then started across the room.

He reached up over the entrance to the stairs, pulled a couple of ties loose, and allowed a canvas curtain to flop down over the doorway. 'Gotta be dark,' he said.

He held the curtain aside long enough for Dougherty to step through. He put a hand on her waist as they mounted the stairs, moving tentatively behind the dancing circle of light. At the top of the stairs, he guided her to the right, into a bare room overlooking the front of the house. He pointed the flashlight beam at the far wall. Moved it back and forth a little. 'The bed must have been right about there,' he said. 'Hubby slept on the left. Mommy on the right.'

'Come on,' Dougherty scoffed. 'Give me a break.'

'Watch,' he said, taking her by the hand and pulling her across the room. He held out the flashlight. 'Hold this.' She took the light. Moved it around the peeling walls, while Warren unzipped the pack and pulled out what looked like an oversized electric flash unit. A little black ray gun was attached to the pack by a three-foot length of telephone cord.

'Turn off the flashlight,' he said. Dougherty thumbed the light, and for a moment they stood in total darkness until, with the flick of a switch, a purple light appeared in his hand. 'Ultraviolet,' he said. He held the light up to the wall. 'Look.' Dougherty stepped in closer. In the ghostly light, a glowing chartreuse stain spread upward along the wall like a galaxy, thick and dark at the bottom, then growing more sparse as it flew upward and outward and finally trailed off in a series of bright yellow dots.

'Blood,' he said. 'You spray a little luminol on it, and it doesn't matter how old it is or how hard anybody tried to scrub it off, luminol will light it up.'

Instinctively she reached out and touched the stain.

'Hubby was laying right here.' He smoothed out a place in the darkness, then walked over next to the imaginary bed. 'The perp stood right here. He or she was right-handed.' He raised his free arm. 'Just hauled off and hit the victim, like this.' He demonstrated a chopping motion, then pointed to another splash on the wall. 'First one didn't kill him,' Warren said. 'So the perp hauled off and belted him again. This is the mark from the second.'

She winced. 'What a bad way to go,' she said.

'Are there any good ways?' he asked. When she didn't answer, he turned the light her way. 'Look behind you,' he said.

The floor showed a ghastly trail of yellow and black blotches leading back to the door, some of the trails wispy, where they'd been painted by hair.

'They go all the way through the house and out the back door. See the black spots?' he said. 'That's where somebody tried to clean up afterward.' He shook his head. 'Waste of time.'

They followed the trail to the head of the stairs, where a river of yellow stains adorned every tread, culminating in a pool of chartreuse at the foot of the stairs. He pointed with the purple light. 'See how the blotches are all over the place? Not in a straight line? On the walls in some places. That suggests the victims were brought to the upper landing and then just kicked down the stairs, one on top of the other, until the perp had them all down there and could drag them out the back door.'

Dougherty looked behind her. Another pair of ghostly trails meandered down from the far end of the dimly lit hallway. Warren pointed the light in that direction. 'Boys' room's down the hall.'

She wandered that way, as if in a trance. Warren followed along on her heels. 'Same blood spatter patterns in there. Their blood's on top of the hubby's, so he must have gone down first.'

He opened the door for her and stepped inside. She stopped in the doorway, unable to force herself any closer to the pair of yellow stains that glowed ominously from the far wall. She turned away, flicked on the flashlight, and walked back down the hall.

She stood at the top of the stairs, seeing the movie of how it had come down. Hearing the wet thunk of the ax as it sliced through flesh and bone. Watching the spray splash along the wall. Eldred writhing in agony, only to take another blow. Seeing the limp bodies cartwheel down the stairs. And although her rational mind knew it wasn't possible, the odor of blood began to creep into her nostrils. That metallic odor of liquid electricity that once encountered seems to weld itself permanently to the olfactory memory. She aimed the flashlight down the stairs. 'Let's get out of here,' she said. 'This is just too creepy.'

She took the stairs at a lope, burst through the blackout curtain into the brightly lit parlor, to find Corso huddled up in the far corner with Fullmer and Dean. The pile of equipment along the front wall was mostly gone now, packed into the vans and about to be carted off.

Claire and a pair of black-jacketed technicians scooped up the rest of the gear. 'See you back in town,' she said to Warren, and then followed the other two out the door. A phone beeped. Dean picked it up and began to listen.

The space heaters had ceased to glow. Outside, the generator had stopped. A couple of minutes later the cables had been rolled up and stowed in one of the vans. Dean moved to the corner of the room so the tables could be folded and carried out the door. Corso wandered over. He nodded at Warren, who winked at Dougherty as he lugged an armload of equipment out the door.

'I think the little guy's sweet on you,' Corso said.

'Warren?' She looked his way. 'He's all right.' She chuckled. 'He knows a little too much about maggots for my taste, but who knows?' she said. 'It's been quite a while. He makes the right moves, he might get lucky.'

Corso sneered. 'All he's missing is a stepladder and delusions of grandeur.'

She waved a cautionary finger in his face. 'You never know, Corso. Sometimes these little guys . . .' She used her hands to measure off a foot and a half of space. 'You'd be amazed,' she said. Before Corso could respond, Fullmer and Dean appeared at his elbow. Dean snapped his phone closed and stuck it into his suit-coat pocket.

'That's it here,' he said. 'Sheriff's gonna send a crew out in the morning to board the place back up.' He tapped the cell phone in his pocket. 'We got a hit on the car the de Groot guy bought. I'm gonna need to get to a land line for the details.'

Fullmer took a last look around the room. 'What a dump,' he said.

'Oh, I don't know,' Dougherty said. 'I'll bet they had it fixed up real cute.'

For the first time all day, everybody smiled at once. Dean led the procession out the door, where the late-afternoon breeze had freshened. Only the blue Chevy Citation and the white van remained.

Warren stood at the back of the van, polishing his glasses.

'You going back into town?' Dougherty shouted at him.

'Yep,' he said with a tentative smile. 'You want a ride?'

'Why not?' she hollered over the wind. 'You can tell me more about those maggots.'

The prospect seemed to cheer Warren no end.

CHAPTER 26

Dougherty used her fork to roll scrambled eggs along the rim of her plate. Corso sipped his coffee. 'Don't play with your food,' he said.

'Didn't I ask for my eggs scrambled soft? You heard me ask her, didn't you?' She jabbed at the eggs. 'These things are hard as a brick.'

'So . . . was it?'

'Was it what?'

Corso leered and held his hands two feet apart. Then three.

She laughed. 'Bigger,' she said, dropping the fork onto the plate. 'Actually, we walked down to the park. They've got a winter carnival kind of thing going on. You know, ice-skating, rides, all that kind of thing. We rode the Ferris wheel.'

'Sounds positively bucolic.'

'He's a really sweet guy. An MIT grad.'

'Lordy be.'

She dabbed at her lips with a paper napkin and then dropped it onto the eggs. 'We gotta get out of here, Corso. We've done what we can with this thing. This place is starting to drive me crazy. Reminds me of where I grew up in Iowa.'

'Midnight tonight,' Corso said, 'the grand jury's term expires. After that I can rent a car on my own credit cards without having those two cowboys show up and haul my ass off to Texas.'

'You owe me a phone.'

'Soon as we get out of here, I'll buy you a dozen.'

Corso covered his cup with his hand, but this time the change in the light wasn't the waitress looking to freshen his cup; it was Special Agents Fullmer and Dean standing in the aisle next to the booth, all showered and shiny.

Corso and Dougherty moved over against the wall. Dean slid in next to Corso. Fullmer opposite. 'We're out of here,' Fullmer announced. 'From now on it's Madison's baby.'

'De Groot's Chevy was found along State Route 83 near Lake Geneva, Michigan,' Dean said. 'Looks like it blew a head gasket and he deserted it.'

'Real close to Chicago,' Fullmer commented. 'Probably cabbed his way into the city. Looking to lose himself in the crowd. We're checking on it now.'

'We'll get him,' Dean promised. 'It's just a question of when. We've got a federal warrant out for him. Interstate flight to avoid prosecution. Whenever he stops wandering around the city, we'll collar him for sure.'

'You really think Madison's going to take the ball and run with it on this Sissy Warwick thing?' Corso asked.

'Nothing to run with,' Fullmer said. 'The one-ton truck was sold fourteen years ago to a guy in Wayne, Indiana. He died in '89. The signature on the change of title reads Sissy Marie Holmes. Truck's been sold three times since. Finally ended up at the bottom of a creek bed on a farm near Davenport, Iowa, which is where it rests to this very day.'

Dean smirked. 'Coupla agents from the Minneapolis office were real upset about having to climb down and verify the VIN number.'

'So that's the end of that lead,' Fullmer said.

'Nothing on the personal items either,' added Dean. 'We blew up pictures of the furniture from the family album. Showed them to every antique and used furniture dealer in the upper Midwest. Nothing. Nobody remembers seeing any of the pieces . . . which, considering the time frame, isn't surprising.'

'Presuming this person named Sissy Warwick is still alive, all we can say for sure is that she hasn't generated a scrap of paperwork since the day in '87 when she signed that title transfer for the truck. Not a credit card receipt, or a library card, or a driver's license. As far as the computer is concerned, she's dropped off the face of the earth.'

'Sounds like we struck out,' Dougherty commented.

The agents passed a glance back and forth. 'Not quite,' Dean said. He reached into the inside pocket of his suit coat, pulled out a black-and-white photograph. He held it close to his chest and took a peek.

'The prints we got from the house,' Fullmer said. 'The computer says they match a young woman busted twice for assault and intent to commit prostitution in Cleveland, Ohio. Five months after you say she ran off from the nuns.'

'Used a straight razor on a couple of johns. Gave one of them eighty stitches.'

'Damn near separated the second guy from his equipment,' said Dean.

'Nitty met gritty, neither of them wanted to press charges,' Fullmer said. 'Both of them married. No way they were going to tell their stories in open court. Bad enough explaining the stitches to the wife.'

'They still don't want to talk about it,' Fullmer said. He looked to his partner. Dean tilted his head as if to say 'why not?' and then dropped the picture on the table in front of Corso. Mug shot. Cleveland Police Department. Number 1258793.

It was like people said. She could have been anything. Greek, Spanish, Puerto Rican, African-American . . . no telling. Fine, even features and a little turned-up nose. Brown wavy hair, looked like it had been given an old-fashioned marcel job. A pair of eyes so light-colored that if you didn't know better you'd swear they had to be tinted contact lenses. A dark bruise covered her badly swollen left cheek and gave her face a mismatched quality, as if it had been hastily assembled from spare parts.

Special Agent Dean couldn't keep the sour look from his face. 'You know, Mr Corso, when you got lucky on the grave, I figured it was just that . . . dumb luck.'

'That's still my theory,' Fullmer said, without a trace of a smile.

His partner waved him off. 'No, Gene,' he said. 'We gotta give credit where credit is due. Rest of the world had fifteen years to figure out what it took Mr Corso here about a week to get a handle on.' He shook his balding head. 'No denying it.'

Dougherty leaned forward across the table. 'So then . . . you guys are satisfied that all these women are the same person?'

'Far back as Allentown anyway,' Fullmer said. 'Sheriff Trask say that's the woman she knew as Sissy Warwick, and the Castigliones were just as certain. That was the girl who called herself Mary Anne Moody.'

'Castigliones?'

Dean nearly smiled. 'The sisters, Agnes and Veronica Castiglione.' He looked to his partner for verification and got it.

'What about New Jersey?' Corso wanted to know.

Dean sighed. 'Home office is working on that,' he said. 'Seems they're having a heck of a time finding anybody who will admit to ever seeing the girl.'

'What about Rodney de Groot?'

'Mr de Groot hasn't returned to his cabin since the day of Dr Rosen's shooting. We're assuming he's still somewhere in the general area, but haven't been able to put a finger on him as yet.'

Fullmer reached out and tapped the mug shot. 'Told the arresting officer her name was Nancy Lee Jamison.'

'Always three names,' Dougherty said. 'First, middle, and last.'

'It's a big extended family thing,' Corso offered, 'where everybody in the family is named after everybody else in the family. It's the middle names that let them sort out exactly who's who.'

Fullmer said, 'So as of right now, there's nothing that ties this person directly to our office's geographic area of responsibility.'

'There's all kinds of things that tie it to New Jersey,' Corso argued.

'Such as?'

'Such as the way the crimes were organized. Except for the hooking beef, these were crimes that took some planning and forethought. The way I see it . . . you're seventeen years old and you figure out a way to off your whole family, make it look like you went up with them, so's nobody's looking for you afterward, you pretty much got your criminal shit together, as far as I'm concerned.'

'There's no profile for somebody who only kills their families,' Dean said.

'Fuck the profiles,' Corso snapped. 'There's an attitude behind all of these crimes. I can feel it. Somebody who truly doesn't give a shit . . . no conscience whatsoever, at least not the way most people have one. Somebody who's been pushed so far that something snapped inside and made it okay for them to do whatever they had to do to survive.' Corso looked from agent to agent. 'Come on . . . you guys have got to feel it too. Help me out here.'

Before they could deny it, the waitress arrived with two more white mugs and a fresh pot of coffee. The FBI declined the offer and slid out of the booth. 'It's not enough,' Fullmer said. 'None of it leads forward. For all we know, she's dead and buried. It's just not the kind of thing we can be spending resources on.'

Corso grabbed the mug shot from the table and offered it to Fullmer.

'Keep it.'

'We sent out a flyer,' Dean said, 'asking for anything in the past fifteen years where a whole family either died or disappeared with the mother turning up missing. We drew a blank. No such animal.'

'What about the ritual behavior?' Corso asked.

'What behavior was that?' Dean asked.

'All the stuff that wasn't necessary for the commission of the crimes.'

'Like?'

'Like standing around and watching your family go up in flames.'

253

'You're talking about the drawings,' Fullmer said.

'And posing the dead sister in an obscene manner. Laying her family out naked in the back-yard. And throwing the family album into the grave with them.' Corso spread his hands. 'None of those things were necessary to the crime. They were necessary to the emotional needs of the perpetrator.'

He looked to the FBI men for agreement but got only stony looks in return. 'None of it leads forward, Mr Corso,' Agent Dean said. 'Maybe back before nine-eleven we could have pursued something like this, but not anymore.'

'It's a dead end,' Fullmer said. 'There's no warrants or wants out on her. We've got no legal reason to pursue the matter.'

'What about her dead family? What about the girl they found in her bed?'

'Bergen County hasn't made up its mind yet, but if you ask me, all they're gonna do is create an open file on the matter.'

'There's a very disturbed woman out there somewhere,' Corso said. 'She's killed eight people that we know about and injured several others.' Corso cut the air with the side of his hand. 'And we've still got gaps in her life. Everyplace she goes, people end up dead.'

Dean shook his head. 'Even if we assume she's still alive, there's no guarantee she's going to hurt anybody else.'

'So you're assuming what? She's seen the error of her ways? She's cleaned up her act and is raising a family somewhere in central Florida?'

'We're not assuming anything,' Dean said. 'Including that she's still out there somewhere.' He pointed at the mug shot. 'She was leading a high-risk lifestyle. You do that kind of thing for thirty years, you generally end up dead before your time.'

Dean squared his shoulders and buttoned his suit jacket. 'I don't know whether you've noticed or not, Mr Corso, but these days we've got a world full of people who want to kill us. People who are sitting around plotting our doom, while you're eating eggs. So I hope you'll excuse us if we get back to doing what we get paid to do.'

They stiffed the waitress. On the way out, Agent Fullmer pinched a piece of honeydew melon from the breakfast bar and popped it in his mouth. He was still chewing contentedly when he turned the corner and disappeared.

Dougherty read Corso's expression. 'This thing's really got a burr under your saddle, doesn't it?' Corso put his nose in his coffee and left it there. 'We're not just trying to waste a week on the lam anymore, now are we?' she prodded.

Corso slid over to the aisle. 'It's like Dr Rosen said about writing his thesis on the Ramapo People. Finding them was like finding some lost Amazon tribe or something.' He looked hard at Dougherty. 'You heard Agent Fullmer. There's no profile for a

255

multiple family killer. As far as we know, nobody's ever done it more than once. There's a unique personality at work here. Something nobody's ever encountered before.' He shook a long finger. 'She's evil the way a shark is evil.'

'A shark's just being a shark,' Dougherty said.

'So's she,' Corso countered.

They got to their feet and started for the cash register.

'A shark's not evil, though.'

'He is if it's your leg in his mouth.'

Nine dollars and seventy-five cents, including a 20 percent gratuity, got them out into what passed for a beautiful late-November morning in Wisconsin. Bright, white, and cold as hell under an acrylic blue sky. Corso was in a full squint, still patting himself down, trying to locate his sunglasses, when a pair of hands grabbed him by the elbows, spun him in a half circle, and plastered him face-first against the front window of the restaurant.

Corso kicked back hard with his right foot. Officer Caruth grunted as Corso's heel made contact with his shin. Caruth's grip loosened completely when Corso threw back his head and made contact with his chin. Had it not been for Deputy Duckett's timely intervention, the outcome might have gone the other way. As it was, it took them the better part of a minute to get the bracelets around Corso's wrists, which settled things down. Inside the restaurant, everyone had deserted their seats and pressed against the inside of the glass, watching the melee outside.

Deputy Caruth's cowboy hat had become dislodged in the scuffle and fallen to the sidewalk. Deputy Duckett retrieved it. 'Mr Frank Corso,' Duckett drawled, 'you are under arrest on a material-witness warrant issued in Dallas County, Texas. It is your right to . . .'

CHAPTER 27

C orso tried to dig in with his heels, but the pressure on his hands kept forcing him forward. 'Come on, guys, give it a rest,' Corso said. 'It's less than fourteen hours until the grand jury's term expires. No way you can get me back to Texas in time.'

'Law says all we gotta do is make the collar in time,' Caruth said.

'It's just a misunderstanding between me and the DA's office, for pity's sake. You guys are treating this like it's a murder warrant or something. What's the deal here? They don't have any real crime in Texas?'

'Guy makes us look bad as many times as you have . . .'

'Makes us look like a pair a dummies,' Caruth said.

'Guy like that . . . we like to put in a little extra effort, if you know what I mean,' Duckett added with a wink to his partner.

Deputy Caruth held on to the handcuff chain as they marched Corso along the street. The first clear day since the storm had brought people into town. Most of the parking spaces were full of dirty pickup trucks. The shoveled sidewalks buzzed with bundled-up humanity, carrying packages and pausing to chat. As Corso and the lawmen approached, the good citizens of Avalon, Wisconsin, stepped aside in wonder, slack-jawed at the incongruity of the scene unfolding before them.

Corso heard somebody say, 'That's that writer guy.'

'I thought he snuck off,' a woman said.

'He did,' said a third voice.

Caruth and Duckett kept nodding and grinning and touching the brims of their hats as they walked along. Corso twisted his head and looked back over his shoulder. They'd picked up an entourage of a dozen kids, who skipped along the sidewalk in their wake playing cops and robbers, bobbing and weaving and blasting away at one another with imaginary guns. Behind the children, a crowd of adults had begun to follow along at a respectful distance.

They stood at the corner of Broad and Main, waiting for the light to change. Traffic crawled along the snow-covered street, the clink of tire chains announcing the passing of car after car. Caruth pushed the button for the third time, but the traffic light paid him no notice. The muted sound of tires on snow pulled Corso's eyes to the curb. A blue Cadillac Seville slid to a halt. The door swung open so hard the big car rocked on its springs.

The first thing out the door was blue steel, cocked and loaded. Clint Richardson's hand shook so badly he brought the other one up to steady himself. Caruth started to reach for his hip. 'Don't!' Richardson screamed. 'I don't want to hurt anybody else. Get away from him.' His face was ashen. His eyes bulging and rimmed with red. 'He killed my boy!' he screamed. 'He killed my boy!'

'Take it easy now, mister,' Duckett said in a low voice. 'No need to get excited here.' He raised a calming hand. Richardson aimed the revolver at Duckett's head. Duckett held his breath and slowly lowered the hand to his side.

In the street, a blue Chevy pickup crunched to a halt. The driver stepped out, keeping his hands in sight. 'Clint,' he said, 'come on now, man . . .'

Richardson threw a glance at the sound. 'Get out of here, Charlie,' he sobbed. 'Get back in the damn truck and go home.'

The guy took a step forward. 'Come on, Clint—' was as far as he got before Richardson swung the wavering gun his way. He froze. Holding his breath. Squeezing his eyes closed. Waiting for the bang.

'Might be best if you got back in the truck,' Duckett suggested.

Charlie didn't need to be told twice. Eyes wide, he backed into the driver's seat, dropped the truck into gear, and went rolling down the street with his foot hanging out the open door.

While Richardson's attention was diverted, Officer Caruth used his hip to bump Corso closer to the steel streetlight pole. The movement caught Clint Richardson's attention. The gun swung back. Waving in a wide arc now.

'Get away from him!' Richardson yelled again.

Nobody moved. Richardson steadied the gun on Caruth.

'Step away!' he screamed.

Caruth raised his hands in surrender. Freed from the officer's grasp, Corso rolled around the light pole, putting the steel standard between Richardson and himself.

'You don't want to be doing this,' Duckett said. 'Nobody'll blame you for how you feel. Not after what you been through. Man loses a son's got a right to feel bad. Just put the gun away, mister, and we'll all just forget about this whole thing.'

Richardson was beginning to sob. 'Shut up!' he screamed. Tears had begun to leak from the corners of his eyes, and his nose had begun to run. He wiped his nose with his sleeve. Aimed at Caruth. 'Get away from him!' he shouted.

Deputy Caruth squared his shoulders. The cords in his neck trembled like cables. 'I'm afraid I can't do that, sir. Mr Corso is in my custody. I can't—'

Richardson took two quick strides forward and pressed the barrel against the young deputy's forehead. 'I warned you . . . I didn't want to hurt . . .' His trigger finger began to quiver. Caruth's

Adam's apple bounced up and down like a tennis ball. Duckett was inching his hand toward the front of his jacket, when Corso stepped out from behind the pole and ambled over to Richardson.

'Don't,' Corso said. 'You want to shoot somebody . . . shoot me. I'm the one you want. No point in anybody else getting hurt, now is there?'

Richardson took the barrel of the gun and jammed it up under Corso's chin. 'I'm gonna kill you, you son of a bitch!' he shouted. 'Just like you killed my boy!'

Corso looked into the man's bloodshot eyes. 'I didn't kill your son,' he said.

'You lying son of a bitch,' Richardson hissed.

Corso watched as the finger began to tighten on the trigger. He held his breath.

'Beg!' Richardson screamed in Corso's face. 'You cowardly bastard . . . go on, beg for your miserable life!'

Corso's gaze was unwavering. 'I told you. I didn't kill your son,' he said. 'So why don't you just go fuck yourself.'

Caruth reached for his hip. Duckett for his breast pocket. Corso closed his eyes.

'Kerpow! Kerpow! Kerpow!' came the noise.

Hands stopped in midair. Breath froze in throats. Corso's eyes popped open.

The kid was about five. A fat little guy with a runny nose, wearing a blue snowsuit and red galoshes. He moved around the sidewalk at an awkward skip, pretending he was riding a horse.

262

His brown mittens were attached to the bottom of his sleeves with safety pins. He pointed a mitten at Corso and dropped the imaginary hammer three times. 'Kerpow! Kerpow! Kerpow!' Clint Richardson began to shake so hard the gun barrel bounced under Corso's chin.

The kid looked up at Richardson and smiled. 'Kerpow!' he said.

Richardson's thumb curled around the hammer. He hesitated for a moment before easing it down and dropping his hand to his side. He began to sob. The gun slipped from his fingers and fell to the sidewalk.

Deputy Duckett took one careful step forward and picked up the revolver. By that time Caruth had his black automatic in his hand, but Duckett waved him off. He took Richardson by the arm. 'Come on now, mister,' he said. 'We'll get you somebody you can talk to here. Somebody to give you a little help with the way you been feeling.'

Richardson sobbed in silence. His shoulders shook uncontrollably, but he uttered no sound. A woman, her hair half in rollers, wearing only a woolly pink sweater and a pair of jeans, rushed forward, scooped up the little boy, and carried him back to the safety of the crowd. Duckett turned their way. 'Anybody here help this man get home?'

There was no shortage of volunteers. After a little conversation, a pair of men stepped forward and led Clint Richardson back up the street.

Another got behind the wheel of the Caddy, swung a U-turn in the middle of the street, and drove it off.

As the crowd receded, Duckett eyed Corso with renewed interest. 'You're a real piece of work, you know that?' He walked a circle around Corso, taking him in, as if for the first time. 'I was thinkin' you were either real brave or real stupid, Mr Corso. But nobody as slippery as you is that stupid, so I'm gonna have to figure you're either a genuine hero or you don't much give a damn whether you live or die.' He wiped the corners of his mouth with his thumb and forefinger. 'Which is it?'

'I ever figure that out, I'll let you know,' Corso said.

Corso turned away and watched the crowd around Clint Richardson as it retreated down the street.

'He was gonna shoot Ray, for sure,' Duckett said, nodding at his partner. 'You hadn't stepped in when you did we were gonna have brains all over the place, sure as I'm standing here.'

'Sometimes they feel like they've just gotta do something crazy,' Corso said. 'So people will know how bad it hurts. They feel like the only thing that will convey their pain is to ruin their own lives in some incredible act of contrition.'

'I can't imagine outliving either of my children,' Duckett said. 'Can't imagine what would get me out of bed in the morning after that.'

He looked to his partner. 'This old boy saved your bacon, son,' he said.

'Yes, sir,' Caruth said.

'I believe the great state of Texas is going to have to do without Mr Corso here, don't you?'

'Seems like it wouldn't be right to arrest him now.'

'Why don't you take those cuffs offa him, then?' Duckett said. 'Seems like the least we can do.'

'Before you do that,' Corso said. 'How about answering a question?'

'What do you want to know?'

'How'd you find me this time? As far as you knew, I was still wanted for murder in this town. Way I figure it, that makes this burg the last place on earth I was likely to be found. How'd you boys know to come here for me?'

Duckett thought it over and then told him.

'That's what I thought,' Corso said. 'Why don't we leave the cuffs on for a while? See if maybe we can't stir up a little trouble.'

CHAPTER 28

Meg Dougherty hugged herself as she watched the cowboy cops march Corso up to the corner and then disappear from sight. Somebody bumped against the inside of the restaurant window, which shimmied and shimmered in the cold sunlight. Feeling the eyes on her, she turned away from the collage of faces plastered against the glass and started up the street toward the Timber Inn Motel.

The toot of a horn scraped her eyes from the sidewalk and drew them to the white van parked across the street. Warren had the window rolled down. He was polishing his glasses with a white paper towel. 'You okay?' he hollered.

Dougherty stepped off the curb and crossed the street to the van.

'What was that about?' Warren asked. She gave him the *Reader's Digest* version, hundred words or less. Across the street the restaurant crowd had begun to spill out onto the sidewalk as the patrons milled about relating their stories to one another in a ritual of repetition, the words and phrases of which floated heavenward on wisps of warm breath.

'You need a ride someplace?' Warren asked.

She thought about it. 'Yeah. I think I do,' she said. 'I guess packing up and getting myself a plane back to Seattle is the next order of business.'

Warren tried to keep the smile off his face. 'I'm headed up to Madison,' he said. 'Why don't I help you pack up and then drive you to the airport?'

'Oh . . . I couldn't,' Dougherty said. 'I'll get a limo to come and—'

'It would be my honor,' Warren insisted. 'Besides, I'm going that way anyway.' He reached over and opened the passenger door.

'I'm sure you've got better things to do than drive me around,' she said.

'Maybe we could have lunch,' he countered.

'On me,' Dougherty insisted.

'Deal,' he said.

She circled the front of the van and got in. Three right turns later they were back at the Timber Inn. Took them just under an hour to pack up Corso's and Dougherty's gear, come up with a plane reservation to Seattle, and check out of the motel. Warren threw Corso's bag into the back of the van and closed the door. 'I guess Mr Corso won't be needing this for a while,' he said.

'With him, you never know,' Dougherty said, buckling her seat belt. 'He keeps a truckload of high-priced lawyers on retainer. Knowing him as I do, he'll find some way to weasel out of it. Probably beat me back to Seattle.'

'You work with him much?' Warren asked as the

van bounced out of the motel driveway into the street.

'For years,' she said. 'Whenever he's got a book coming out, I do the pictures and help with the research.' She shrugged. 'He pays me way more than I deserve, and I put up with his bullshit.'

Something in her bravado caught Warren's attention. 'So then you and him aren't . . . you know . . .' He colored slightly.

'Not anymore,' she said. 'We used to be an item. Years ago. But that's over. These days Corso and I are strictly business.'

Dougherty could see his brain working up another question, so she changed the subject. 'You think the Madison field office is going to follow up on this Holmes family thing?' she asked.

'Only if it shows up on *America's Most Wanted*.'

Warren turned right at the courthouse, nosing the van down a wide, tree-lined street bordered on either side by stout Prairie Style homes, their square columns and insistent horizontal planes rooting them inexorably to the dark earth. No attic, no basement; no heaven, no hell. Just a broad overhanging roof to protect it from evil.

'Your friend Mr Corso,' Warren began, 'he really the recluse the press makes him out to be?'

'Frank likes to bill himself as an artist in reticence.'

'That's good,' Warren said, chuckling. 'Artist in reticence.'

At the end of the street the van turned left, running due north and parallel to Main Street.

On the right, the wooden sign read 'McCauley Park.' What looked to be about twenty acres of America's rural past rolled by, snow-covered grass beneath an ancient grove of trees, its benches empty, its playground deserted and silent as the stark white gazebo out in the middle of the park, where Dougherty imagined a military band playing before a packed house on summer nights. She could almost see the women, sitting in the humid evening air, fanning themselves with the program, while children, wild with summer, ran willy-nilly about the grass.

The Avalon Parks Department Building, with its neat piles of sand and gravel, separated McCauley Park from Avalon Gardens, the town cemetery. Another well-tended, tree-shaded twenty acres whose level ground, dappled by sunlight and shadow, ran away from the eye and disappeared over the brow of a narrow hill.

'Lately, I always seem to end up at the grave-yard,' Dougherty said. 'I hope to god it's not an omen.'

Warren was horrified and assured her that no such portent was likely in her immediate future.

'How do you know?' she asked.

'I've just got a feeling,' he said with a grin.

'Corso's got a feeling that all these women and girls are the same person, and you guys assure me he's wrong. How do I know you're not wrong too?'

'I'm just a technician, not an investigator or anything, but it's the lack of a consistent modus that bothers everybody,' he said. 'Contrary to what you see on television, criminals aren't generally the brightest people in the world. They find something that works, they stick with it. That's why modus is such an important part of the protocol in a homicide investigation. It's individual, like a signature, or a fingerprint. For Corso to be correct, I'd have to be able to accept the fact that a multiple murderer used a different modus every time out the gate. Poisoned her first family and then set them on fire, used a knife on a couple of johns, pushed a nun down a flight of stairs, chopped holes in the heads of her second family . . .' He took one hand off the wheel. 'It just doesn't make sense,' he said. 'If it ain't broke, you don't fix it.'

'It's possible, though.'

'I guess,' he said. 'Something like that would demand a completely new investigation protocol and a completely new psychological profile. Neither of which is very darn likely.'

Dougherty reached out and put a hand on Warren's arm. 'What did you just say?'

'I said it wasn't very darn likely that—'

'Before that.'

'I said . . . if something works for a perpetrator, they tend to repeat it because there's no reason to change something that already works.'

Ahead, on the side of the mountain, a steady line of 18-wheelers crept up the freeway grade, nose-to-tail like a herd of metal elephants. Dougherty looked back over her shoulder. The surrounding forest had swallowed Avalon whole.

'Warren . . .' she said. 'I need a favor.'

'Like what?' he said.

'Take me back to town.'

He pulled the van to the side of the road. Jammed it into Park.

'I need to get back to Madison,' he said. 'I've got to be at the lab at seven tomorrow morning.'

'Please.'

He shook his head. 'By now I've already got people wondering where I am.'

'Come on,' she pleaded.

'Tell you what.'

'What?'

He told her.

A deep laugh rolled from her chest. 'You little pervert you,' she chuckled. 'And here I was thinking you were the last of the Mr Nice Guys.'

'Sometimes you just need to see things under a microscope,' he said with a grin. 'They're usually clearer that way. Deal?'

She laughed, harder this time. 'I feel like I'm nine again,' she said. 'Back in the corn crib with Jimmy Crabtree.'

CHAPTER 29

I'm going down swinging,' he announced.
Sheriff Trask looked over at the handcuffed
Corso and smiled. 'Not in your present condition, you're not.' She closed the top drawer of the
file cabinet and opened the next one down. 'Soon
as Barbara gets the extradition papers put together
and signed, I'm afraid the only place you're going
is Texas.'

Corso bumped himself off the wall and
meandered over by the sheriff, who was refiling
a stack of case folders. Her secretary, Barbara,
had made filing easy for her by color coding the
drawers – red, yellow, green, and blue – top to
bottom. All Trask had to do was keep each drawer
alphabetized.

'What say we go for the daily double?'

'What's that?'

'What say you get me out of these cuffs and let
me out the back door. All I've got to do is stay
lost till midnight. What do you say?'

'You know I can't do that, Mr Corso. I lose track
of you a second time, people are gonna start to
think I've got Alzheimer's.'

'Even if they catch me, I won't say a word. Not about any of it.'

She heaved a sigh and turned his way for a moment. 'You want to tell people I let you go the first time, you go right ahead. I'll deny the hell out of it.'

She went back to filing. Corso ambled to the other side of the room, put one cheek up on the sheriff's desk, and crossed his feet in front of him on the floor. Behind his back, his hands were busy.

'I'm not talking about you letting me go, Sheriff. I'm talking about you knowing damn well what happened to Cole Richardson,' he said.

She was good. Her hands only paused for an instant before resuming her task. 'That doesn't even deserve a response, Mr Corso.' She put the folders on top of the file cabinet and turned his way. 'And if you don't mind me saying, that kind of lie is pretty low.' She looked him up and down. 'I misjudged you, Mr Corso. Turns out you're exactly the kind of irresponsible skunk folks say you are.'

'I've known it was you ever since you told Special Agent Molina you weren't sure whether or not Cole Richardson was wearing his tie that day.' He shook his head in wonder. 'That spit-and-polish SOB wore his tie to bed, and we both know it. Told me right away you knew something the rest of us didn't. Something you needed to keep under your hat at all costs.'

She closed the second drawer and slid the third

open. 'How you do go on,' she said with an over-the-shoulder smirk. 'A man with your credibility history really ought to be careful about throwing stones, if you know what I mean.'

'They don't have to believe me,' Corso said. 'All they've got to do is check the serial number on the piece you're carrying right now against the serial number that's listed for your piece in your own files. Number one-seven-five-three-three-nine-eight-SWA-ten. That's what the file says.' He paused. 'Let's see what's on that piece you're carrying, Sheriff.'

She ignored him. Kept filing. Corso went on. 'Because there's no way in hell they match. No way you're still carrying the piece that put a slug in Cole Richardson's head. You told me that much yourself. The Wisconsin State Police tested every gun in the department, including yours, and came up empty. Come on, Sheriff, show me your piece, and I'll shut up and go off to Texas like a good boy.'

Her face began to color. 'You shut your filthy mouth, you hear me?'

'Just show me the piece.'

'I'm not going to tell you again,' she snapped. 'Close your mouth.'

'What happened? He figure out you let me skip and threatened to go public on you? That it? He threaten to tell his daddy? Get your ass fired for dereliction of duty? You can tell old Uncle Frank,' Corso taunted. 'Confession is tonic for the soul.'

She straightened up and checked her office door.

Walked over and pushed on it to make sure it was latched all the way, and then stalked over and put her face in Corso's. 'You shut your lying mouth,' she whispered. 'I've got enough problems around here without you getting everybody riled up with ridiculous lies like that.'

'Show me the serial number.'

'You're starting to annoy me, Mr Corso.'

'I annoy everybody. It's a gift. Show me the gun.'

'You don't understand,' she said.

'Enlighten me.'

'You don't know what you're talking about.'

'So . . . straighten me out.'

She checked the door again. 'The dumb son of a bitch tried to arrest me. Soon as I let him up, he made a grab for my gun.' Her eyes relived the moment. 'We didn't even really struggle. Soon as he grabbed my hand . . . it just . . . the gun just went off. And . . . then he was dead . . . and . . .' She hardened herself. 'It was an accident, pure and simple. And if you think anybody's gonna take the word of a lying dog, fired reporter, convicted felon, over mine . . . well, you've got another think coming.'

She grabbed him by the shirtfront, swung him in a circle, and was about to propel him toward the door when the light caught her attention. She stopped in midswing, let go of Corso's shirt, and slowly dropped her hand to her side. Open-mouthed and disbelieving, she stared at the brightly lit red button on her phone.

Corso kept backing up until he reached the door, where his manacled hands found the handle and pulled it open a crack so his foot could swing it the rest of the way.

Maria Trask wouldn't look that way. It was as if she knew what was there but figured if she didn't look at it, it couldn't be real. As if by power of will, her withheld acknowledgment could make the pair of Wisconsin state policemen go up in smoke. She gave it a try. Straightened up and got all haughty. 'Is there a problem here?' she wanted to know. The sound of her own amplified voice coming from the outer room let the air out of her in a hurry and finally moved her eyes to the doorway.

She looked from one trooper to the other, then over their shoulders to Deputies Caruth and Duckett standing grim-lipped along the wall. 'It was—' she stammered.

'Don't say anything,' Corso said. 'Call a lawyer.'

She glanced helplessly about. 'I didn't mean for—'

'Call a lawyer,' Corso said again. He nodded at the red button on the phone. 'I've got some doubts about whether information obtained this way is usable in court. Not only that, but if things came down the way you say they did . . . well, it was just an accident. With a clean record and a good lawyer, you ought to pretty much walk.'

'I shouldn't have—' she started, then clamped her jaw and looked over at Corso. 'I shouldn't have—' she started again.

Corso interrupted. 'What you shouldn't have done was tell those Dallas boys where to find me, this time. You had no call to do that, unless, of course, you were worried I'd keep mucking around in things until I turned something up. All that told me was that I was right about what I was thinking about you . . . and that, contrary to something else I'd been thinking, I didn't owe you a goddamn thing.'

CHAPTER 30

'Y ou're a caution, you are, Mr Corso,' Duckett said. 'I'm gonna have to sit down and have a couple of fingers of bourbon when I get back home . . . see if maybe I can't make sense outta you.'

'Personally, I don't bother,' Corso said.

'You got this real interesting way of putting two and two together and coming up with nine. Then getting everybody else to agree with you. Don't think I've ever seen quite the like of it.' Deputy Duckett rubbed his hands together and stamped his boots. 'I'll surely be grateful for some Dallas weather,' he said. 'Never been so dang cold in all my life.'

'Your young partner there's gonna turn out to be a hell of a cop.'

'Caruth? He's a damn good boy . . . that's for sure.'

'Guy puts a muzzle on your forehead and tells you to move . . . most folks just ask how far and how fast. The kid showed big balls,' Corso said.

Duckett snorted. 'As I recall, under very similar circumstances, you told the same gentleman to go fuck himself.'

'I don't like being called a liar.'

Duckett chewed on the idea for a moment. 'I can understand how a man might take serious offense at something like that,' he said. 'I surely can.'

A maroon Crown Victoria crunched up to the curb in front of the police station. Deputy Caruth got out and stood in the open doorway. Corso waved.

'Go home and get warm,' Corso said to Duckett.

They shook hands for a bit longer than was comfortable, and then Duckett started down the stairs. Corso shouted a good-bye to Caruth, who doffed his hat in salute, before climbing back in, shifting the Chevy into Drive, and rolling out into the street.

Corso buttoned his overcoat all the way up to his chin and turned up the collar. He hunched his shoulders against the cold and started down the gray granite steps.

'Hey,' a familiar voice called.

The sound pulled his eyes across the street to the police station parking lot. He slipped a hand from his pocket and shaded his eyes against the red glare of the gathering sunset. Dougherty and Warren stood side by side at the rear of an unmarked white van. He barely came up to her shoulder. Looked like he'd been captured by vampires and was being kept as a pet.

As Corso approached, Dougherty turned to her companion. 'Told you,' she said. 'He weaseled out somehow. One minute he's under arrest and on his way to Texas. Next minute he's sharing a male-bonding moment with one of his captors, who then proceeds to drive off into the sunset without his prisoner. It's absolutely amazing.'

'Pretty slick,' Warren agreed.

'What are you doing here?' Corso asked her. 'I figured you'd be back in Seattle catching a little of that liquid sunshine by now.'

'I had some good news, so we stopped by the cop shop to see if you were still here. The woman at the desk said she didn't think you were under arrest anymore. Said there was something going on she couldn't talk about, but that if we hung around you'd probably be waltzing out on your own sometime this afternoon.'

'Looked like a big day at the Avalon Police Department,' Warren commented. 'People coming and going all afternoon. Lotta real grim looks.'

'Yeah. We had a little excitement, we did.'

He told them the story. Started back with Clint Richardson and the scene in the street and worked his way up to about five minutes earlier, when Duckett, Caruth, and he finally signed their statements and were shown the door.

'No shit,' Dougherty said. 'The sheriff herself.'

'Not anymore she isn't,' Corso said with a shiver.

'What the hell are we standing out here for?' Dougherty wanted to know. She pulled open the van's sliding door and stepped up into the rear seat. Warren slid the door closed and walked around toward the driver's side as Corso climbed into the passenger seat and pulled the door shut.

It was fifty degrees warmer inside the van. Corso looked from Dougherty to Warren and back as he unbuttoned his coat. They were having trouble keeping smug looks from taking over their faces. 'So . . .' Corso said, 'what was this good news?' He watched as they shared a look. Waited as Dougherty decided whether to blurt it out or to torture him some first, as she usually did. She opted for the former.

'We found her,' she said.

'Sissy?'

'Nancy Anne Goff.'

'Who's that?'

'That's who Sissy became after she left Avalon,' Warren said. Corso repeated the name. 'And would we have any idea where Nancy Anne got to from here?' Corso asked.

'We would,' Dougherty said with a smirk.

'You're going to make me suffer, aren't you?'

'Count on it,' she said.

'Midland, Michigan,' Warren offered.

Corso folded his arms across his chest and looked from one to the other. 'Okay, I'll bite . . . how'd you two find all this out?'

'Warren was driving me to the airport. He said something that gave me an idea. We turned around and checked it out, and lo and behold, I was right. Got her on the first try.'

'What'd he say?'

'He was talking about how modus operandi was so important to investigations because criminals generally find something that works and stick with it.'

'If it ain't broke, don't fix it,' Corso said. 'And?'

'He was talking about the way the murders were committed and how no two of the methods were the same.' She leaned forward in the seat. 'Right then we were driving past the town graveyard. I told Warren it seemed like I was spending a lot of time in cemeteries lately.' She put her hand on Corso's shoulder. 'And that's when it hit me. Maybe the murder methods didn't match, but what about the way she came up with new identities? What if she used the same method of identity theft as she did the last time?' She waved a hand. 'At least the last time we know about anyway.'

'So?'

'So we went to the courthouse and checked the death records for the year preceding her disappearance from the area. Women. Late twenties to late thirties.'

'How many?' Corso prodded.

'Two,' she said. 'One of them had two names, the other had three. You wanna guess which one I tried first? The county had a request for a birth certificate seven weeks after Nancy Anne Goff's funeral. The Social Security Administration sent her a new Social Security card a month after that. By the time she disappeared, Sissy Warwick had a complete new set of identification, including a driver's license and two credit cards.'

'Everything sent to a P.O. box in Midland, Michigan.'

'Dude,' Corso said. He slapped high fives with both of them. 'Hell of a job! Hell of a job!'

'What next?' Dougherty asked.

'You come up with a copy of the license?'

'No picture,' Warren said. 'Wisconsin didn't start putting pictures on their driver's licenses until '89.'

'Shit.'

'We've still got the mug shot,' Dougherty said.

'What we've got is a twenty-five-year-old shot of a seventeen-year-old hooker with one side of her face swollen up the size of a grapefruit. We turn anything from that shot, we'll have to get real lucky.'

'So . . . what? We're gonna give up and go crawling back to Seattle?'

'Of course not. That'd be way too sensible.'

'What then?'

Corso thought it over. 'Where's Midland?' he asked.

'Northern part of the state,' Warren said. 'Want to see a map?'

'Love to,' Corso replied.

Warren rummaged around in the glove box and found a packet of road maps held together by a red rubber band. He handed it to Corso, who spread the map across his knees. Warren snapped on the overhead light.

'Near the base of what I think they call the Upper Peninsula,' Dougherty said as Corso found his way to Midland with his finger.

Corso nodded. 'That figures,' he said. 'Someplace away from people. But where there's enough bodies to get lost in.'

'Good place to hide out,' Dougherty said.

'Actually, she'd be better off in Chicago, where folks come and go all the time and nobody gives a shit anyway. Get herself lost in the crowd.' He tapped the map with his fingertip. 'Place like Midland, it's big enough to blend in but small enough to find a place out of town where you can have a little space.'

'Which is why she's not someplace like Chicago,' she said.

'Big city like that's way too out of control for her,' Corso said. He looked over the seat at Dougherty. 'You remember what that county shrink said about her back in New Jersey?'

'What?'

'She tries to control everything in her environment. Anything she can't control, she sees as a threat and has to do something about. In a place like Chicago, you can only control things as long as you stay inside. The minute you step out into the street, it's a zoo.' He folded the map in two. 'Too scary for her. For her, this is all about control. About creating a nice safe little haven for herself where she can pull all the strings and deal with other people as little as possible.'

284

'But she seeks out people,' Dougherty argued. 'She slept with half of Avalon. She married a guy. Had a family.'

Corso handed the map back to Warren. 'That's the other thing the shrink said. She's psychologically attached to her roots. She can't imagine living in any situation where she's not surrounded by some sort of family. That's all she knows. It's the only lifestyle that makes any sense to her, so she tries to duplicate it.'

'Then why kill them?'

'Because they get out of control. For one reason or another, things start to go haywire, and she gets this terrific urge to start all over again. To take it from the top so she can get back in charge of everything. That's what the angels were doing in those pictures she drew. Cleaning up loose ends before moving on to whatever was next.'

'Kids grow up,' she said.

'And become teenagers . . . and get out of control and crash the family truck . . . and get arrested, bring a lot of unwanted attention to the happy little haven.'

'They start building a freeway in your backyard.'

'Time to flap your wings and fly off,' Corso said.

'But she leaves alone,' Dougherty said. 'In the pictures, it's always two angels flying off together.'

'So who's the other angel?' Warren asked.

'No idea,' Corso said. 'Maybe some kind of alter ego she walks around with or something. With her psychological profile, god only knows.'

'Like an imaginary friend.'

'Something like that maybe. Or some imaginary character who comes to her rescue when things get tough.'

'Or the other way around,' Warren chipped in. 'Maybe she sees herself as the rescuer rather than the rescued.'

'Rescuing who?' Dougherty asked.

'She's got no real family left other than Rodney and Tommie,' Corso said.

'And *they* think she's dead.'

'So . . . who's left to rescue?'

'Who knows,' Corso said with a shrug. 'Maybe . . .' And then he stopped, as if listening to distant voices. 'You got a map of the whole United States?' he asked Warren.

Warren said he thought so, and after half a minute of rummaging around in the driver's door pocket, produced another map. Unfolded, it covered most of the dashboard. A minute later, Corso grunted and laughed a private laugh.

'What a bunch of dummies we are,' he said.

'What'd you find?' she asked.

'An angel.' He pointed at the map. Dougherty leaned over the seat to see: New Jersey. 'Look,' Corso said. 'It starts here, in north Jersey. Right?'

'Yeah.'

He ran his finger across the map. Westward, along the southern shores of the Great Lakes. 'Tommie de Groot stole a set of license plates here in Elgin, Illinois. Right?' When nobody disagreed,

286

he went on. 'They found the car abandoned here.'
He pointed again. North and west. 'Lake Geneva,
Michigan. State Route 83.'

'Holy shit,' Dougherty said.

Corso's finger moved again. 'You follow 83
north . . . and where are you?'

'Midland, Michigan,' they said in unison.

Her father lay on his back, his head stuck up under the stove. 'Hand me the big orange wrench,' he said. Sarah rooted around in the toolbox and came out with a heavy pipe wrench. 'This one?'

'That's it.'

She handed the wrench to her father. When she straightened up and looked out the kitchen window toward the highway, the blue-and-white mail truck was pulling away from their mailbox. She bent at the waist and shook his foot. 'Mail's here, Papa,' she said. 'Can I take the car down and get it?'

He set the wrench on the floor and pushed himself out from under the stove. He looked around. 'Where's your mama?' he asked.

Sarah jerked her finger over her shoulder. 'She's out in the barn with Pinhead.'

'You better not let her hear you say that.'

'Can I?'

'You hear me?'

'I heard.' She hopped from one foot to the other. 'Can I?'

'Yeah,' he said. 'Why not?'

She skipped across the floor and plucked the keys from their hook next to the refrigerator. 'Hey,' her father said.

'I know . . . be careful.'

'I don't want to be havin' to listen to her if you put a dent in that old car.'

'I don't want to listen to her at all.'

He wagged a grimy finger at the girl. 'She's your mama. You don't talk about her that way . . . you understand me?'

'Yes, Papa,' she said before running out the door.

He watched as Sarah got into the car and rolled slowly down the driveway toward the mailbox half a mile away, then lay back down and grabbed the wrench.

The kitchen door burst open. She stepped into the room. Hands on hips.

'What did I tell you about letting that damn girl drive the car?'

He got to his feet. 'She's a good little driver,' he said.

'She's not old enough.'

'She will be soon enough.'

'I told you before . . .'

'Yeah,' he said. 'And before that and before that . . .'

He looked out the window again. Sarah was on her way back. 'Look,' he said, pointing, 'she's doin' just fine.'

She stormed from the room, slamming the door

hard on her way out. He walked over to the door and gazed out. He watched as Sarah brought the car to a halt in the yard. Watched her make it halfway to the door before his wife snatched the keys from her hand and began shouting at her. When she raised her hand, he turned away.

A minute later, Sarah burst into the kitchen. A bright red blotch covered her left cheek. 'I hate her,' Sarah said. 'I wish, she was dead.'

He started to say something but changed his mind.

CHAPTER 31

Corso had a map of Michigan spread out over the dashboard. 'So,' he began, 'you never told me how it was you managed to induce an FBI employee to call in sick and help you with your little investigation.'

'I showed him my artwork.'

'You what?'

'You heard me. I showed him my tattoos.'

'All of them?'

'As much as I could in a van . . . in broad daylight.' She took a hand off the wheel and waved it. 'You know . . . without getting gyno and all.'

'Why in god's name would you do a thing like that?'

'Because he wanted to see them.'

'You bribed—'

'I traded.'

'You seduced an FBI field operative into helping you . . . by exposing yourself to him. Is that what you're telling me?'

'What I'm telling you is that without Warren making some calls, we wouldn't know a damn thing about Nancy Anne Goff, and we sure as hell wouldn't be here in Michigan looking to find her ass.'

'I don't believe it.'

She shot him a sneer. 'Ooooh . . . what is that I detect there?'

'Don't be ridiculous. I've seen the show . . . remember?'

'Uh-huh.'

'Don't be uh-huhing me.'

'Uh-huh.'

Corso folded the map. Didn't get it right, so he unfolded it and tried again. When he failed a second time, he left it that way and stuffed it into the console.

To the west, out over the fields and the trees and the houses and barns, out at the extremes of eyesight, a line of power towers marched north and south down the middle of the peninsula, their steel stanchions shimmering in the cold dry distance.

'You given any thought to how it is Tommie de Groot knew his sister was still alive?' Dougherty asked a couple of miles later.

'At some point she must have come back to New Jersey for him. Nothing else makes sense. He was four years old the night the family burned up. Rodney said the kid lived in a foster home for a couple of years before he took him in. The foster family undoubtedly knew the story of how the de Groot family went up, so there's no way she approaches them about seeing her little brother.

At that point she's supposed to have been dead for a couple of years. Got to be after he was living with Rodney that she shows up back in Jersey.'

'Had to be after she ran off from the Sisters too,' Dougherty added.

'So . . . it was either during that three and a half years we haven't accounted for, or she went back and made herself known to him while she was living in Avalon.'

'Either way, Rodney had to know.'

'Absolutely.'

'So all that nonsense about Tommie going off every summer to visit friends in Idaho was just a smoke screen for visits to his sister.'

'For sure.'

'Why him?' Dougherty asked.

'Rodney?'

'No . . . why Tommie? She had two other brothers and a mother and father she poisoned and then burned to cinders. Why all the effort to keep in touch with a brother who's thirteen or fourteen years her junior?'

'Maybe it's that family thing of hers again,' Corso said.

'Hell of a risk, just to see somebody who was four years old the last time you laid eyes on them. Who might not even remember who in hell you are.' She looked over at Corso. 'Happens to me all the time with my nieces and nephews back in Iowa. They barely recall me from year to year. Have to be prompted to remember my name.'

'Maybe, because of his age, Tommie was the only one she didn't identify as being one of her abusers.' Corso winced. 'Or maybe he was a victim too.'

'At four?'

'God only knows with that family.'

They drove in silence, until Dougherty broke the spell. 'Or maybe little Tommie being in the hospital on the night of the fire wasn't a coincidence after all.'

'You mean . . . like she arranged it?'

'Just a little touch of whatever she was about to feed the rest of the family. Off to the hospital and out of the way, so's she can set up the rest of the scene.'

'Interesting thought . . . but like you said before, it's a hell of a lot of trouble over a four-year-old kid she'd probably be better off without.'

'Not like she's the most nostalgic person in the world either.'

'No kidding.'

'Who knows,' she said with a shrug.

A black-and-white road sign read 'Midland 3 Miles.'

'What do we know about Midland, Michigan?'

'Can you say "Dow"?'

'As in chemical?'

'As in . . . owns the whole damn town.'

'Really?'

'Believe it or not, I've been here before,' Corso said. 'Back in '89, I was working in North Carolina.

Some sort of chemical spill killed a bunch of fish. Everybody thought it must have come from the new Dow Chemical plant. The *Charlotte Observer* sent me up to Midland to interview Dow corporate types.'

'You get anything from them?'

'Lunch.'

Dougherty eased the car into the right-hand lane and took the Route 20, Midland exit. A mile later, they hit the city limits. Midland: An All-American City, the sign said. 'Take a left here,' Corso said. 'Main Street is down that way. Down along the river.'

'What river is that?'

'The Tittabawassee,' Corso said. 'I remember 'cause I could never spell the damn thing. Drove my editor nuts. Midland is where the Tittabawassee and the Chippewa Rivers converge. They got this weird bridge downtown, right at the confluence of the two rivers. Y shaped. Call it a tridge instead of a bridge because it forks out in the middle and you can go in either direction.'

She pulled the car to a stop at a traffic light. Pointed at a collection of signs on a light pole. Blue and white. Pointing in all directions. To the right: Dow Chemical Corporate Center. To the left: Dow Corning Michigan Site. Ahead: Alden B. Dow Home and Studio. Back behind them: Dow Gardens, Dow High School, and the Dow Library. 'You weren't kidding about the Dow connection, now were you?' she said.

'The last of the great company towns,' Corso said. 'Turn right on Main.'

'What are we looking for?'

'Something little and out of the way. Something seedy. At least two stories, so we don't have to be on the ground floor. Something where you're either coming in through the door or you're not coming in at all.'

'Sounds like another Timber Inn,' she said with a sneer.

'We're not taking any chances this time,' Corso said. 'These people kill the way other folks change their socks. We're going to keep our distance. We turn anything, we call Molina and let the feds handle it.'

Downtown consisted of six blocks of renovated brick buildings running parallel to the river. Restaurants, gift shops, antique dealers, two banks, the Chamber of Commerce. Anyplace, USA.

The river's rippled surface gleamed like fire in the late-afternoon sun. Dougherty pulled the visor down and used one hand to shade her eyes from the glare as she wheeled through the sparse traffic.

Corso pointed toward the far end of town. 'Keep going,' he directed.

They found it a mile down. Across the street from a little green glen called Emerson Park. The Pine Tree Motor Inn and Café. Senior discount. Cable TV.

Room 223. Second floor back. Off the street. A

nonsmoking room that smelled of smoke. Long black burn marks graced both end tables. Dougherty checked the facilities. Wrinkled her nose. 'I'd kill for my own bathroom,' she said.

Corso had both hands inside his bag. He looked up and nodded in agreement.

'Couple more days,' he said. 'One way or the other.'

He came out with the mug shot and closed the bag.

'I'm going to make copies for tomorrow,' he announced.

Dougherty was putting her hair up behind her head. 'Keys are on the dresser,' she said. 'I'm gonna take a shower before dinner.'

'You can't stay here,' she said. 'Gordie won't put up with it. You been here three days and he's already bitching. Wants to know when you're gonna leave.'

'I got no place else to go,' he whined. 'I was thinkin' maybe I could get on with the company. Like maybe Gordie could help me.'

She spit a bitter laugh. 'Hell, that fool can't hardly help himself, let alone you. He's been with Dow for nineteen years and he's still so low on the totem pole he'd have to look up to see dirt.' She cut the air with the side of her hand. 'Spends all day down inside the vats, scrubbing with a brush, that's what Mr Big Shot does. That's how come he's got that smell to him. Been at it so

297

long, the smell sunk right into his flesh. Can't even wash it off no more. It's enough to make me sick.'

'What am I gonna do?'

'How much money you got?'

'Eighteen hundred dollars.'

'We'll go into town in the morning. We'll—'

'Plus I get my check every month,' he interrupted.

'No more you don't,' she said. 'You try to cash one of those government checks, they'll find you in a day.' She shook her head. 'Nope. Time for you to fly away. Tomorrow morning we go into town. Do a little work. Make Tommie de Groot disappear off the face of the earth.'

He reached in his back pocket and pulled out a baggie of loose tobacco.

'Do that outside,' she said. 'You know how smoke pisses Gordie off. Son of a bitch can smell it before he gets out of the damn car.'

'Fuck Gordie,' he said sullenly. 'Who needs him anyway.'

She poked him in the chest with a finger. 'I do,' she said. 'At least for right now.' He opened his mouth to speak, but she brought her finger to his lips. 'I'm dug in here. You hear me? Don't need anything messing it up, so you just mind your p's and q's, and don't be making us any more trouble than we already got.'

'He gets in my face again I'm gonna fuck him up.'

She poked him hard enough to back him up one

step. 'You'll do no such goddamn thing. Wasn't for me you wouldn't be here at all. You remember that.'

Dougherty held the wineglass to her lips and watched as Corso threw his napkin onto the table. 'Not bad,' he announced.

'Hard to mess up a steak,' she said.

'It's been done. Believe me.'

Her throat worked slowly as she swallowed the Meursault. She set the wineglass on the table, pulled the bottle from the ice bucket, and poured out the last drops.

'Another dead soldier,' she said, returning the empty bottle to the ice bucket. 'I think we're over our limit tonight.'

'We deserve it. It's been a rough week.'

She downed the wine. Wiped her lips with the napkin.

'You ready?' he asked.

She answered by sliding out of the booth. Corso threw a pile of twenties on the table, got to his feet, and followed her out the door.

A frozen wind rocked the door on its hinges. Corso had to use both hands to force it closed. Dougherty hooked her arm in his, and together they started up the sidewalk.

Three blocks up, the Pine Tree Motor Inn's red neon vacancy sign glimmered in the night air. Dougherty leaned her head against his shoulder as they walked along.

'You ever wonder how we turned out like this?' she asked.

'Like what?'

'Like a couple of adults who . . . for whatever reason just can't seem to maintain a personal relationship with each other.'

'As I recall, that was your idea.' Corso threw an arm around her shoulders. 'I believe you said I was "emotionally unavailable" and therefore banned from the garden of earthly delights.'

'You are.'

'Lotta people can't maintain relationships with each other,' he said, pulling her closer. 'That's what keeps therapists in business.'

'Yeah, but it usually doesn't happen to people who are as fond of one another as you and I are.' She waved her free hand in the air. 'Relationships aren't perfect. Everybody has trouble now and then, but—'

'Are we fond of each other?'

'Stick it, Corso.'

They crossed the empty street against the light. 'Downtown really clears out after dark,' Corso said. 'Everybody lives out in the burbs. Just comes down here to work and shop.'

'Don't change the subject.'

Corso sighed. 'If I admit it's all my fault, can we talk about something else?'

'Nope.'

'Then I deny everything.'

'You're like a turtle, Corso. You only come out

of your shell long enough to make love. Then it's right back inside.' Again she waved her hand. 'It's just not enough, Frank. I need more than that.'

'You ever seen a turtle without his shell?'

'I'm not kidding, damn it.'

'Me neither,' Corso said. 'There's no more pathetic-looking creature on earth than a turtle without his shell. Just this little sack of gristle with a head attached. Looks like it wasn't properly gestated.'

'When have you ever seen a turtle without the shell?'

'In the Bahamas. He was about to become soup.'

'That's disgusting.'

'It's life in the food chain is what it is.'

They turned right, into the motel entrance. On the left, a minivan danced on its springs as a quartet of children screamed and scurried about the interior like crazed rodents. The father was inside registering. The mother leaned her head against the side window, her puffy eyes closed, seemingly oblivious to the din behind her.

'How long have we known each other?' Dougherty asked.

'Five, six years . . . why?'

'Where were you born?'

'What's that got to do with anything?'

'It's got everything to do with anything. I've known you for over five years. We were lovers for almost two years, and you know what?'

The muscles along his jawline rippled. She went on.

'I don't know where you were born. I don't know your mother's name. You slipped once and said something about a brother. That's the only way I ever find out anything about you. All this time. The countless hours we've spent in each other's company and I still don't know one goddamn thing about you.'

'What's your point?'

She stopped walking, disengaged herself, and took a step away from Corso. 'That hand pump in Rodney de Groot's yard.' Her voice carried the slightest of slurs. 'How did you know how to make that thing work? How did you know you had to pour water in it?' She raised both hands in wonder. 'I'm from bumfuck-dirt-farmer Iowa and I've never even seen one of those things before. How come you knew?'

Corso turned his back to her and looked up at the night sky. He could make out Orion's belt and, higher in the sky, the North Star.

'Well?'

He spun on the balls of his feet. 'That's how we got water when I was a kid,' he said. 'You've got to prime the pump or it will just suck air.'

She cocked her head, looking for signs that he was kidding. He laid a hand on her back and guided her toward the stairs. He could feel her eyes on the side of his face as they climbed. Halfway up, she wobbled slightly and leaned harder into him, until he propped her against the wall, opened the door, and snapped on the overhead light.

'Come on,' he said.

Once inside, she walked a wavy line to the bathroom. Corso sat on the edge of his bed and pulled off his boots. He padded over to the TV, played with the buttons until he found CNN, and got it closed-captioned.

He pulled both pillows out from under the spread, piled them against the headboard, and stretched out with a long, audible sigh. The clock in the lower-left-hand corner of the screen read 9:54 ET. George Bush senior was making a speech. Corso closed his eyes for a minute. When he opened them again, the clock read 10:09, and college football scores were scrolling down the screen.

Suddenly, the overhead light went out, leaving the room bathed only in the flickering, multihued flashes of the television screen.

He didn't see her until her hand reached out and turned off the television. He was blind. He blinked several times, trying to get his eyes to adjust to the total darkness.

He felt her weight on the bed next to him. Reached out and put a hand on her side. His fingers could feel the raised whorls and words etched on her skin.

She leaned over and kissed him. Her heavy breasts flattened against his chest. His hands could feel the yellow lightning bolts on her back.

'You're going to regret this tomorrow,' he whispered.

'I know' was her response.

'You'll take it out on me for days.'

He could feel her smile in the darkness.

'It's how I square it with myself afterward.'

'Is it worth it?'

'We'll find out, won't we?' she said without hesitation, and kissed him again, harder this time, then stood up. Corso pulled his shirt over his head. And then, before he could do anything about his pants, she was on him again flesh to flesh.

'You'll be gentle with me now, won't you?' he joked.

'No,' she said, without the slightest trace of humor.

CHAPTER 32

The old guy put his glasses up on top of his head and squinted at the poster. Above the swollen face of Nancy Anne Goff it read: 'Reward.' Beneath the face: 'Have You Seen This Woman? 346–9987.'

'Quite a puss there,' the old guy said. 'This used to be a mug shot?'

'Just a bad picture,' Corso assured him, as he had everyone who'd asked that same question all day long. 'You seen her?'

'Don't believe I have,' he said, handing the picture back to Corso.

Corso plucked the poster from his fingers. 'Be all right if I put this in the window?' he asked. The old guy looked toward the front of the store.

'Take that orange flyer offa the door,' he said. 'Elks Pancake Breakfast was last Sunday. Don't expect they'll be needing the space anymore.'

Corso removed the BPOE breakfast flyer and replaced it with his own. The old man wished him luck. Corso gave him a wink as he closed the door.

The day had started slowly. They'd languished in bed till nearly nine. Made love twice and then headed for the shower. Corso first, so he could run a few errands.

Dougherty was still fluffing her hair with a towel when Corso returned with a pair of cell phones, a couple of staplers, and coffee and bagels for breakfast. They'd wolfed down the coffee and bagels, divided the pile of posters in half, agreed that Dougherty would take the east end of town and Corso the west, and headed out together, leaving one of the cell phones plugged into the wall for messages and pocketing the other.

Corso checked his watch. Three thirty-four. What had started out as two hundred and fifty posters was now a rolled-up wad of no more than twenty-five. The rest decorated every Laundromat, beauty parlor, antique shop, and café in Midland, Michigan.

He pulled the stapler from his pocket and tacked a poster onto the nearest telephone pole. Satisfied, he threw the last of the posters into a sidewalk trash bin. On this day in Midland, Michigan, no matter which way you turned, Nancy Anne Goff's battered countenance stared defiantly at you.

The river wind blew the tails of his coat out behind him as he strode down Prospect Street, making his way south toward Main and the motel. Scattered clouds, lined up end to end like dirty box-cars, moved east across a blue sky. He'd walked about four blocks when he heard her whistle. He stopped and looked around. Dougherty was behind him, ambling down the sidewalk in his direction.

'Any luck?' he asked as she drew near.

She grabbed his arm and pulled him down the street. 'A woman at the discount food market thought she'd seen her before. Says she's got blond spiky hair these days. Thinks she's married to somebody who works for the company.'

'That narrows it down,' Corso said sarcastically.

'You?'

'Nada,' he said, pulling her closer as they walked. 'Everybody was pleasant, but nobody recognized the face.'

'What now?'

'You eat?'

'Just the bagels.'

'You want to do lunch?'

'Something light.'

'After that we return to our sumptuous room and await calls.'

'Can we do that naked?'

'I believe we can,' he said.

She eased the big Pontiac into the diagonal parking slot and got out. She fed three quarters into the meter and then hustled south along Midland Avenue, the click of her narrow heels echoing off the buildings. Tommie de Groot had to stretch his legs to keep up. 'Where we going?' he asked as they hurried along.

'To the courthouse,' she said. 'That's where we start.'

'That how you done it?' he wanted to know.

307

'It's—' And suddenly the words froze in her throat. She stopped. Stood still staring at the front door of Guzman's Gallery. He watched the blood drain from her face until she was the blue-white color of skim milk. The cords in her neck trembled. She looked around. She spotted something halfway up the block and ran head-long in that direction, leaving Tommie to stumble along in her wake.

A moment later she stood nose-to-nose with her own likeness stapled to a telephone pole on the corner of Midland and Trice. She gagged twice, and for a moment it seemed she might vomit. She reached out and steadied herself on the pole, as the street swirled before her eyes. Then used her fingernails to pick at the staples until the poster came loose in her hands.

'That's you,' Tommie said. 'How'd—'

'Shut up,' she hissed. Her chest heaved like a marathon runner's, sending violent streams of breath whooshing out into the air. She looked around again and then, without a word, began to retrace her steps back to the car. Quicker now, nearly at a run, she moved across the concrete on the balls of her feet.

By the time Tommie made the car, she had the engine running and the poster spread out across the steering wheel. When he opened his mouth to speak, she hit him.

A straight right to the mouth. And then another and another. Tommie buried his bloodied face in his arms and took the punches in silence.

She was panting now, her breath coming in gasps. 'You stupid son of a bitch. You brought them here with you. You brought them to me.'

Tommie had tears in his eyes and blood on his teeth when he looked up. 'Nobody followed me. Swear to god. No way anybody followed me here.'

She hit him in the mouth again, and again he buried his head. She jammed the car into reverse. Horns blared as she careened out into the street and roared off.

She was screaming now, the inside of the car filled with her voice. 'I should killed you with the rest of them when I had the chance!' she screamed. 'Swear to god, you wasn't my own flesh and blood, I'd kill you now.'

Beneath his arms, Tommie wept. 'I didn't,' he blubbered. 'You gotta believe me . . . I didn't . . .'

The car fishtailed around a corner, tires howling. She stared out over the long hood, her face hard as stone. Tommie peeked out from under his arms and then sat up in the seat. She began breathing deeper now and eased her foot off the gas pedal.

At the corner of Midland and Main she braked the Pontiac to a stop, drumming her fingers on the steering wheel as she waited for the light to change. A couple crossed in front of the car, walking arm in arm, engaged in animated conversation.

'You gotta believe me,' Tommie said through the blood in his mouth. 'I didn't—' And then he stopped and stared out the side window. 'That's them,' he said. 'The ones come to Rodney's house asking about us. I'd know that big tall son of a bitch anywhere.' He pointed to the couple on the corner. 'That's them right there.'

'We try to get the information over the phone,' Corso was saying. 'Anybody wants to meet in person, we do it in broad daylight in some public place.'

'You sound pretty confident we're going to stir up some action,' she said.

'A reward always brings the loonies out of the woodwork,' Corso assured her. 'Yeah . . . we'll get some action. No doubt about it.'

Horns began to sound in the street. They turned their heads to see what the commotion was. A battered '69 Pontiac blocked the intersection. Impatient engines raced. An 18-wheeler, five cars back, sounded its air horn. By the time the Pontiac lurched around the corner and disappeared from sight, the light had changed to red again. First in line now, a guy in a white BMW slapped the steering wheel with the flat of his hand.

Corso and Dougherty walked slowly up the street. Occasionally spreading out, allowing passersby to pass between them, and then coming back together.

'Last night was cool,' Corso said as they bumped shoulders.

'This morning wasn't so bad either,' she said.

Corso agreed. They divided again to let a skate-boarder hurl himself down the block on plastic wheels. 'I think maybe I'm through beating myself

310

up over you,' Dougherty said. 'Like maybe I can just appreciate you for what you are and not let all the other crap I've got stored up get in the way of a good time.'

'Sounds good to me.'

'Of course it sounds good to you.'

Halfway up the block, the Pontiac slid to a stop. She pulled a wad of tissues from a box attached to the visor. Handed them to Tommie, who dabbed at his broken mouth.

'You sure that's the same people?'

Tommie nodded. 'Dead positive. That's them right there.'

'Follow them,' she said. 'Find out where they're staying.'

He opened his mouth to speak, but she cut him off. 'It's all over here,' she said. 'Time to fly away.' She jerked a thumb back over her shoulder. 'How we gonna do that depends on who else other than those two knows we're here. Now get going. I'll drive around the block and catch up with you.'

Tommie jogged up the sidewalk and peeked around the corner. They were a block away, walking north on Main, shoulder to shoulder, all kissy-face-like.

He crossed the street, dodging cars like a matador, until he got to the river side, where he began to follow along as they ambled up the sidewalk together. On his left, the river steamed in the late-afternoon sunshine. On his right, the orange glare of the sun reflected off shop windows, forcing him to squint as he watched the pair cross Dexter Avenue and begin to meander out of the downtown core.

He stepped behind the row of hedges separating Emerson Park from the street. In the center of the grassy lawn, a pair of teenage boys tossed a red Frisbee back and forth as a golden retriever ran from one to the other, frantically following the disk, leaping now and then, snapping at the spinning red blur they kept just out of reach.

When the lovebirds turned right into the driveway of the Pine Tree Motor Inn, he scurried out from behind the hedge and ran into the street. Half a block back, she had the Pontiac nestled against the curb as he dodged a furniture truck on his way across.

The couple walked hand in hand to the stairs at the back of the U, climbed to the second floor, and disappeared through the first door on the left. He followed until he could read the numbers on the door. Room 223.

When he turned toward the street, the nose of the Pontiac was visible along the south edge of the driveway. He hurried over.

'They're in two twenty-three,' he announced.

'Okay.' She took several deep breaths. 'Better stop at the drugstore and the bank,' she said. 'Then we'll run back to the farm.'

She didn't look panicked anymore. She was wearing that stony face he'd seen before. The one she wore when bad things needed to be done. Like when she handed him the ax in Wisconsin and told him what to do. He breathed a sigh of relief. Everything was going to be all better now. She'd see to it, like she always did. And this time, no matter what they had to do, at least they'd be together when it was over.

CHAPTER 33

'We gotta hurry,' she said. 'The girls'll be home from school in twenty minutes. We gotta have everything together by then.'

She threw a roll of duct tape into the brown canvas bag on the kitchen table.

'I'm telling Gordie I'm taking you to the airport in Chicago,' she said. 'Gonna have to spend the night. That way he won't be looking for me till he gets home tomorrow night and wants his dinner.' She waved a hand. 'Even then, he won't worry none. He'll just figure I broke down or something and go over to his mama's for supper.' She looked over at Tommie. 'You bring your gun?'

'Two.'

'Better bring 'em along,' she said. 'We gotta try to wipe the slate clean before we fly away. Best as we can anyway.'

'We gonna kill 'em?'

'Not till we find out who else knows I'm here. Then we're gonna take 'em out in the woods and bury 'em deep, where nobody's ever gonna find 'em.'

'We gonna leave Gordie and the kids be?'

'We're not organized enough to do anything about them. His nosy-ass mother'll know something's wrong in a minute we mess with any of them.' She looked around the kitchen. 'This is Mama May's house. Mama May's land.' Her eyes darkened. 'And she never let either of us forget it. Not for all these years. Brought it up every damn time money was mentioned.' She caught herself. 'Besides that, even if we did . . . you know . . . there's no way to cover our trail. Nope. We take care of those other two busybodies, and then Gordie and the girls just wake up tomorrow morning and find me gone.' She rubbed the back of her neck. 'Way things been going around here lately, I expect they'll be glad to see me gone. God knows his mama will.'

She crossed the kitchen to the phone on the wall. Dialed. 'Mama May,' she said after a moment. 'I'm taking my brother to the airport in Chicago tonight. He got a good deal on a midnight flight.' She listened. 'Yes,' she said. 'I will.' Listened again. 'I need you to look after the girls. Send 'em off to school in the morning.' She rolled her eyes. 'Yes. Yes. I'll leave him a note. I'll have them ready.' She hung up and headed for the stairs.

'I'm gonna pack a bag,' she said. 'You get your stuff together, and then we'll load the car.'

The voice on the phone was a hoarse whisper. 'How much is the reward?'

'Depends,' Corso said.

315

'I wanna see the money up front.'

'You give me the information. I check it out. Then you get the money.'

'By then she'll fly away.'

Corso sat up straight. Pointed at the phone. Dougherty stopped painting her nails and held her breath.

'Fly away, you say?'

'Sure,' the voice rasped. 'Like a bird.'

Dougherty set the nail polish on the nightstand. The arrows and vines and words that decorated her shoulders and chest gleamed Technicolor in the harsh overhead light.

'How's she gonna do that?' Corso asked.

As he listened, Corso's face moved from rapt attention to mild amusement.

'I see,' he said finally. 'Thanks for calling. No. No. Yeah. I'm taking it down, don't worry. We'll be in touch. Yeah.' He used his thumb to break the connection. Dougherty resumed breathing and cocked an eyebrow. 'She's one of a coven of witches living way up on the peninsula,' Corso said. 'We got to be careful or she'll fly away on us. Seems she's got this magic broom.' He pointed at the phone. 'He's personally seen her do it.'

'Where do these people come from?'

'*The Jerry Springer Show,*' Corso said.

The phone rang. Corso picked it up and pushed the TALK button.

A woman's voice. 'You the one's looking for that woman?'

316

'Yes.'

'I know her,' she said. 'You meet me ten o'clock tonight. Downtown. Out at the back of Emerson Park. Down by the river. Bring the money.' Dial tone.

She stood with the phone in her hand, looking out through the dirty front window as Sarah and Emily walked down the half-mile driveway toward the house.

Something in the ditch had attracted Emily's attention. She'd fallen behind her sister, who returned now and pulled the little girl upright. She watched as Sarah wagged a finger in Emily's face and then slapped her hard; she turned away as the girls again began trudging in her direction, Sarah striding out ahead with a smile on her face, Emily wiping the tears from her cheeks.

Dougherty puckered her lips and blew on her nails. 'Another loony?'

'Could have been her,' he said.

'She say something?'

'Just a feeling.'

'So?'

'She wants to meet across the street at ten tonight.'

'In the park?'

'All the way at the back, by the river.'

'I thought we were only meeting in broad daylight in public places.'

'She didn't give me a chance.'

'We don't have to show.'

'No . . . we don't.'

'But what if it's genuine?'

'Could be the only lead we get,' Corso mused.

'You figure that's just a coincidence?' She waved her bright red nails. 'You know, being right across the street from our motel and all.'

'What else could it be?'

'You tell me.'

Corso paced as he mulled it over. 'Maybe it's the only secluded place in the downtown area,' he offered. 'Maybe it's—'

'This place is a graveyard after dark. Besides that, why down-town? Why not somewhere out in the boonies?'

'You might be right,' he said. 'We'll get ourselves out there real early. Get the lay of the land. Make sure we're not walking into anything we can't handle. We see anything remotely scary, we hit the road and call Molina.'

She eyed him. 'You're really spooked, aren't you?'

His eyes got hard. 'All we've done so far is find out who she used to be. Her past is scary enough. Imagine who she is now.'

'I don't want to go to Grandma's,' Emily whined.

'Stop your sniveling,' her mother said. 'Mama May will be here in just a minute to get you two.'

'I wanna stay here and see Papa.'

Her mother grabbed her by the shoulders and gave her a shake, sending the child's head bouncing back and forth like it was on a string. The woman raised her hand but stopped short of using it when a loud bang startled her.

She turned her head. The new stove inlet pipe lay on the floor at Sarah's feet.

'How many times do I have to tell you? Leave that damn thing alone before I bash your damn head in with it!' she yelled.

Sarah reached to pick it up, but her mother was on her before she could close her fingers around the cold metal. Sarah took a step backward and watched her mother snatch the pipe from the floor, carry it across the room, and lean it against the wall, where it would be behind the door when it opened.

'There,' she said. 'It's out of the way now.' She pointed at Sarah. 'Get your coat on. Mama May's coming to get you.'

'Where you going?' the girl wanted to know.

'I'm taking Uncle Tommie to the airport in Chicago.'

'Good.'

When her mother started across the room toward her, Sarah turned and ran up the stairs. 'I'll smack your mouth,' her mother said to her back. Emily scampered upstairs after her sister. 'You get your coat on,' their mother shouted.

When the girls disappeared around the upstairs corner, she turned back toward the kitchen window just in time to see Mama May's blue Ford Torino bouncing to a stop in the yard.

She watched impassively as the older woman struggled out of the car and limped her way up the walk toward the door. Mama May had undergone hip replacement surgery three years earlier and, even with a new ceramic joint, had never regained her normal gait.

She'd seen the pictures. Three dead husbands ago. Way back in the fifties when May and Homer had first inherited the farm from his parents. May Galindo hadn't been attractive then, and she wasn't attractive now. A tall, hawk-faced, wide-hipped woman whose puckered, disapproving mouth and glowering countenance spoke of a lifetime of dour disapproval.

She always entered without knocking. The house belonged to her; she didn't want anyone to forget. Once inside, she gazed at her daughter-in-law with all the warmth of a snake. 'Gordon working late again?' she asked.

'Till midnight.'

She had immovable Margaret Thatcher hair and a look of contempt strong enough to wilt flowers. 'It's good your brother's leaving.'

She swallowed the wave of anger that flooded her. 'He needs to get back.'

'The girls don't like him. They say he touches them. They tell you that?'

She shrugged. 'You know how they are. Especially that Sarah.'

'That's no way to be talking about your own kids.'

'Why don't you let me worry about that? I was going to be taking parenting lessons, it sure as hell wouldn't be from you.'

The women stood a yard apart on the worn linoleum, locked in mutual loathing, until the younger woman broke away and walked over to the foot of the stairs.

'Let's go, you two. Mama May's here.'

'Name's Teresa Fulbrook. Least that's what she calls herself now.'

Dougherty held her breath. 'Oh?'

'I don't mind other people's business. I'm not that kind.'

'Of course not,' Dougherty said.

'This is something different, though.'

Dougherty reached over and slapped Corso on his bare stomach. He sat bolt upright in bed. She pointed at the cell phone pressed to her ear, bobbed her head up and down. 'This is different,' she said softly. As Corso swung his legs over the edge of the bed and got to his feet, the woman went on.

'Like I said . . . woman you're looking for calls herself Teresa Fulbrook now. Got white spiky hair sticking straight up. Got a couple of little girls. Seven and fourteen. That's who I'm worried about here . . . those girls.' The voice cleared its throat. 'Couldn't give a damn about that Fulbrook woman.'

Dougherty used her thumb to jack the earpiece volume all the way up. Corso leaned in close, resting his head against hers, listening to the tinny amplified voice.

'How do you know her?' Dougherty asked.

'Her oldest girl – Sarah's her name – she's in the same class as my son Billy. Southshore Junior High. They're at that age . . . you know . . . where boys start noticing girls and the other way around.' Dougherty could sense her discomfort. 'Anyway,' the woman continued, 'I guess this woman – I seen her there a few times before – I guess she sees Billy and her Sarah holding hands.' She hesitated, as if to keep herself under control. 'To hear my Billy tell it, she come running down the sidewalk like a banshee, starts screaming at the two of them, drags the girls back to the car, and drives off.'

'Really?'

'That's not the part, though. Girl don't come to school for a week. She gets back, and somebody's cut all her hair off. Right down to the nubs. Sarah tells Billy it was her mama done it.'

'For holding hands?'

'What kind of woman would do a thing like that to a teenage girl? All the problems girls that age got anyway, and you cut off all their hair?'

'You know where this woman lives?'

'Out east someplace on Route 10. I gotta go,' she said suddenly. 'Kids are home.'

A soft click announced the terminated connection.

'Bingo,' Dougherty said.

'The hair bit sounds about right.' He made a face. 'Eyewitnesses are always dicey, though.'

'The name's right.'

'Teresa Fulbrook?'

'Teresa Thomes. That was the other woman who died back in Avalon about the time Sissy disappeared. I never followed up on her, because I struck it rich on the Nancy Anne Goff alias. I'm betting we do a little checking, we find out she took over both identities at the same time.'

'Smart,' Corso said. 'One name to leave town with. Another to settle in under. Make it doubly hard for anybody to trace you.'

'What now?'

He held out his open palm. 'Molina.'

CHAPTER 34

Teresa Fulbrook ran her fingers through her hair as she used the blow-dryer. Her platinum spikes had given way to soft curls of a deep black that, as best she could recall, approximated the natural color of her hair. She smoothed the hair, pulled a pair of scissors from the kitchen drawer, and, using her reflection in the kitchen window, snipped a few minor adjustments. She patted her head in several places and then returned the scissors to the drawer.

Tommie de Groot spun the open cylinder of the Colt revolver. 'Kill two birds with one stone,' he was saying. 'Get these busybodies off your back, and get rid of the only two people seen me shoot that professor guy. Pretty neat if you ask me.'

Teresa opened her mouth to speak, but a movement in her peripheral vision held the words captive in her throat. She walked quickly to the window.

'Gordie's home,' she said.

Tommie stopped fiddling with the revolver and stashed the gun in his bag.

He walked to her side. 'Thought he was working tonight.'

'Maybe he's sick,' she said. 'He's been under the weather lately.'

They stood hip to hip and watched the white Ford pickup truck roll to a stop thirty feet away. Gordie got out, heading for the side door in a crablike shuffle.

Gordon Fulbrook was fifty-six, eleven years her senior. Bald in front except for a wiry black circle that clung stubbornly to the front of his scalp. An awkward man and a lifetime bachelor, he'd succumbed easily to her tender ministrations. At the time, she'd never met Mama May and assumed that Gordie owned the farm, a misconception her prospective husband never bothered to correct. By the time Mama May returned from wintering in Florida, they'd been married for a month and a half. The fountain of carnal delights in which Gordie had been bathing dried up in a hurry when his new bride learned that all six thousand acres belonged to his shovel-faced mother, with whom she shared a mutual hatred far beyond the scope of their actual relationship.

Unlike his mother, he was small. 'Small all over!' Teresa used to shout at him in moments of rage. Five foot six, same as her. Maybe a hundred fifty pounds dripping wet. Lost a couple more pounds every year.

He burst through the kitchen door. Stopped dead in his tracks.

'You done your hair.'

'Yeah.'

'I never liked that other shit anyway. Kinda thing didn't look right on a family woman your age.'

'So you said.'

'Where's the girls?'

'At your mama's.'

He turned his head. Took in Tommie standing next to the two bags on the kitchen table. 'Goin' somewhere?'

'Taking Tommie to the Chicago airport.'

'That so?'

'He got a good deal on a midnight flight.'

'Good deal, huh?'

'Yeah.'

'That how come there's no money in the bank? He got such a good deal.'

'What?'

'You heard me. I decided to go out to lunch with Perry and the boys. Didn't have enough for lunch and the cake I promised the girls, so I stopped by the ATM for a little cash. Machine wouldn't give me a damn thing.' He looked at the bags again. 'I go inside, they tell me you closed out both accounts.'

'I made you lunch.'

He crossed the floor. 'Where's the money?' he demanded. 'Twelve hundred from the checking account. Eight thousand four hundred from savings.'

'I don't know what you're talking about.'

326

He looked over at Tommie. 'You and your pinhead brother here think you're gonna walk out of here with—'

She slapped him in the face. Hard. Sending him staggering backward. He touched his cheek and then folded both hands into fists. Whatever he was planning next was stopped by the push of cold steel behind his ear.

'Go ahead,' Tommie breathed. 'Do somethin' stupid.' He grabbed Gordie by the collar and forced his face down onto the kitchen counter. He looked to Teresa for encouragement but found only veiled caution in her eyes.

Face pressed against the counter, Gordie began to prattle. 'Jesus, Teresa . . . come on now . . . make him put that gun away. Somebody could get hurt here.'

'Shut up,' she said.

'The money's not a problem. If you need the money—'

'You remember Doug?' she asked.

'Doug?' Gordie stammered. 'I don't know any—'

'In Omaha?' Tommie asked.

'That's the one,' she said.

Gordie started to blubber again. Tommie dug the barrel in harder behind his ear.

'Nobody knows nothin' about that one but us,' she said. 'This one gotta be just like that. Nice and clean.'

Tommie nodded his understanding. He put more pressure on the back of Gordie's neck.

'Don't you move, you son of a bitch. I'll blow your brains all over the damn wall, don't you think I won't.'

Teresa walked quickly to the refrigerator; she got up on tiptoe to reach into the cabinet above. Came out with a white plastic bag. Meijer's Markets. Brought it to her mouth and blew inside, checking that it was airtight, then pulled the duct tape from her bag and walked over to the counter, where Gordie was still mumbling. 'Ain't no need for any of this, Reecee,' he was saying. 'You want the money, it's yours. Ain't no need to go and do something—'

With one hand, Tommie grabbed Gordie by the back of the hair and jerked him upright. He used the other to stuff the revolver into his own back pocket before looping his arms around Gordie, pinning the smaller man's arms against his sides.

When Teresa slipped the Meijer's bag over his head, Gordie went wild, thrashing so violently he sent both Tommie and himself crashing to the floor, where they rolled about in a frenzy of straining limbs until Tommie finally got his legs around Gordie and rolled him chest-up. Teresa dropped quickly, landing on Gordie's sternum with her knees, driving the air from his lungs with a whoosh. As he fought for breath, she ripped off a piece of tape and wound it tight along the lower edge of the bag, sealing the plastic around his throat. And then another. Then a third. Two deep breaths and he was out of air. The white plastic was plastered against his face now. Drawn into his nose and mouth cavities by his desperate attempts to breathe, the plastic welded itself to the contours of his face, making it possible to watch his final moments of bug-eyed agony through the thin plastic veneer.

Another futile breath, and his nervous system went on automatic pilot. Flopping across the floor like a fish on a riverbank, Tommie welded to his back, Teresa riding his heaving chest like a bronc rider, until finally he stiffened and, with a sound not unlike a rueful sigh, suddenly lay still. Above their labored breathing, the refrigerator clicked on, scaring the hell out of both of them. Took a minute before anybody breathed.

Tommie unlocked his ankles and dropped his feet to the floor. She looked down into Gordie's purple, contorted face. He'd vomited all over the inside of the bag.

'Might have been better if you'd just ate that lunch I packed,' she said.

'What do you mean it's not enough?'

'He says it's too tenuous. Thinks we need to see the woman for ourselves before he starts sending agents our way.'

Corso set the phone on the nightstand. He checked the clock. Nine minutes after eight. It had taken an hour and a half to get themselves patched through to Special Agent Molina's pager. He'd called back immediately. He'd been in Nyack, New York, attending a retirement dinner with his wife and, thus interrupted, had been somewhat less than enthused by Corso's information. 'Nothing I can do with that,' he'd said. 'Not even the same name. It's too much of a stretch. Plane flights coming out of my budget, you're going to have to do better than that.' When Corso began to protest, Molina interrupted him. 'I'm not careful, I end up with a credibility problem, like some people who shall remain nameless.' Nothing much Corso could say to that, so he mumbled an apology and broke the connection.

Corso breathed a sigh. He looked over at Dougherty. 'So we try to get a peek at whoever shows up in the park tonight.'

'Be best if we got there first,' Dougherty said.

Corso retrieved his jeans from the floor and buckled them around his waist.

'No contact,' he said. 'We're just going to look.'

'Absolutely.'

'Dress warm. We're going to be out there for a while.'

'I don't like it.'

'Me neither.'

CHAPTER 35

The sky was a blanket of gray. The air fifteen degrees warmer than the night before. The change in temperature must have been what sent the fog rolling in from Lake Huron, forming a moving carpet above the river and wrapping the town in gauze. Beneath the muted glow of the street-lights, Main Street, Midland, Michigan, was little more than a series of glowing pools, strung along the river like pearls, winding south with the fog and the water for as far as the eye could penetrate.

The well-tended shrubs and bushes of Emerson Park stood tentative and unsure of themselves, like half-finished sketches, as Corso and Dougherty moved slowly down the park's long central path, their heads swiveling, their eyes searching for patterns among surrounding greenery.

'Feels like one of those English horror flicks,' Dougherty whispered.

'Yeah . . . except I'm way more scared than that,' Corso said.

She jerked hard on his elbow. 'Don't say that, Corso. I start hearing a guy with a death wish saying he's scared, it makes me nervous.'

He stopped. Looked hard into her eyes. 'I'll walk you back to the room.'

She shook her head. 'Anyplace you're going, I'm going.'

He knew better than to argue. Instead he took her by the hand and pulled her off the path, angling away from the lights out into the semi-darkness of the lawn, and then finally into the deep gloom among the shrubs that separated the family picnic area from the river. They duckwalked their way among the twisted roots until they had a clear view of the path, then squatted in the darkness, surveying the concrete walkway running along the edge of the water.

Their hideaway was at the high point of the path. To the right, they could see for forty yards. The path was deserted. To the left, for twice that distance, nobody was in sight. 'We wait,' Corso whispered. Dougherty pulled her cape beneath her and sat down on it.

Tommie de Groot lowered the binoculars. Two hundred yards across the foggy park, the pair of outlines beneath the bushes sat invisible to the naked eye. If he hadn't watched them creep into place, even with his deer-hunting binoculars he might never have found them in the gloom. He closed one eye, as if aiming. 'I had my rifle, I'd put one right through her into him.'

'We need 'em alive, remember?' Teresa whispered. 'Else we'll never know what's behind us.'

She leaned in and whispered in his ear. 'You don't know what's coming for you, you don't know what to do next. How deep to dig in. How far to run.' She put a hand on his shoulder. 'I been running all my life,' she whispered. 'Running away from people and the things they done to me. Running away from the things they made me do. It's all the same. You just take out the garbage and move on.'

When Corso reached out and squeezed her arm, Dougherty moved nothing but her eyes. To the south, a solitary figure emerged from the haze, walking fast like she was out for some exercise. As she passed under the wooden stanchion that marked the park's boundary, she slowed her pace, as if impeded by the slight incline.

Corso bent until his chest was scraping the damp ground, peering out from under the branches at the approaching woman, whose loose-fitting jacket and raised hood made it difficult to see her features.

As she moved along, she gazed out at the river, leaving Corso to peer at the side of her hood as she walked closer and closer to their hiding place. Twenty feet from where they crouched, she turned and began to walk back the other way. Kept going until she disappeared into the fog again. They waited in the darkness. The river gurgled twice, the blatt of a truck rolled in from the road, and then all was silent.

Corso started to rise. Her hand on his arm held him down. The stroller was back. Her dark silhouette displaced the silvery air. She came their way again, still gazing at the ruffled black water as she ambled back up the incline. She stopped and leaned out over the rail. Checked her watch and looked upriver. Corso checked his. Five after ten.

The sound of voices split the air. Something about a doctor's appointment on Tuesday. When the woman turned toward the sound, Corso got a brief glance at the side of her head. Whatever color her hair was, it wasn't white. Either the caller had been mistaken, or this wasn't her. A cold wave of disappointment rushed through his body.

An elderly couple gradually emerged from the fog, chatting as they walked along at a brisk pace. The woman at the rail turned her back on them as they passed.

'Evening,' said the older woman as she walked by. No answer. They walked a dozen paces before she leaned close and whispered something in the man's ear. As they disappeared around the bend, the man looked questioningly back over his shoulder at the solitary figure standing at the river's edge.

The odors of stale sweat and nicotine came to Corso's nostrils in the moment before he heard Dougherty whimper and felt her shift her weight on the ground. He saw the gun first, pressed against her temple, and the hand across her mouth, the

334

long fingers seeming to wind completely around her head. The face took him a minute. Wasn't until he heard 'Don't you fucking move' that he recognized the shaven and shorn version of Tommie de Groot. 'Get out,' de Groot told him. 'Get out from under here right now.'

When Corso didn't move, de Groot cocked the hammer. Dougherty's eyes got to be the size of saucers. 'I'm going,' Corso said.

He crawled out onto the strip of grass separating the path from the shrubbery. She had her hood down now. Her hair wasn't blond. Wasn't spiked. But it was her all right. Her small exotic features had aged gracefully. Mrs Ethnic Housewife, Anyplace, USA. Only the shark in her eyes and the gun in her hand said otherwise.

'Over there,' she said. 'Lean against the rail.'

'Move it,' Tommie growled from behind.

Corso felt the icy touch of fear running up and down his spine like steel ball bearings. He had no doubts. The only way they were coming out of this was dead. They had nothing to lose.

He put his hands on the icy rail, just as Dougherty was slammed in next to him. Her mouth hung open. Her eyes were beginning to fill. Corso heard a ripping sound and looked back over his shoulder. Tommie de Groot stood a pace back, his revolver aimed at Corso's head. Teresa Fulbrook had her hands around a roll of duct tape and was about to tear a five-foot section with her teeth.

Corso looked over at Dougherty. She read the terror and desperation in his eyes.

'No,' Corso said. 'We can't let them take us.'

Before she could process the information, Corso had thrust himself off the rail and was rushing toward the barrel of the unwavering gun.

'No,' Teresa Fulbrook screamed, dropping the tape and reaching for her gun. She'd only moved a few feet when Tommie shot Corso about a foot above the left knee. The sound of the report was swallowed whole by the fog. Corso went down in a pile of arms and legs. When Teresa snapped her head around, all she saw was the back of a cape fluttering in the breeze as Meg Dougherty vaulted the rail and splashed into the dark river below.

And then it was silent. Nothing but the cold and the darkness and the pressure in her ears as the current bumped her along the bottom, where her hands could find no purchase among the slimy rocks, where she struggled to get her feet beneath her, to push, to kick, anything to get her head above the rushing water, out of the cold blackness and into the light, to stop the scream that was building in her ears and the red-hot coals that filled her lungs as she rolled along the river bottom, banging a knee and then her head as she somersaulted through the inky water, out of control . . . out of air . . . In her final throes, she began to flail . . . felt a hand break water and splash . . . felt the cold night air on her wet skin . . . felt . . .

She used her teeth to rip off another yard of duct tape. Used it to bring Corso's elbows together behind his back, then rolled him over and checked the tape covering his eyes and mouth again. Didn't want him to bleed to death, so she wound two more strips tight around the hole in his leg. The sounds of boots brought her eyes up.

Tommie was out of breath. He rested his hands on his knees and worked some oxygen through his lungs before he spoke. 'She never come up. I followed her all the way till I heard people. Never seen a sign of her at all.'

'Just another tourist fell in the river and drowned. Happens all the time,' she said, getting to her feet. She kicked the unconscious Corso in the ribs. 'Tape or no tape, this one's gonna be trouble once he wakes up.' She looked around. 'We'll drag him in the bushes. You stay with him. I'll get the car.'

. . . a hand on her wrist, pulling, slipping off, losing its grip, then another set of fingers entwined in her hair, breaking her momentum, spinning her in the water until her knees scraped across the top of a rock and she could use the last of her strength to lever herself upward, gasping, spitting water, her breath coming in convulsions as the hands dragged her from the current until only her feet remained in the water and she began to gag and choke on the night air as the voices swirled about her.

'You go call for an ambulance,' a woman's voice said. 'I'll stay with her until you get back.' She listened to the sound of shoes crunching across the gravel riverbank and felt the steadying hand on her back. 'Help is on the way, honey,' the voice said. 'You just relax and we'll get you to the hospital. Everything's going to be just fine.'

Corso lay facedown on the floor of the car. Backseat, with the transmission hump squeezing the air from his lungs with every bump. Tommie de Groot had his feet resting in the middle of Corso's back. 'This is done,' he asked, 'where we gonna go?'

'One step at a time,' she said from behind the wheel. 'Don't want to get ahead of yourself here. Don't want to be thinking too far down the line. Just take things one step at a time. First thing we do is we find out from Mr Nosey Parker here who he is and what it is he knows about us.'

'You think he'll tell us?'

She laughed a laugh he'd only heard once before. Back when he was little. Back when she'd described how she'd gotten the nun to tell her where the money was hidden. The sound sent a shiver running down Tommie's spine.

'Oh, he'll tell us all right,' she chuckled. 'He most surely will.'

★ ★ ★

Dougherty ran her tongue across her teeth and then spit on the ground beside her face. After a moment, she pulled one knee under herself and then the other. The woman's hand on her back pressed harder now. 'You just stay still till the ambulance gets here, honey,' the woman cooed. 'Everything's gonna be all right.'

Dougherty lurched to her feet, reeling and nearly going down on the rough stones. She swayed as she looked around. The woman was a blur – sixty-something, short and solid, wearing something bright blue. Some kind of hat on her head. 'Oh, honey,' she pleaded as Dougherty used the metal handrail to pull herself up the four steps to the walkway. 'Come on now, honey. Jack's at the phone by now . . .'

Dougherty lost whatever the woman said next in the rasping and rattling of her own breath as she staggered north along the river. She tried to pick it up, to move from a walk to a jog to a run, but instead tripped herself and fell hard on the asphalt.

Four minutes and two falls later, she was back at the apex of the trail. Knees bleeding, breathing like a locomotive, she looked over into the gloom beneath the oversized bushes and then walked over to the spot where she'd gone over the rail. Nothing. Not a sound. She checked the river. The path. All the way till it disappeared into the fog. No blood, no nothing. Not a sign of Corso.

Trotting now, she skirted the bushes to the left

and, once in the open, began to run across the grass toward the lights on Main Street. The picture brought her heart to her throat. Spinning tires had clawed a pair of seeping ruts into the grass. Her eyes followed the tracks across the ravaged lawn, out through the gate, to the street beyond. 'She's got him,' she said out loud, and then began to sprint. 'Oh, Jesus, she's got him.'

CHAPTER 36

Dougherty burst through the motel room door, slamming it into the wall so hard the knob punched a hole in the plaster-board. The mirror at the far end of the room showed what a pitiful sight she was. Blotches of brown mud all over her body, one shoe gone, her hair caked with mud and hanging in her face, a pair of bloody knees visible through the holes in her jeans.

She kicked off the remaining shoe and ran to the nightstand, where the blinking red light on the cell phone was telling her they had messages. She snatched the phone from the charger. Held it to the side of her head before she realized she didn't know the number. Took her a full minute to figure it out; then she brought the receiver down and pushed Redial. Seven rings. A sleepy voice. 'Molina.'

'We found her,' she yelled.

'Found—?'

'The de Groot woman. We found her.' The connection was so good she could hear the rustling of linens as he sat up in bed.

'Are you sure—' he began.

'It's her,' she shouted into the mouthpiece. 'She's got Corso.'

'Slow down,' Molina said. 'What's the—'

'We found her. She calls herself Teresa Fulbrook. She lives somewhere east of Midland, Michigan, on Route 10. Please . . . you gotta—'

'Call nine-one-one.'

'No time,' she panted. 'Tommie de Groot's here. He shot Corso. Took him off someplace. Please . . . please . . . you gotta send help.'

'Okay . . . okay . . . okay,' he chanted. 'I'll—'

She didn't wait for the rest of it. Instead broke the connection and threw the phone onto the bed. She stood for a moment, staring stupidly at the walls, before crossing the room to the desk and pulling the phone book from the drawer. Her hands shook as she leafed through the white pages. Skipped from *D* to *H*. Went back, found *G*, and moved backward to *F* from there. *Fu*. One *l* or two? Then she found it. One *l*. Two listings. M. L. Fulbrook 27654 RFD 10. G. F. Fulbrook 24788 RFD 10.

She tore the page from the book, grabbed the car keys from the desk, and started for the door. Stopped and turned around. Grabbed the phone from the bed. Back to the phone book. Leafed through the front of the book until she found the local map. Tore that out too and ran out of the room.

★   ★   ★

342

'Papa's home,' Sarah said. Emily rushed to her sister's side at the windowsill. Three-quarters of a mile away across the winter fields, the lights of their house were visible from Mama May's upstairs window, as was the white pickup truck parked by the kitchen door. 'Let's go see Papa,' Emily cried.

'Mama don't like surprises.'

Emily's lower lip trembled. 'I want to see Papa,' she whined.

'Tomorrow,' Sarah said.

'He said he'd bring us ice-cream cake.'

'We leave here, she'll skin us.'

'Not if Papa's there,' the little girl said. 'Papa won't let her.'

'Papa goes to work,' Sarah cautioned, but Emily wasn't listening. Instead she skipped across the room to the closet. Pulled her red jacket from the hanger and put it on. 'I'm going to see my papa,' she announced.

'Mama gonna make you wish you didn't,' her big sister said, but the little girl was undeterred. She hurried back to the window, pushed the bottom sash as far up as it would go, and climbed out onto the back-porch roof.

Sarah stood in the bedroom they shared and watched as her younger sister climbed down the latticework to the ground below, just like Sarah had taught her to do last summer. Sarah looked out over the fields at the glowing spark in the distance. At the white pickup in the yard. Thought about ice-cream cake and could feel the cool creaminess in her mouth, just as Emily came into view, riding her new bike away from Mama May's house, the white beam of the headlight bouncing crazily along in front of her as she pedaled down the tractor path that wound across the fields.

Sarah smiled. Smiled for the beating Emily was sure to get the first time she was alone with the witch. Smiled as she reached for the phone and dialed. Something she was never allowed to do in her own house. At least not when the witch was home. Billy's father answered. 'Yeah,' the gruff voice said.

'Could I talk to Billy, please?'

'Just a sec.'

She watched Emily's little red tail-light bounce into the distance and smiled again.

A woman's voice crackled in her ear. 'This Sarah?' it wanted to know.

'Yes, ma'am,' she said.

'Listen,' Billy's mother said. A short silence ensued before the woman went on. 'I'm sure you're a very nice girl and all, Sarah, but our Billy isn't ready for . . .' She stopped again. 'What with your mother and all . . .' the woman began again. 'Please don't call here anymore,' the voice finally said, before hanging up.

Tommie de Groot took one last hit on the hand-rolled cigarette before grinding it out on Corso's bare shoulder. Naked to the waist and taped to the kitchen chair, Corso could do little more than

344

squirm in the seat and groan behind the duct tape covering his mouth. Despite several layers of tightly wrapped tape, the wound in his right leg had begun to seep, dripping a pool of blood on the floor around his foot.

Teresa Fulbrook tore off the strip of silver tape covering Corso's mouth. Left the end hanging down over the series of burn marks covering Corso's shoulders and chest.

'Tell me again,' she said to Corso. 'Just you and the drowned girl. That's it. Right? That what you been telling me? You found us all on your own.'

Tommie slapped Corso's face, the impact painting the images of his long fingers on Corso's cheek. 'You answer her, god damn you,' he said.

Corso kept his mouth shut and his head bowed. Tommie grabbed him by the back of the hair, tilting Corso's face toward the ceiling. 'You hear me?' He put his face right in Corso's. 'I'm talking to you, boy!' he screamed. 'You hear me?'

'He hears,' she said. 'This . . .' She reached over on the table where the contents of Corso's wallet were spread out over the surface. Picked up his driver's license. 'This Frank Corso character here fancies himself a hard case.'

'You lemme have a knife and we'll see about that,' Tommie said.

She bent at the waist and put her mouth next to Corso's ear. 'You want me to do that?' she asked. 'You want me to give Tommie here a steak knife and let him have a little fun with you?'

Corso raised his head and looked into her nearly colorless eyes. 'Just the two of us,' he said. 'We checked the death records back in Avalon. Figured it out on our own.'

Tommie drew back his hand to slap Corso's face again, but a shake of her head stopped him in midswing. 'Smart,' she said. She looked over at Tommie. 'You'd think a man smart enough to run us down . . . a man that smart would know what's coming for him here, now wouldn't you?' she asked. 'Figure he'd know he ain't coming out of this alive. Figure it was just a matter of how he went out . . . easy or hard.'

She ambled over to the new stove and opened the red toolbox sitting on the floor. Corso watched as she pulled out the top tray and set it on the floor. When her hand appeared again, Corso began to make noises in his chest like a gored animal. He began to struggle against his bonds, throwing himself desperately from side to side, trying to tip the chair over, pulling so hard at the tape it felt as if his arms would be broken loose from their sockets. The look of terror on his face seemed to cheer her.

CHAPTER 37

Meg Dougherty didn't realize she was barefoot until she jumped out of the car and ran across both lanes of Route 10 to check the numbers on the mailboxes. By the time she got back into the driver's seat, she was hobbling, as half a dozen jagged pieces of gravel threatened to work their way through the soles of her feet. She scraped her feet on the car's carpet and roared off down the road, talking out loud to herself now: 'One-nine-six-four-two,' she mumbled. She reached down and brought the page from the phone book up close to her eyes. 'Two-four-seven-eight-eight,' she chanted as she floored the car and went fishtailing up the road.

Route 10, on this side of the river, had started out suburban, neatly trimmed houses and lawns. Numbers in the one-four-four-five-something range. Mailboxes along both sides of the road. Five miles later, things were strictly rural, and all the mailboxes were along the eastbound lane, allowing the RFD carrier to drive along the right shoulder while making his appointed rounds.

She drove nearly a mile before another clump

of mailboxes appeared along the shoulder. Unable to skid to a stop in time, she threw the car into Reverse and burned rubber backward. The mailbox for two-one-four-six-eight was painted to look like a barn. An arrow on the top pointed to the right, up the long driveway to the farmhouse in the distance. 'Even numbers on the right,' she muttered to herself, throwing the car back into Drive. 'Close,' she breathed. 'Getting close.'

Sarah Fulbrook ran both hands through the stubs of her hair. She pulled a tissue from the box on the desk and wiped first her eyes and then her nose. Billy's mother's words still echoed in her mind. 'Don't call here no more.' She heard it over and over. What had started as a tiny amplified voice on the phone had risen to a shout inside her head. She dropped the wadded-up tissue on the desk and held her head in her hands, rocking back and forth in the chair, humming to herself, louder and louder, finding some inner rhythm of sound and motion to block out the words that tormented her soul.

As the humming got louder and the rocking more frenzied, the room began to fall away . . . She could see blue sky and a swing . . . She was swinging . . . at school. Somebody was pushing her, but she couldn't see who it was. Each push lifted her higher into the sky, until finally her head nearly reached the level of the bar, and the seat began to get airborne, snapping the chains each time she began her descent. Above her own laughter, she could hear the whoosh of the air and the sounds of birds. 'Higher,' she cried. 'Push me higher.'

She swung for what seemed an eternity, and then, without warning, the pushes stopped. When she looked back over her shoulder at the ground, no one was there. The arcs of her swing got smaller and smaller, until finally she was still, and the air around her was silent.

Sarah rose from the chair, walked slowly to the closet, and retrieved her coat. She was still humming as she climbed out the window onto the porch roof.

Teresa Fulbrook turned the little brass knob on the blowtorch. The sound of rushing gas filled the room. In a single expert motion, Tommie pulled a kitchen match from his pocket, flicked the top with his fingernail, and lit the pressurized gas. She fiddled with the knob until she had a roaring blue flame and then looked up at Corso.

'This is *your* doing. Don't you forget it.' She took a step his way. Corso began to thrash about in the chair. Only Tommie's hands on top of the seat back prevented Corso from toppling over onto his side. 'You hadn'ta lied to me, none of this woulda happened, so don't be pushing the blame my way.'

She kept talking as she waved the hissing flame in front of Corso's face. 'All I wanted from you was the truth. After that I'da had Tommie put you out of your misery.' She ran the torch across the front of his hair. Corso heard the crackle and smelled the acrid odor of burning protein. He struggled harder now, but could only move himself to and fro in the seat. 'See, this talk about how it was just the two of you that found me here sounds good and all, but . . .' She took three steps over to the kitchen table. Came back with the poster with her face on it. 'But that don't say nothing about how you all got your hands on this picture, see . . . 'cause I know where this picture come from, and I know who took it.' She took the torch and set the corner of the poster on fire. Held it gingerly in her fingers, tilting it this way and that until only the blackened shard in her fingers remained. The charred remains floated to the ground at her feet. She reached over and put the tape back over Corso's mouth. Smoothed it down hard with her free hand. 'So here's what we're gonna do,' she said. 'I'm gonna burn off your right ear, and then we're gonna have us another little talk. If that don't get your attention, I'm gonna burn off the other one.' She looked up at Tommie. 'Hold his head,' she said.

Tommie laced his fingers in the hair at the top of Corso's head and slipped his other hand under Corso's chin. He leaned hard against the back of the chair as Corso began to go wild in the seat. Corso was screaming through the tape, shaking uncontrollably as she brought the torch to bear. Again he heard the crackle of his hair, and then, as she moved again, he could feel the heat of the flame on his flesh. A scream rose and fell in his chest. Without willing it so, a high-pitched keening noise began to escape from behind the tape. Blood splashed in a wide arc as his feet took on a life of their own, beating a frantic rhythm against the floor. A siren wailed full blast in Corso's ears.

And then Tommie let go of his head and straightened up and the siren began to wind down, more of a moan now. Corso opened his eyes to see Tommie pointing out over Teresa's shoulder. Out into the darkened field where a bright white light was bouncing their way. 'What in hell is that?' Tommie asked.

She snapped her head around. 'One of those goddamned girls,' she said. She shut off the torch and then pointed to the swinging door separating the kitchen from the living room. 'Take him in the other room with Gordie,' she said.

The quavering light was less than a hundred yards away when Tommie grabbed the chair by the top rail and began to back his way across the floor, towing the struggling Corso, chair and all, out of the room.

Emily leaned her bike against the kitchen steps and bounded into the house. 'Papa,' she yelled as she ran to the kitchen. Three steps inside, she looked over toward the sink and came to a sliding halt. Her mother stood leaning against the counter, arms folded across her chest. The look

351

on her face was like none that Emily had ever seen before. She swallowed hard and asked, 'Where's Papa?' Her mother looked out through the window at the pickup truck in the yard.

'What are you doing here?' her mother demanded. 'You're supposed to be at Mama May's. What the hell are you doing back here?'

'I wanna see—'

When her mother started across the room toward her, Emily made a dash for the swinging door. 'Papa,' she cried. 'Papa.'

Papa didn't answer. The first slap nearly knocked her from her feet. The second sent her reeling backward so violently she hit her head on the refrigerator and slid to the floor.

'Get upstairs!' her mother screamed. 'Right now! Get upstairs!'

Even in her dazed condition, Emily knew better than to disobey at a time like this. She brought a hand to the red welts on her cheek, then scrambled to her feet and darted for the stairs, using her hands and feet to climb as quickly as possible, her mother following along behind. As she reached the landing, the little girl was swept off her feet and carried down the hall. She used her arms to cover her head, but the anticipated blows never arrived. Instead her mother carried her into the room and threw her on her bed.

'Get undressed. Get in bed,' her mother said through her teeth. 'You move outta this bed, I'll make you wish you were never born.' Emily threw her jacket on the floor and pulled her sweatshirt over her head. 'Hurry up, damn it!' her mother screamed. 'Get in that damn bed.' Emily jumped in and pulled the covers over her head.

She listened to the echo of her mother's steps. Heard the sound of a banging door and the sudden rush of water. And then her mama came back into the room.

'Sit up,' she said.

Emily poked her head out from beneath the covers. Her mother was standing with two white pills in one hand and a glass of water in the other. 'Take these,' she said, holding out the pills. Emily sat up and did as she was told. Placing the pills on her tongue and then washing them down with water.

Teresa Fulbrook left the bedroom door open when she left. Back at the landing, she found Tommie standing at the bottom of the stairs. She motioned him back into the kitchen and then followed him through the door. 'Damn kid changes everything,' she said. 'We're gonna have to buy ourselves a little time. Gonna have to give 'em something to think about.' She looked around the room until her eyes came to rest on the new stove. She turned to Tommie.

'You take that Corso fella out and put him in the trunk of the Pontiac. Make sure you bring a pick and shovel along. We'll bury him out by Evers Marsh where Gordie takes the kids camping.'

Tommie started across the room. 'Gordie's got

him some gas cans in the barn we keep for emergencies,' she said. 'There's a big old funnel hanging on a nail. Fill the Pontiac up with as much gas as'll fit. Get us a long way down the road before we need to stop for anything.'

354

CHAPTER 38

Sarah threw her bike on top of her sister's and started up the kitchen stairs. Two steps up, she stopped. The inside door hung open. She opened her mouth to call but quickly changed her mind. Instead she stood still, cocked an ear, and listened. Nothing. Not a sound. And then . . . she heard her mother's voice coming from down the hall, talking to herself in that singsong voice Sarah hated so much, the one she used when she thought nobody else could hear. Only this time it was different, like she was doing something else at the same time. Something hard. Something she was straining to do. 'Come on now,' she was saying. 'Just gonna move you out here. Come on now. Easy does it. That's it. Come on . . .'

When the words suddenly got louder, Sarah panicked and stepped behind the kitchen door. She waited for a second and then peeked around the corner; her mother was bent over, backing into the room, dragging something. Somebody! Dragging somebody by the feet. The air stuck in Sarah's throat. She clapped a hand over her mouth and watched in horror as her mother pulled the rest of the body into the room and the door swung shut with a clatter. She shrank back into the corner. As she flattened herself against the wall, her hand came into contact with something cold and hard. She looked to the left and saw the big pipe Papa made for the new stove leaning against the wall. Then she peeked around the door again.

The body had a white Meijer's bag taped over its head. No matter, though. She knew the shirt. Mama May had given it to Papa last Christmas. Sarah choked back a sob and pulled her head back behind the door. Mama was talking again. 'Just gonna lay you down right here,' she was saying. 'Make it look like you was working on the stove when something went wrong. Something with the gas. Just a terrible tragedy. Killed the both of you.'

As she listened to the sound of her mother's voice, Sarah could feel her anger rising. Feel the heat as it colored her neck and then her ears, until she could hear the power of her own blood and feel her heart beating in her temples like a drum.

And then the noise. The loud hissing. And almost at once the stink of gas filling the room. Sarah peeked again. Her mother had her back to Sarah's hiding place. She had a dish towel mashed against her face as she pulled tools from the red metal box. Sarah's eyes began to water. She stifled a cough.

When Tommie de Groot bent down to heave his captive into the trunk, Corso uncoiled himself and headbutted him in the face, sending Tommie down onto the seat of his pants. Tommie got to his feet, rubbed his face, then kicked Corso in the head. 'You gonna pay for that later, you son of a bitch,' he said. 'As god is my witness you will.' He pulled back his foot again and kicked Corso in the solar plexus, driving the air from his lungs, sending Corso into near convulsions as he gasped for air through his tape-covered mouth. Tommie grabbed the shuddering Corso by the lapels and managed to heave the upper half of his body into the trunk of the car. He paused to rub his face again, then grabbed Corso's feet and swung the rest of the body over the rim. The car rocked on its springs as Corso fell down into the cavernous trunk.

She was running blind. No headlights. Flying down the long washboard driveway. One hand on the wheel, the other pressing the cell phone to the side of her head. 'Could I have your name, please?' the police dispatcher said for the third time.

'Please,' Dougherty said, 'it's an emergency. I'm at two-seven-six-five-four RFD Ten. M. Fulbrook is on the mailbox. Send somebody please.'

'I can't dispatch until I—'

Dougherty dropped the phone onto the seat. The tinny voice coming through the speaker grew more urgent in its squawking. She reached over and pushed STOP until the light went out.

Another quarter-mile and the house came into

view. Wasn't until she saw the house that she realized she didn't have a plan. Didn't have a clue what she might be walking into, so she turned off the engine and silently coasted the last hundred yards. She used the last of her momentum to wheel the car in a wide circle. Grabbed the poster from the passenger seat and left the car facing back toward the road. Just in case. Got out and carefully pressed the door closed. Lights were on both upstairs and down. The room at the downstairs front of the house showed the flickering kaleidoscopic images of a television bouncing off the ceiling and walls. She moved that way. Wincing as the rocks in the driveway cut into her bare feet.

She stepped over a brick border into a flower bed, got up on tiptoe, and peeked into the room. The gas fire burning in the fireplace added to the flickering in the dimly lit parlor, where an older woman lay stretched out in a black La-Z-Boy, her mouth hanging open, her arms limp. Dougherty took two steps to her right and checked the TV.

Survivor.

Corso lay on his side, staring up at the gray night sky. His senses were fading. He knew he was in danger of drifting off into a blank nothingness from which he would never return, so he worked hard to hear the gurgling of gasoline being poured into the tank. Forced himself to count the number of times the gas cans spewed their contents down the hole. And forced himself to notice the sound of the empty cans being tossed aside, and the tuneless whistle and the scrape of boots on the ground. He flared his nostrils and inhaled the heady gasoline fumes, hoping the odor would help bring him around. He had no doubt whatsoever. To drift off was to die. And then the light wavered, and Tommy de Groot was there looking out from his little head, down into the trunk at Corso, before tossing in a pick and shovel and slamming the lid.

CHAPTER 39

Emily's throat was on fire. Her eyes burned like the time she rubbed poison oak into them on a camping trip. The room was sideways. Spinning. Everything seemed like it might come apart and float off like in the cartoons. She stuck one foot out of bed, and before she knew it, she fell on the floor, dragging her bedcovers with her. She lay on the floor, trying to blink her vision back to normal, but the room still looked like a fun house. Her head spun as she thrashed her way out of the covers and crawled across the carpet to the door. From downstairs, she could hear a loud roaring and the sound of her mother's voice. She tried to get to her feet but couldn't, so she crawled down the hall on her hands and knees. At the top of the stairs, she again tried to rise and again was unable to get her legs to co-operate. 'Papa,' she croaked. The roaring from the kitchen seemed to get louder. Louder even than the roaring in her ears as she tried to back down the stairs on her hands and knees, only to lose her grip and go sliding to the bottom on her belly, where she

360

landed in a tangle of arms and legs. Her lungs felt as if they were frozen. Tears rolled down her face. She couldn't stop coughing as she crawled toward the back door.

The limp was gone. Mama May came down the stairs at a lope. 'They're not upstairs,' she said, her face a mask of concern. 'Must have snuck back home while I was napping.' She shouldered her way out onto the porch and stood beside Dougherty. She pointed out over the fields at a brightly lit house in the distance.

'That's my son's place over there.'

Dougherty didn't wait. She turned and began running for the car, with the older woman hard on her heels. They jumped into the rental car together. Mama May was still trying to close the passenger door when Dougherty threw the car into Drive and went peeling out toward the highway. Wasn't until they bounced out onto Route 10 that Mama May realized she was still clutching the poster in her gnarled hand.

Sarah tiptoed out from behind the door, holding the pipe in front of her like an offering. The sound of rushing gas filled the room, masking her footsteps as she crept across the linoleum. The smell of the propane was overwhelming now. It burned in her chest like cold fire as she moved across the room. Her mother was coughing and wheezing as she worked. Her hands shook as she peeled the tape from the bottom of the Meijer's bag and pulled the plastic sack from Papa's head.

Must have been a change in the light. Or maybe some vestigial survival instinct kicked in right at the last moment. Either way, Teresa Fulbrook looked up for the last time and made eye contact with her oldest daughter just as the pipe began its swift descent. The first blow seemed merely to stun her. She rocked back and then reached for the top of her head as if to assess the damage. She was still in that position when the second blow hit her full in the face, shattering her nose and both cheekbones, sending her sprawling to the floor with a look of disbelief etched on her bloody face. Sarah brought the pipe down again and again, beating her mother's head to jelly, until she was no longer able to breathe. At that point she used one hand to clutch the pipe to her chest and the other to cover her nose and mouth as she grabbed the car keys from the hook next to the refrigerator and staggered off toward her bike in the backyard.

Tommie de Groot dusted his hands together. He pulled open the driver's door on the Pontiac and got into the car. The seat was set for Teresa, so he had to find the handle and move it back to accommodate his long legs. Wasn't until he reached to start the engine that he realized he didn't have the keys. 'Dumb shit,' he muttered to himself as he got back out, slamming the door hard in frustration. He stopped alongside the car and pulled a plastic baggie of tobacco out of his back pocket. He pulled a rolling paper from the baggie and shook it full of tobacco. He set the baggie on the trunk lid and used his free hand to tamp the tobacco into place before running his tongue along the edge and using the side of his finger to roll the package into a perfect cigarette. He stuffed the baggie back into his pocket and started for the house. 'Be smokin' wherever the hell I want now, won't I, Gordie baby,' he said to himself with a chuckle as he walked up the flagstone walk toward the kitchen door. 'Don't gotta listen to none of your no-smokin' bullshit no more, now do we?' He bounced the hand-rolled cigarette in his palm as he walked. 'Son of a bitch got what was comin' to him,' he said with a smile.

CHAPTER 40

Sarah burst through the back door and threw herself onto the brown winter grass, her chest heaving, her eyes burning and so full of water the world was little more than a kaleidoscope of broken glass. She gulped air like a marathon runner. Wiped her eyes with her sleeve just in time to notice she wasn't alone. Emily.

Clad only in a T-shirt and underpants, her sister tottered around the corner of the house and disappeared from view. The question screamed in Sarah's brain. 'Did she see? Did she see?' Over and over. Each time louder than the time before, until Sarah scrambled to her feet and started after Emily. Then stopped and ran back. Picked up the car keys and thrust them in her pocket. Then picked up the pipe and followed her sister around the corner.

As he strutted up the walk, Tommie de Groot tried to remember what movie the line came from. Something he'd seen while he was in the marines. In his mind's eye, he could see the crazy guy's face. Famous guy. Big muckety-muck movie star.

Had an ax in his hands. Head stuck through a hole in a door saying, 'Honey . . . I'm home.' Who the hell was that? he wondered as he pulled open the screen door and stepped into the kitchen. In one smooth motion, he flipped the cigarette into the corner of his mouth and flicked the top of the match with his thumb. His central nervous system had an instant to record the scene . . . to see the woman, her head a pulp of blood and broken bone, stretched out on her back beside Gordie on the floor. Just enough time to send a message to his brain before the world exploded and the terrible wave of blue flame washed over him like the lava fires of hell. His last thought and his last word were the same.

'Mama,' he cried as he burst into flame. 'Oh, Mama.'

Dougherty jerked the wheel violently to the right, sending the car skidding onto the loose gravel. Wasn't until she regained control that she noticed the bank of red lights glued to her back bumper and heard the screaming of the police car siren above the engine noise. The old woman sat ramrod straight in the passenger seat, holding the over-head handle in a death grip, her face the color of cement.

When Meg Dougherty snapped her attention back to the driveway, she had only a second to take it all in. The car with the trunk open. The white pickup truck. What was that at the rear of the car? Girls? And then – in an instant – the scene erupted – the house went up in a ball of blue flame. The force of the explosion sent a tall figure staggering backward out the side door. Completely engulfed in flames, the figure ran in a tight circle, wildly flapping his arms, like he was trying to take off, and then falling to the ground where he continued to burn. Wasn't until the police car killed the siren that she could hear the continuous high-pitched scream coming from the burning ember of a man writhing in the driveway. And the hissing . . . the awful hissing of frying meat. Dougherty began to sob.

CHAPTER 41

Dougherty struggled with the wheelchair. As she pushed Corso along, wiry tufts of winter grass sent the front wheels spinning, changing her course, forcing her to lean her weight on the handles and make constant corrections.

'At first I thought it was you,' she said. 'Burning to death, right there before my eyes.' He heard her breath catch. 'You actually could hear him hiss . . . like frying bacon. It was . . .' The words escaped her.

Corso closed his eyes. He could see it all . . . feel it all . . . like it was naked and pressed against his skin. The warmth spreading all over his body as he lay in the darkness. The sound of Tommie de Groot talking to himself as he walked away from the car. Then the trunk lid unexpectedly opening, blinking his eyes, and the girl looking down at him in amazement. The way her face changed from fear to wonder and then to – what was that look on her face as she raised her arms above her head? Was it terror? At the time it had seemed the most malignant expression Corso had ever seen, feral and full of fury as she raised what seemed a silver sword, trembling with anticipation, fey with the prospect of splitting Corso's skull like a piece of rotten fruit. And then the whoosh of the explosion swept her away, like the swipe of a giant hand, rocking the car, clattering debris all over the metal skin, before the tempest gave way to the wail of the siren and finally to the single high-pitched scream of agony that seemed to linger in the air like cannon smoke.

'I came to terms with it,' Corso said out of the blue.

'With what?'

'Dying.' He could feel the hitch in her stride. 'Lying there in the trunk . . . I don't know how to say it, but I had some sort of cosmic experience . . . something where it was okay with me that I was about to die. Like I was going somewhere I'd been before, and it was okay with me. As long as it didn't hurt too much or take too long, I was ready to go.'

She didn't trust herself to say anything. For the past week, he'd been more morose and withdrawn than she'd ever seen him. She'd attributed it to the effects of shock and trauma, but somewhere in her heart, she'd had a niggling that Corso had been forever changed in some fundamental way. That the man they'd pulled from the trunk of that old car was not the same man who'd gone in.

'Don't talk like that,' she said finally. 'It scares me.'

'No . . . it's a good thing,' he said. 'There's a kind of peace to it . . . like maybe everything's going to be all right after all . . . like . . .' He stopped. Laughed at himself. 'Listen to me,' he said bitterly. 'I should know better. The only experts on death are the dead, and they been kind of quiet lately.'

She pushed harder now, forcing the chair forward across the uneven ground. They crested a small rise. The graveside assembly came into view. Dougherty stopped.

'We keep ending up in the graveyard,' she said.

'Almost like we belong here,' Corso added.

She smacked him in the back of the head. 'Cut that out.'

A gathering of about fifty people stood sad and stately beneath the trees. The grave diggers had lined the hole in the ground with canvas. A flower-strewn bronze casket was to be Gordon Fulbrook's final vault. The crowd parted for Special Agent Molina, who detached himself from the gathering and ambled over to Corso and Dougherty. 'Good to see you're still with us,' he said to Corso.

'What are you hearing?' Corso wanted to know.

'I'm hearing it's the damnedest crime scene anybody's ever processed.'

'How's that?'

Molina checked the area. Bent at the waist and spoke into Corso's ear. 'Nothing makes sense,' he said. 'The hubby died of asphyxiation. No burning of the lungs, which means he was dead before the place went up. No scarring either, which means he didn't breathe propane before the place blew up.'

'You're saying the husband was dead before the whole thing even started?' Dougherty said.

'That's exactly what I'm saying,' Molina said. He looked around again. 'With our girl Sissy, or Teresa, or Louise, or' – he waved a disgusted hand – 'whoever the hell she is, things get even weirder. She had four separate skull fractures, a broken nose, and both her cheekbones collapsed.'

'Somebody beat her to death,' Corso said.

'Somebody beat her bad enough to kill her, but ended up just leaving her unconscious. Official cause of death was having her lungs incinerated by breathing burning propane.' Dougherty winced. 'No . . . no . . .' Molina chided her. 'Now we get to the good part.' He pointed at Corso. 'The car he was in, right, that old Pontiac . . .'

'Yeah,' she said.

'Out behind the car, they find a four-foot length of galvanized pipe, fittings at each end. A real sturdy piece of plumbing, about the size and weight of a baseball bat. The local supplier says Gordon Fulbrook was do-it-yourselfing himself a new stove.' He waved a hand. 'Anyway, the lab goes over the pipe, and guess what they find?'

'It's what caved in Mommy's skull,' Corso said.

'Bingo,' Molina said. He looked up at Dougherty and furrowed his brow. 'Did I mention the younger daughter? Emily?'

'I don't believe you did,' Dougherty said.

'She was found unconscious in the grass. Right behind the car Corso was in. Big-time skull fracture to the top of her head. Forensics says she was dragged around the side of the house to the position she was found in.' He held up a finger. 'Her blood and hair were also present on the piece of pipe.'

'How's that work?' Corso asked.

'You tell me,' Molina said.

'She well enough to talk?'

'Spoke to her myself.'

'What's she say?'

'She says she sneaked home from Grandma's to see her papa. Says her mother made her take a couple of pills and sent her to bed. All she remembers after that is waking up, not being able to breathe. She thinks she fell down the stairs. Last thing she remembers is coming around in the backyard. After that, it's all a blank to her.'

'Get any prints off the pipe?'

'Everybody's – Papa, Mama, Tommie, the older daughter, the salesman who sold it . . .' He threw up his hands in resignation. 'Seventy-some-odd prints on the damn thing.'

'What about the older daughter?'

'Sarah.'

'What about her?' Dougherty asked.

'She's the hero. Saved her little sister from the fire. Had her picture on the front page of the local paper the other day. I hear she's got a CNN interview scheduled for tomorrow.'

'What's the official version gonna be?'

'We're leaving that to local authorities,' Molina said.

'Which means what?'

'Which means we can't come up with a scenario that satisfies us, so we're gonna keep out of it. We've closed the Rosen case. That was our end of the business.'

'What are the locals saying?'

'They like Tommie de Groot for the pipe wielder. They're thinking he had a falling-out with his sister and clubbed her to death. They're thinking Tommie maybe thought the little girl had seen and tried to off her too. Maybe broke a gas pipe in the process. Next thing he knows, the whole thing goes kablooie.'

'I don't think so,' Corso said. 'Tommie was outside with me. Gassing up the car. Unless I passed out or something, I don't think he had the time.'

Molina studied the horizon. 'Tell the locals.'

'I'll be here another month.'

Molina shrugged. 'The holidays in the heartland,' he said with a smile.

'It's starting,' Dougherty whispered.

She was right. A priest in full regalia had arrived at the gravesite and begun to read from a Bible. Molina gestured toward the wheelchair.

'May I?' he asked Dougherty. She stepped back and allowed Molina to take hold of the handles. The three of them arrived at the graveside just as the priest was getting warmed up. His voice rose as he described the heavenly paradise for which Gordon Fulbrook was bound. Across the semicircle of mourners, May Fulbrook was seated in a metal folding chair. She held a lace hankie to her face as the priest spoke. On her right, seated in an identical chair, her grand-daughter Sarah was holding up remarkably well for a kid who had just lost both her parents. As the priest droned on, her head turned toward the newly arrived trio. Corso removed his sunglasses and set them in his lap. When he looked up again, Sarah Fulbrook was staring at him, her pale eyes cold and steady. Not a hint of grief. Not a hint of anything.

Could be he was wrong. Could be the strain of the past week had colored his vision, but . . . in that thirty seconds of eye contact before she turned her head away, Corso could feel her disdain. Feel her mocking them all for their weakness and stupidity. A chill ran down his spine like a mouse. It got worse when she turned those white eyes on him again and nearly smiled. This time, it was Corso who turned away.

Twenty minutes later it was over. The mourners drifted away in threes and fours, until only Molina, Dougherty, and Corso remained. A pair of grave diggers arrived on an orange backhoe.

'Nice service,' Molina said. They all agreed. He shook hands with Dougherty first and then Corso. 'I'm betting this is going to be a book,' he said as he shook Corso's hand.

For the first time in a week, Corso smiled. 'Count on it.'

Corso and Dougherty watched as Molina walked down the drive and disappeared from view. Corso bent forward in the chair and scooped a pair of acorns from the ground. The driver raced the backhoe's engine, sending a plume of oily diesel smoke into the air. Dougherty grabbed the handles and began to push Corso across the grass.

She watched as he picked the outer shell from one of the acorns, until all he had left was a smooth little oval with a pointy top. 'Storing nuts for the winter?' she asked.

He shook his head. 'I was thinking how acorns never fall far from the tree.'

He knows. I can see it in his eyes when he looks at me. Sittin' there in that wheelchair throwing hard looks my way while the preacher runs on at the mouth. Hell with him. He didn't look so tough laying there in the trunk of Mama's car, now did he? Looked like he was gonna start bawling all over himself like a little girl or something. Don't matter what he thinks, though. If he had anything to say, he'd have said it by now. Must have his own reasons for shutting up.

People are like that. You think you know what's going on inside their heads, but you don't. They tell themselves they know how other people feel, when really they don't have a clue. 'Cause everybody does things for their own reasons. They do what they gotta do to survive. No matter how crazy it might look to somebody on the outside, to them it makes perfect sense.

Mama May says Papa's life insurance from the company will take care of Emily and me for a long time. Says we can split the money as we grow up and go off to college. Says it'll give us a good start in life. Maybe even buy each of us our first house. If I had the money all to myself, I could buy a big old fancy house someplace far away and never come back here again.

'Course I didn't say that to her.